BOOK 2

CAPTURE
THE
WIND

WENDY DOLCH

CAPTURE THE WIND

Copyright © 2021 by Wendy Dolch.

For information contact :

info@wendydolch.com

https://www.wendydolch.com

Cover design by MoorBooks Design

ISBN : 978-1-7341455-5-7

First Edition: October 5, 2021

BOOK 2

CAPTURE
THE
WIND

WENDY DOLCH

ALSO BY
WENDY DOLCH

THE HEED THE WIND SERIES:

HEED THE WIND

CAPTURE THE WIND

FEAR THE WIND

SIGN UP FOR MY
AUTHOR NEWSLETTER

Be the first to learn about new releases, updates, giveaways, and get exclusive insights that are reserved just for my email besties! If you want to join the party, come on over, Bestie!

https://www.wendydolch.com/join-the-club/

Delhi •

Grand Trunk Ro

India

Legend

River ~

Road – – –

City •

Nepal

Tirhut District

Bihar District

Ganges

Danapur

...d

Jamshedpur

Fort William, Calcutta

Hoogly

Bay of Bengal

Prologue

July 1847, England

Daylight filtered through the barred windows of the carriage, slashing across Pól's downcast face. He sat on the floor of the carriage across from Peadar, picking at the flaking paint. Peadar rubbed his shoe against the floor, noticing his big toe poking through a rip in the seam. He looked back to his brother and cleared his throat. When Pól refused to look up, Peadar kicked his foot with his own.

Pól ceased picking at the paint, glancing up at Peadar, his head rocking back against the carriage wall as they passed over a rough patch in the road.

Peadar fixed his eyes to Pól's, pleading. "What are we going to do?"

Pól returned his question with a blank stare and a helpless shrug.

"Say something." Throat tightening, Peadar pursed his lips, grasping the knees of his trousers with trembling hands.

Rolling his eyes, Pól brought his knees up to his chest, shrugging again. "What do you want me to say?"

"Say it was my fault," Peadar glared, speaking through gritted teeth. "Say I lost her. Say I failed."

"I will not," Pól glowered, looking away with a shake of his head.

Peadar frowned, kicking Pól's foot harder than before. Pól furrowed his brow in anger, and a sense of satisfaction gripped Peadar's chest. "Say it." His lower lip trembled as his throat tightened once more and his eyes burned.

Pól kicked back even harder, clipping him on the Achilles tendon. Peadar winced and closed his eyes, focusing on the pain in his foot, hoping it would ease the ache in his chest. His head knocked back against the carriage as they passed over a large hole in the ground, reminding him once more of their situation.

"Kick me again."

"No, Peadar."

"Do it," Peadar snarled, balling his fists and sitting up straight. He breathed in deeply, quickly, a cloud filling his mind, threatening to rain, but he was not going to let it. The pressure built, squeezing his chest. "Kick me."

"I am not playing this game," Pól grumbled, sitting up straighter and glaring at him in disbelief.

Peader snarled as the pressure broke and the rain fell. Launching himself at Pól, he kneed him in the thigh and punched him in the gut. The sound of Pól grunting as he rained blows down upon him in a furry, brought fresh tears to his eyes. His fists paused long enough for Pól to grasp his arms. Then he renewed his punches, but Pól's grasp was firm, keeping his arms locked down despite his flailing.

"It's okay, Peadar."

Peadar closed his eyes, panting for breath, still trying to fight against Pól's grasp. "Hit me back, you coward."

Wincing in anticipation of a blow to his chin, Peadar flinched as his brother released his arms and wrapped him in a hug.

"It's okay, Peadar."

Easing into the tightness of his brother's arms around his shoulders, he sobbed, burying his face in his shirt sleeve. "I lost her."

"I lost her, too," Pól squeezed harder, fingernails clawing his shoulder.

"And Seamus..." Peadar shivered, remembering the look of pain in his brother's eyes as the convulsions gripped him, writhing on the floorboards of the ship.

"It's not your fault, Peadar."

Unconvinced, Peadar took deep breaths and nodded his head, easing back from his brother's arms.

"Alright?"

He nodded, righting himself. Cheeks burning from shame, Peadar rested his cheek on the cold side of the carriage, refusing to look at Pól. Bringing his knees up to his chest, he buried his face in his kneecaps, covering his head with his arms.

He did not look up until the carriage rolled to a stop and the iron door screeched as it opened, allowing the bright sunshine to flood the carriage.

They had been locked inside for days and the light was an assault upon their eyes. Peadar blinked as he stretched out his limbs and stood to a crouch.

Mr. Scotts stepped in the door, grabbing them each by the arm and dragging them out of the carriage without a word.

Peadar oriented himself to the world outside of the carriage. They had arrived in a city much like Liverpool. The streets were busy with horse drawn carriages and filthy with dung and mud. People rushed along the sidewalks and darted in between the passing carriages. A shove on his back told him to start walking. He tripped over the curb, but Mr. Scotts grabbed the back of his shirt and kept him from falling.

"Get walking," he growled, shoving him towards the door of a brick building.

"Where are we?" Pól dared ask, moving to walk beside Peadar.

Mr. Scotts opened the door. "Shut up."

"What about our sister?" Peadar stopped in the doorway, fixing him with a hard stare.

"I don't know and I don't care, so shut up," Mr. Scotts replied roughly. Then to himself he mumbled, "'nother five minutes and I'll be rid of this vermin. 'nother five minutes..."

"You do know," Peadar glared.

Mr. Scotts sighed and pushed them through the doorway, thrusting them towards a man sitting at the front desk. Peadar stumbled, then righted himself, glancing nervously at the guard stationed next to the desk and the man behind it.

"There you are, two dirt boys," Mr. Scotts sidled up to the desk, leaning his elbows on the counter. "Now, where's my money?"

The man raised an eyebrow and took out a small purse filled with coin. He dropped it into the man's hand. "Pleasure as always, Mr. Scotts."

Mr. Scotts turned to leave, not giving the boys a second glance.

Spinning on his heel, Peadar launched himself at Mr. Scotts. "Tell us where she was taken."

A hand fell on his arm and tightened, holding him back.

Mr. Scotts paused in the doorway, turning towards him slightly. "Forget her, dirt boy. You will never see her again."

Peadar blanched. Next to him, Pól balled his fists and took a step forward, only to be accosted by the guard. The guard swung them around, pushing them up against the desk where sat patiently the sallow-faced man.

"Names?" He drawled in a low, bored voice.

"Peadar and Pól Burns," Peadar replied.

The man sighed, raising an eyebrow at them, then lowering it slowly. "How do you spell those names?"

Peadar shrugged, glancing at Pól. "I don't know."

The man peered at them, frowning. "You will be known as Peter and Paul then." After writing the names down on the paper in front of him, he asked without looking up, "Place of birth?"

Peter shifted his eyes to his feet, mumbling, "Dublin, Ireland."

"Dates of birth?" The man continued.

Peter cleared his throat, and, avoiding the question, asked instead, "Sir, is there any chance we can leave this place if we don't wish to be here?"

The man looked up from the papers and pointed his long nose at him. "You are orphans. Where else would an orphan be but an orphanage?"

"We can work, sir. We can get jobs easily enough to

support ourselves," Peter continued.

"Yes, yes, the workhouse, all in good time. Dates of birth?" The man asked impatiently.

"Sir, we need to find our sister. She was taken from us. May we be permitted to leave and find her, Sir?" Peter asked, his voice becoming more harassed by the minute.

The man made a disgusting noise in his throat and squinted at Peter. "Girls are not allowed in a boy's orphanage. And children are not permitted to leave this establishment under any circumstance except by leave of adoption, joining the army, or until they come of age. Now...dates of birth?"

With a sinking heart, Peter relented and passed on the requested information until the man had filled out their forms. The guard took him and Paul into a suite of rooms on the upper level; a long, narrow room with iron bunk beds lining each side of the wall.

"What are we supposed to do?" Paul asked as the guard started walking away.

"Unpack your belongings and wait for your attendant."

"We were kidnapped," Peter snapped at the guard with a curl of his lip. "We don't have any *belongings*."

"Then sit and wait," the guard sniffed, walking away.

Hearing the tell-tale squeak of a rat, Peter turned

to inspect the room, grimacing at the sight of roaches in the bedclothes.

"It stinks in here." Paul wrinkled his nose, inspecting the brown-smeared walls.

"No worse than our shack on the streets, is it?" Peter kicked the foot of a bed. "At least we have a bed here."

"I'm starving," Paul crossed his arms over his stomach and sat down on a bed. "Where are the other orphans?"

Peter shrugged his lips in reply.

"What would they do to us if we left this room?" Paul raised one side of his mouth, standing, and moving towards the door.

"Don't try it, I don't want to get in trouble," Peter held up a hand to steady him.

Paul raised his eyebrows temptingly and opened the door.

Shaking his head, Peter followed along behind, stepping out into the long, empty corridor. Softening their footfalls by walking on tiptoe, they moved towards the staircase, then on down to the bottom.

The boys met the bottom of the stairs and began to explore the first floor, avoiding, of course, the guard and the man at the front desk. They quickly rounded a corner and stopped short. A man with a cane stood before them.

Peter closed his eyes momentarily, then raised them to the man, smiling as if they had done nothing wrong.

"What are you doing down here?" The man glowered down at them. "Are you Peter and Paul? You were told to wait for me upstairs."

"We were hungry," Paul exclaimed, clutching his stomach. "We haven't eaten in two days, Sir."

"You haven't eaten, have you?" The man said sarcastically, puffing his lip out. "So, you thought you would come downstairs and steal from the kitchens, is that it?" His eyes narrowed, brows scowling at them heavily. "Instead of waiting until the proper time?"

"Not steal. We thought we might ask the kitchen workers for a snack, bread or something," Peter responded.

"Stealing will not be permitted on these grounds," The man said strictly. "We are here to provide education and housing to orphans, not raise criminals. You will be punished. Hold out your hands."

"What?" Peter declared. "We haven't done anything wrong. We haven't stolen anything."

"Hold out your hands and stop talking in that thick accent of yours, I can't understand you," The man yelled. "And you would be wise to address me as Mr. Marks from this point on."

Peter pursed his lips into a thin line, tentatively

holding out his hands, palms facing down. Mr. Mark raised his cane and brought it down hard. Peter pulled his hands back, shaking them, then holding them against his stomach.

"Now you," Mr. Marks addressed Paul.

"No," Paul exclaimed, tucking his hands beneath his arm pits.

Mr. Marks raised his cane and brought the end of it clean across Paul's cheek, leaving a thick, stinging welt.

Paul yelped, slapping both hands across the wound, and falling to his knees.

Flames leaped in Peter's eyes. Reaching into his pocket he pulled out a jack knife, holding it out in a shaky hand. "Leave us alone!"

Mr. Marks flicked his head pompously and stepped back smugly. With a flick of his wrist, the cane flew up and smacked into Peter's wrist, sending the knife flying out of his hand.

Crying out, Peter clutched his wrist, holding it between his legs.

"I'll have to confiscate that." He smirked, tossing his head at the knife. "Get going. You will not want to miss the last lesson of the day. Come on then."

Mr. Marks indicated they turn around and head back down the hall, the cane flicking at their backsides as if they were cattle herded to slaughter.

Peter turned around to look back as Mr. Marks

picked up his knife and slipped it into his pocket.

"I said get going!" He growled, pushing them into a room filled with boys from six years old to sixteen, lined up in rows with their shirts off. Four guardians walked down each row, administering a stinging lash to each of their bare backs.

"What lesson is this?" Peter hissed, taking a step back, his voice quavering with barely restrained emotion.

Mr. Marks smiled. "Lesson in morality," he said matter-of-factly. "When a boy in the community sins everyone in the community suffers because of it. You'll do well to remember that."

Mr. Marks herded them into line. A flick of the cane indicated they should remove their shirts.

Still clasping his cheek, Paul struggled out of his shirt, brushing Peter with his elbow.

An overwhelming feeling of failure washed over Peter as he helped his brother out of his shirt. He choked on a lump growing in his throat. "I'm sorry, this is all my fault."

As the lash lanced across his back, he balled his fists, sucking in his breath, and squashed every instinct to cry out in pain. Instead, he felt the sting, felt it race across every nerve, and embraced it.

"We don't belong here," Paul wrung the bars covering the window in their room. "We're nothing more than prisoners.

"We have to get out of here," Peter whispered under his breath, not wanting the other boys to hear.

"You heard what the man said, no one leaves here unless they are adopted or age out," Paul slumped onto his bed.

"Or we join the army," Peter sat down opposite, a sudden fire giving him hope.

"I'm only eleven. Are we even old enough to join the army?"

Peter sighed. "I don't know."

Paul eyed him warily. "Even if we join the army, what is there for us but death? We would be giving our lives to a country that is not our own. We would surely die. What would happen to Réalta then?"

Peter gulped. "I don't know. But we must do something. I cannot sit here, imagining what Réalta is going through right now. Can you? At least, if we are working for the government, we might be able to find out about Réalta. You know, military people have access to all sorts of information, don't they?"

"We could also die," Paul reiterated sarcastically. "I say we run away, get some job like before until we have earned enough to go search for her."

Peter paused to breathe in deeply and exhale

loudly. "Where would we begin searching?"

"I don't know." Paul gritted his teeth. "It's hopeless. Like Scotts said, we'll never see her again."

Snorting, Peter shook his head and shrugged. "Then I have failed."

"This pitying yourself," Paul spat. "Pa would be ashamed. You're the leader here. You better start acting like it. I am not going to waste away in this God-forsaken place so you better find a way to get us out of here."

"I know you are right," Peter breathed in deep, "though I don't wish to admit it. Ma and Da put me in charge of protecting you all and look where I have gotten us. Seamus dead before we even got here, Réalta stolen from us, and us, no more than prisoners. There seems no hope. The army is our only option as far as I can see."

"We are just kids. Are we ready to die? Are we ready to go to war?"

Peter blinked at the maturity evident in those words. He nodded his head and gave his brother an ironic smile. He placed his elbows on his knees and leaned forward, piercing him with his eyes.

"We are already soldiers fighting in a war that we did not ask for, that we have no control over, and we are losing far too quickly. We have faced death more than once. Why stop now? Let us go out fighting to the bitter end."

Paul nodded fervently, tightening his jaw. "Now you are talking like a leader."

Peter crossed his arms. "We're joining the army."

Paul breathed in through his nose and relaxed his shoulders. "Alright."

Peter leaned back, breathing in deep. "I will not give up hope. I will not fail you as I failed the others."

Reaching out a hand, Paul nodded his agreement. "For Réalta."

Peter slapped his hand in Paul's and squeezed. "For Réalta."

In the darkness covering the room, Peter focused on the image of his sister, the one star bright enough to illumine the path ahead.

September 1849

"Get up, Paul," Peter jumped into his brother's bed, shaking him vigorously. "Today, we get our freedom."

Groaning, Paul rolled over, blinking slowly. "What are you on about?"

"Today, we are no longer prisoners. Today, we begin the search for our lost sister. Today, we leave this orphanage as boys and become men."

"Ohhh...that," Paul grinned, elbowing him in the ribs. "Almost forgot," he said playfully.

Peter sat up, feeling giddiness in his stomach and a quickness to his heart. Quickly, the boys laced up their boots and slipped into their shirts, making up their beds hastily before the guardian came to inspect.

Mr. Marks showed up not seconds later, tossing a coin into the air. Without a word, he went to each bed, bouncing it off the mattress and nodding in approval when it landed back into his hand.

When he reached Paul, he smirked, moving around him to the bed. Limply, he dropped the coin onto the hastily made bed and it did not bounce back. Smiling, Mr. Marks sighed, tapping his cane on the floor with enthusiasm. "Oops, somebody was sloppy this morning. For somebody endeavoring to join the army, you are going to have to do much better than that."

Mr. Marks moved in front of him, smirking. His smirk fell when he saw Paul smiling. Mr. Marks scowled, thrusting the cane into his abdomen. Paul doubled over, clutching his stomach, gasping. Mr. Marks smirked, but the smirk quickly fell away as Paul stood straight, laughing in his face.

"You insolent brat," he spat, face going red. He lifted his cane and brought it back across his abdomen, then down on the back of his neck, until Paul crumpled to the floor. The cane came down on his nose with a sickening crack. Pulling back, Mr. Marks breathed heavily, straightening his jacket.

Peter's fists balled, turning white at the knuckles as his gut clenched in horror at the blood pooling out of Paul's nose. Paul continued to laugh, looking Mr. Marks right in the eye.

"You can' hu't me an'mor," he mumbled through the thick blood pooling down his lips.

Infuriated, Mr. Marks snorted, then stalked out of the room, forgetting to check the other beds altogether.

Peter reached down, clapping arms with his brother, hauling him up. "That was stupid, Paul."

"I know." Paul stripped off his shirt and used it to wipe his face. "But it sure was fun," he winked.

Later that morning, the guardians gathered the boys into the cafeteria. Peter and Paul sat at the edge of their seats. They had waited two years for this day. The day that Paul would come of age. The day they could finally join the army.

General Elkhert strode into the cafeteria, a cap firmly balanced upon his bald head, a gold watch swinging from his breast pocket, a pipe in his mouth profusely blowing out smoke, and a parchment in his hand. He slapped the parchment down on the table in front of the assembly of boys.

"I am here," the general said as he waved his pipe

in the air after having plucked it out of his mouth. His shifty eyes focused on each face in the crowd. "...to call the strong youth of our great nation to join Her Majesty's Army. All you need do is step forth and sign on this line." The general plopped a meaty finger on the parchment.

Peter and Paul hopped from their chairs, smirking over at Mr. Marks who scowled and rolled his eyes.

"General, I would not allow these dirt boys into the army. They are Irish. Not good for much more than digging up rotten potatoes." Mr. Marks turned up his lips.

The General eyed him, poking the pipe back into his mouth and smooshing it to one side. "Look here, no man can tell me who is and who is not allowed into my own regiment. No, thank you, Sir. Any man who wishes to fight for a good cause is welcome to join. I do not see you lining up, eager to join. A weak weasel that cowers behind a beating stick would never have the guts, though, would he?"

Mr. Marks turned pale and then red, stepping back, mouth gaping wordlessly like a fish. The boys stifled their laughter, smiled pleasantly at the officer, and shook his hand with enthusiasm.

"Welcome to the army, boys," he said, after which he scrutinized Paul's broken nose closely, and then inquired, "Not a trouble-maker, are you?"

"Only to the enemy, Sir," he replied with confidence, not batting an eyelash.

General Elkhart nodded. "You two are brothers?"

"Yes, Sir," Peter replied, "Peter and Paul Burns."

The General nodded his head. "I look forward to serving with you both. You may sign the roster."

"Thank you, Sir," Peter considered his words, took the proffered pen, and after a quick glance at Paul, signed the roster. He handed the pen to his brother and stepped aside. Paul bent, scratching out his name, smiling as he dropped the pen.

Peter watched as the General pulled a jack knife and an apple out of his pocket. His eyes followed the knife as it sliced off a piece of the apple.

"You like it?" The General asked.

Peter broke his eyes away, shy at being caught staring. "I had a similar knife, but he took it away the first day we arrived." Peter nodded at Mr. Marks.

"Is that so?" the General peered over at Mr. Marks, narrowing his eyes. "Mr. Marks, would you come here, please?"

Straightening his suit jacket, Mr. Marks stepped close, face pinched in dislike.

"This boy says you confiscated his knife. As he no longer belongs here, it would be good of you to return it to him."

Mr. Marks' face twitched and he shrugged his

shoulders. "That was many years ago. It was probably given away a long time ago."

The General's face tightened, and he held out his hand. "The knife, Mr. Marks."

Straightening his jacket aggressively, Mr. Marks' cheeks blazed red. "I will have to go search for it." Then he turned on his heel and left the room.

While they waited, two more boys signed. When it was clear that no one else was going to sign, the General picked up the roster.

"Follow me," he declared.

The boys followed him out of the dark orphanage doors and out into the bright light of the Yorkshire street.

Freedom.

Peter smiled up at the sky and at the road ahead, nudging Paul with a grin. The grin fell away as Mr. Marks pushed through the door and headed towards them.

He pushed the knife into Peter's hand. "Good riddance."

Peter grinned at his fleeing back, then looked down at his jack knife. His Pa's knife. He gripped it tightly, tightened his jaw, and nodded his head.

"We'll get you on a train first thing tomorrow morning to be shipped out to join your regiment for basic training," the General spoke.

"And where will the train be taking us, Sir?" Peter asked, feeling excitement well up inside at the idea of this new adventure.

"To London. A great city, that." The officer opened the door to a carriage waiting patiently on the street. They clambered inside and listened eagerly as the officer talked incessantly of the rules, obligations, and expectations of the army.

For the first time in their lives, the boys felt as though they had a purpose, something more than growing potatoes in Irish soil, or delving deep into the English soil to mine for coal. They were becoming true men who fought for their freedom as they fought for their lives, men who would be respected and honored, men who were far better than the dirt from which they came.

1

June 1858, London

The warm scent of bread baking in the oven filled the small apartment. Staletta sang, *"Hear the wind blow love, hear the wind blow. Lean your head over and hear the wind blow,"* as she danced around the kitchen in a floral dress and an apron. Her bare feet skipped lightly around the floor as she dried and put away the dishes.

"The currachs are sailing way out on the blue, laden with herring of silvery hue. Silver the herring and silver the sea, and soon there'll be silver for baby and me."

Modestly sized, Daniel and Staletta's apartment boasted two bedrooms, a kitchen, small dining room, and a small sitting room with a staircase leading down to Daniel's new carpentry shop. Two months in and it already felt like home, like she had been living there forever and never did she wish to leave.

She put a dish away in the cabinet, then closed the door, noticing Daniel staring at her from the bedroom doorway.

Having just arisen from bed, Daniel's brown hair was tousled and his eyes still sleepy.

"How long have you been watching me," she threw the towel at him in exasperation, but smiled, her eyes twinkling in the dim morning light.

"Not long," he chuckled. "I was admiring your form."

"Oh, were you?" She said, handing him a plate to put away.

"You were up early this morning," he walked to the cabinet and put the plate away. "Could you not sleep?"

"It's my brothers," she moved back to the pile of dishes on the counter, gazing out the small window that looked down over the row of buildings cloistered next to them. She wrinkled her brow at a slight pain in her abdomen, unconsciously placing a hand over the area. "I'm getting close and yet, not getting anywhere." She sighed, dropping her hand and turning back to face him.

Staletta referred to the great mystery of her long-lost brothers. They had been separated as children when they were orphans living on the streets of Liverpool. In an effort to deport the Irish immigrants, the government had come to clean them out of Liverpool. Staletta was taken to London, where she had escaped from her captors. Her brothers were also taken. To where, she never knew.

Up until two months ago, that is. She had received a tip from her old boss, Smitherton Bobs, that her two brothers had been taken to an orphanage in Yorkshire and from there they had both enlisted in the army.

The last few months had been hectic and new to her. She and Daniel had been married, they had moved out of the house of Mr. and Mrs. Winchelsley, and they had started this carpentry business. That had left little chance for searching or doing any further research.

Staletta had finally found a rhythm over the last few weeks and had settled in well enough she could afford to do some research down at Mudie's Lending library. Of course, she couldn't read, but with the help of the librarian, she had been able to discover no Peter or Paul Burns had died in the army in the last ten years, according to the number of fatality records they sifted through.

That discovery had come with great relief for Staletta and gave her the hope to continue looking. The last time she had been at the library, she had made up a mental list of the places a soldier in the Queen's army could possibly be: dead, retired from the army and living who knows where, fighting in the 2nd China war, or fighting in the Indian rebellion. Add to the list, severely wounded and recuperating in a hospital somewhere, or worse, missing in action. But Staletta was not going to worry about such things as that.

She knew she was missing something or not looking in quite the right place. But surely the records had been better kept and finding a soldier, not so difficult.

"I'm going back to the library today," she told Daniel.

"I need to do more digging...if that's alright with you, of course."

"Of course," he said, and wrapped an arm around her waist. "If you want, I'll go with you."

"But who will tend to the shop?"

"I have an apprentice, remember? This will be a good exercise to see how he does on his own. Besides, it will only be for a few hours."

"Okay then, Danny-boy," Staletta said, leaning into him. "I could use the help."

Daniel laughed and pulled her closer in front of him, putting his hands around her waist, and sliding them over her belly.

Whispering in her ear, he said, "I need to teach you how to read then you can read to our little one someday."

She turned her head to look at him and nodded. "Would you?"

Daniel breathed happily in her ear, tickling her. "Of course. It's weird, though, isn't it?"

"What do you mean?"

"Thinking about being parents, don't you think?"

"It's downright frightening, Danny-boy," she said with no hesitation.

"You'll be a great mother; I have no doubt of that."

Staletta smiled and shooed him away. "You better go to work. I will come collect you when I am ready to leave."

"Yes, ma'am," Daniel replied, heading back into the bedroom to change and comb his hair.

Staletta smiled at his back, then let her gaze wander back to the window, ignoring another sharp pain in her stomach.

2

Staletta walked hurriedly to New Oxford Street, Daniel by her side. She weaved through the crowded sidewalks and streets, remarking to Daniel how temperate the summer day was. The great stone building soon loomed before them, and after pushing through the crowd thronging outside, they arrived.

Daniel opened the door for Staletta, and she moved into the great square room with practiced ease. Awed by how large the library was, Daniel paused, looking around in wonder at the shelves of books lining the first floor. His eyes travelled up the staircase leading to a second-floor landing likewise stocked with bookshelves.

Placing her hand on his arm, Staletta pulled him towards the back of the room. "Army records are back here along with immigration records, marriage records, birth records, and death records. I've already searched the death records. That leaves everything else."

Daniel's eyes poured over the sections Staletta showed to him. "It will take ages to go through every document here. Let's try and narrow it down." Daniel held a finger to his chin in thought. "Is there a specific section for regiment lists?"

"Hmm?" Staletta blinked, looking at him blankly. "I don't know, is there?"

Half-smiling, Daniel took her hand. "Let's find out, shall we?"

Daniel set to searching, scanning the shelves of each section. Staletta followed in his wake, one hand on her stomach. It did not take long before Daniel exclaimed, "Haha," and pulled a book with black binding and gold lettering off the shelf. "Here they are. Volumes organized by year; these should contain lists of the regiments."

Staletta rushed over, grabbing a similar book off the shelf, staring down at it in wonder. "Which year should we look in first?"

Daniel thought aloud, "We should start with the current year. I don't know if these records are for year of enlistment or active-duty lists, but we can start with the most recent and move on down the line if we don't find anything."

"Which one is the current year?"

Daniel pointed to the book labelled 1858, "That one there, the ones before it are the preceding years."

Staletta nodded, scooping the first ten books into her arms. Daniel hid a smile by wiping his nose.

"Can I help you with those?" He remarked, taking a few out of her arms.

"We're close, Danny," her eyes sparkled. "I can feel it."

Daniel smiled, following her over to a table and chairs in the center of the room. The books tumbled out of Staletta's arms and feeling suddenly tired, she sat in the chair, feeling her stomach clench.

"Are you alright?" Daniel knelt beside her; concern etched on his brow.

"Just morning sickness," she gritted her teeth and forced a smile.

Narrowing his eyes, Daniel shook his head. "We should go home."

"I'm fine," Staletta straightened as the pain passed. She wiped a cold sweat from her brow, then started for the books. "Where did that current year book run off too?"

Concern still evident in his features, Daniel reluctantly rose and reached for the 1858 book, thumbing through the table-of-contents. "Looks like we'll have to thumb through each page until we find their names."

"Might as well get started, then," she flashed him a lopsided grin as he took a seat opposite her and began to inspect each page. Staletta reached for a different book. Shifting in her seat to get more comfortable, she laid the book flat on the table, opening it to reveal pages filled with words she could not read. Furrowing her brow, she placed one hand on her chin, chewing on her pinky nail. The other hand began flipping pages, looking for the only words she could read: Peter and Paul Burns.

3

With a sigh, Staletta closed a book and shoved it aside. Her eyes flicked up to Daniel and she bit her lip at the glazed look in his eyes. They had been at it for hours. She sighed again, reaching for yet another book. Pulling it over to herself, Staletta flipped a page and another page, running her finger down each one.

The sound of footsteps and an intentional clearing of the throat caused her to look up. The library attendant nodded his head at Staletta and Daniel, and with hands crossed behind his back, he cleared his throat again, then remarked, "the library will be closing in ten minutes."

As the attendant walked on to the next table, Staletta's shoulders sagged. "Oh bother." She frowned at Daniel. "But we haven't found them yet."

Daniel closed the book he had been perusing and

shrugged. "We'll check them out at the front desk and continue at home."

"I suppose you're right," she mumbled, looking at the stack of books yet to go through. Reaching forward to the book she had been going through, she took hold of the pages to close them and froze.

Peter and Paul Burns. Staletta gasped as she read their names. She dropped the book, then picked it back up, stared at it and blinked several times, then dropped it again.

"What is it?" Daniel rose and rushed to her side of the table. "Did you find them?" He asked, peering over her shoulder. He laughed slightly. "You did. There they are. You found them!"

She sat dumbly for a moment, fingers trembling, while the discovery sank in. Mouth open in shock, she looked one last time, then jumped up, crushing Daniel in a tight embrace. "I found them. I found them. Haha!" In a much softer tone, she repeated, "I found them." Breaking away from Daniel, she picked up the book, holding it out in front of them with trembling hands.

Daniel took her by the shoulders, looking over her shoulder once more. He moved around to face her and she watched as a smile spread on his face. "Look, it says they are enlisted in the 19th foot regiment."

"The 19th foot," Staletta breathed out and let the information sink in. Rapping her fingers against the book, she bit her lip, not understanding what the 19th Foot was or where they were and not sure how that information would help them at all. "Alright..." she looked to Daniel and shrugged "...what now?"

4

A week later and Staletta had gotten no closer to knowing where her brothers were. After tidying up around the apartment, she grabbed her bag, and started down the stairs. Stopping off at the workshop, she peeked inside to find Daniel deep into a discussion about proper sanding techniques with his new apprentice, Henry James, who was about fourteen years of age.

Henry looked up at her arrival. "Hiya, Mrs. May," he waved.

"Hello, Mr. James," she smiled for the lad was always in such good humor. "Danny isn't working you too hard, is he?"

"Not at all, ma'am," he replied, "haven't even touched hammer to wood yet."

"Oh, Danny, let the boy build something already," Staletta knew how seriously Daniel took his carpentry. He was a perfectionist and in training up this young lad, he needed to impart the knowledge he possessed. Nothing would be overlooked. Nothing would be done with half a spirit.

"I've got him for ten years," Daniel replied, looking over his shoulder at her. "What's the rush? He'll get to build something, oh maybe, half-way through his apprenticeship-"

Henry's face sagged.

"-the first fews years are basics and techniques," Daniel continued. For a moment Staletta thought he was serious, until he winked at her.

"Don't take him too seriously, Henry," Staletta said conspiratorially. "He is a terrible tease."

Henry's shoulders relaxed as Daniel laughed, clapping him on the shoulder.

"Almost had me considering a different career there, boss." Henry shook his head and chuckled.

"Star, are you heading out?" Daniel asked.

"I'm going back to the library. I received a notice the muster roll archives we ordered have arrived. I am going to go check them out."

"If you need help searching through the archives, you should take them to my mother," Daniel supplied eagerly. "It would be a great reading exercise for the kids."

"That's a great idea, Danny-boy, thank you," Staletta beamed. "Alright, I'm off. You boys have fun."

"We will," Daniel and Henry said in unison.

Staletta turned to leave, but Daniel caught her arm and walked her to the door, whispering in her ear: "You're pale. Is you're stomach still bothering you?"

Sighing, Staletta reluctantly nodded. "Morning sickness is worse than I thought it would be." She half-smiled, trying to make for the door, but stopped as Daniel's hand held her back.

"Perhaps it isn't morning sickness, Star." He loosened his grip on her arm, but his eyes held her fast. "Please, consult my mother when you see her. She'll know what to do."

"I will, Danny-boy," Staletta stroked his face, kissed him, and smiled as she closed the door behind her.

5

Staletta arrived at the house of Mr. and Mrs. May with a box of archival documents in her arms. Ever a curiosity, the children had swarmed in upon her, unloaded the box, and swept her right into the house before she even knew she had arrived. They placed her in a chair and brought her a cup of tea.

Mrs. May entered shortly after and quickly put the kids to work. "Otilly, it's your turn to do the dishes; Eberhard the garden needs your attention please, the rest of you go clean your room. Staletta dear, it is good of you to come."

"Mrs. May, if it's not too much trouble, I have a job for the children."

"What's that, dear?"

"As you know, I have been looking for my brothers and all we knew was they were in the army," Staletta paused for Mrs. May to acknowledge she did know that much. "Recently, Danny and I discovered they are in the 19th foot regiment. I ordered this box of muster rolls from Mudie's to discover where in the world they might be stationed right now."

"I see." Mrs. May exclaimed. "That is exciting news."

"Danny suggested the children could help me look through the records; there are so many, it would take me ages by myself."

"A splendid idea," Mrs. May agreed. "Children assemble." She called out in her strong, clear voice and eight children appeared in a great flurry around her. "Children, would you mind helping your sister-in-law find the 19th foot regiment in the documents in this box?"

"Yes, ma'am," the kids replied and set to immediately.

"Be careful with the papers," Staletta said, "they don't belong to me and I must return them in near perfect condition."

"Yes, ma'am," the kids replied again.

Mrs. May looked at Staletta with concern on her face. "My dear, you are quite pale. Is everything alright?"

Staletta winced, clenching her stomach. "I admit I don't feel the best. This pregnancy has not been easy on me. The morning sickness has been dreadful. I believe that is what ails me, but Danny disagrees."

"You should lie down for a while, let the kids work."

Staletta took a deep breath and looked longingly at the pile of papers. A sharp stab caused her to catch her breath and clutch her stomach again. "I think you are right,

Mrs. May."

Mrs. May's face turned ashen. "Right this way, dear," she said as she grabbed Staletta's arm and led her to the spare room.

"I'm sorry for the trouble," Staletta winced, concentrating on staying upright. "I don't know what's wrong with me."

"No trouble at all, dear, although I am quite certain I know the problem."

"Is this normal?" Staletta said as she collapsed into the bed, face drained of color.

"Indeed it is," she replied in a low voice. "Take off your dress, dear, you'll be more comfortable." Mrs. May said, helping her to undo the closures and lift it over her head, then loosened the ties on her corset.

Staletta settled back into the pillows as a wave of pain clutched her gut. Writhing, she held her stomach, then looked down to find blood seeping out from between her legs.

6

"Daniel, you must come right away," Eberhard hurtled into the workshop, grabbing Daniel's hand. "Come on, no time to lose. We must hurry."

"What is it?" Daniel exclaimed, pulling against Eberhard's hand.

"It's Staletta, she's at our house. She is unwell."

Daniel cursed under his breath, "I knew I shouldn't have let her leave this morning." He put his tools down, sharing a look with Henry.

"Daniel, you must come right away," Eberhard took his hand again and pulled. "There is blood."

"Blood?" Daniel froze as his stomach plummeted to the floor.

"A miscarriage," Eberhard said. "She lost the baby."

Daniel thrust a hand into his hair, then brought it down to cover his mouth.

"We need to go right now," Eberhard pressed.

Daniel tore off his tool belt. Heading for the door, he called back over his shoulder. "Henry, take over the shop. I don't know when I'll be back."

Henry nodded. "I'll be fine, just go."

Daniel and Eberhard arrived at Staletta's bedside twenty minutes later. She lay curled up on her side, her face wet with tears.

Daniel kneeled by the bed, grasping her hand. "Star-" he started, but could not find any words. He had never seen her like this before: grief-stricken, without any spirit at all.

She said nothing. She closed her eyes and pressed her face into the pillow. Daniel kissed her head and reached to rub her back. He heard the door open and looked up to find his mother standing there.

"Is she going to be okay, mother?" He asked.

"In a day or two," she nodded. "Best to leave her alone for now."

Daniel nodded, kissing Staletta's head again. "I'll be right outside if you need anything," he whispered in her ear. She gave him a slight nod in return.

Standing slowly, Daniel followed his mother out the door where he collapsed in the sofa in the sitting room. He placed his elbows on his knees, dropped his face in his hands and rubbed vigorously, then leaned back and flopped his head against the sofa.

"Thank you for taking care of her, mother," he finally

said. "I'm glad it happened here. I would not have known what to do."

His mother nodded. "Poor dear girl, this will be quite a shock for her, but she'll be okay in time. We'll keep her here until she is ready to be moved."

Otillie jumped up excitedly, brandishing a piece of paper in the air. "Look, I think I found it."

"You found the 19th foot, dear?" Mrs. May said happily. "Let's see then. Give it to your brother."

Daniel took the paper from her hand. "There it is. Well done, Otillie. The 19th foot, Peter and Paul Burns are listed right there. Stationed in –" Daniel raised his eyes towards his mother. "India."

"The Rebellion?" His mother asked.

"She won't be able to go see them, but," Daniel replied, a smile growing on his face. "She will be happy to know where they are."

Mrs. May smiled sadly. "Best wait until tomorrow to tell her."

"Shouldn't we tell her now?" Daniel asked, confused. "It might cheer her up."

Mrs. May shook her head. "The poor girl needs to grieve. The grief she feels cannot be relieved by good news."

Daniel nodded. "What should I do?"

"You'll do nothing," Mrs. May said firmly. "Tomorrow you can sit with her for awhile and we'll see how she does with you and then we'll go from there."

"What do you mean, 'see how she does with me'?"

"Don't take this the wrong way, dear, but she might not wish to see you right away," Mrs. May replied carefully.

"I'm her husband," Daniel said aghast. "Why wouldn't she wish to see me?"

Mrs. May sighed. "Other than owning your own carpentry shop, what has been your one great desire?"

"To be a -" Daniel paused, understanding flooding him. "- a father."

"Exactly, and she believes she has failed you in that," Mrs. May said quietly.

"Did she say that to you?" Daniel said in a small voice.

Mrs. May shook her head. "She doesn't need to."

"But I don't blame her," Daniel exclaimed. "I would never think ill of her."

"I know, son, but grief has a way of blinding the truth and twisting it into an evil thing."

Daniel closed his eyes, rubbing his face again. "What am I going to do?"

"Don't despair," Mrs. May said. "She will come around in time."

7

The next day, Daniel slowly opened the door to Staletta's room and peeked inside. He paused as he saw her sitting up in bed, her arms lying in her lap, eyes red and swollen. She lifted her eyes at the movement of the door and when she saw it was him, gave a slight smile.

"Hi, there," he said warmly. "May I come inside?"

She nodded. Pushing the door open, he walked inside, closed the door behind him, and sat on the bed next to her.

"How are you feeling?" He asked tentatively.

"Fine," she said faintly.

He nodded in understanding. "Is there much pain?"

"Not so much now," Staletta fidgeted, looking down at her hands.

"I cannot believe this happened-"

Staletta looked off to the side. Her face obscured from him, she continued bitterly, "Why not? I always lose my family, do I not?"

"Do not think that way," Daniel reached forward to grab her hand. "You've got me. I won't ever leave you, no matter what."

Looking up at him, her blue eyes pierced into him. "We both know life doesn't work that way."

Remembering the advice of his mother, Daniel figured it was best to hold his tongue, and not argue with her at this moment, though he longed to cry out and refute her. Instead, he squeezed her hand reassuringly. "I don't know what to say to ease your grief."

"Say nothing," she whispered, giving him a humorless smile. "It is *our* grief. We will bear it together."

Daniel reached forward to stroke her chin with his finger. "Deal."

"It's funny..." Staletta looked back down at her fingers.

"What is?"

"How quickly your whole attitude can change."

Daniel furrowed his brow. "What do you mean?"

"Yesterday, nothing mattered so much as finding my brothers and being a mother. Now both are gone. Stolen from me."

"No," Daniel leaned forward. "You mustn't think like this."

"Yesterday I was a mother and in two seconds, I was no longer," Staletta snapped.

The acidity in her voice forced Daniel to lean back.

He bit his tongue, inspecting her with a frown.

Staletta covered her mouth, eyes widening in shock at her own outburst. "I'm so sorry, Danny."

He breathed out, expression softening. "You have every right to be upset."

"But not with you," she whispered, tears pooling in the corners of her eyes. "I am angry at God. I don't want him to take away anymore of my family."

Daniel watched the tears break from her eyes and slip down her cheeks. "I understand."

"What can I do to keep from losing everyone I love?"

Swallowing a lump in his throat, Daniel leaned forward. "The tough answer is: there is nothing you can do."

Her lips parted and she nodded, blinking back more tears.

"But I do have some news for you, about your brothers. Perhaps it will ease your grief?"

Wiping her tears away, Staletta took a steadying breath. "What news?"

"Otillie found something in the muster rolls yesterday. Star, we know where they are."

Staletta sat up straighter, eyes widening. She wiped the tears away from her cheeks and looked at him eagerly. "Where? Where are my brothers?"

"They are in India."

Staletta leaned back against the pillows, her head resting against the headboard. She closed her eyes. "So far away."

Daniel watched her face with rapt attention, and continued, "I couldn't sleep last night, so I did more looking.

I found they were deployed last year."

"Are they still there now?" Staletta asked, opening her eyes and concentrating on him.

"I don't know for certain, but I assume so."

Staletta twisted her lips in thought and grew silent, looking off at the wall on the opposite side of the room.

"After you knew their location," Daniel asked carefully, "did you ever think of what you would do next?"

Staletta avoided his gaze. "I was going to go meet them, but India-" she shrugged. "It's so far away."

"Not to mention impossible," Daniel lifted his eyebrows, nodding. "Staletta, they are in the middle of a rebellion over there."

"A rebellion?" She narrowed her eyes. "What do you mean?"

"India is in rebellion against British rule. Last year there was a mutiny-an uprising of the Indian troops against the rule of the British East India Company. I would bet that's exactly when your brothers were sent there."

"I see..." She bit her lip, looking down at her hands.

"It would be utterly foolish to run off to India in the middle of that turbulence," Daniel continued. "Besides that, we would not have a way to get there, we would not have any one to go with, and in your condition – it would never do."

"But, there are British citizens living there?" Staletta turned her gaze back to him, a light of hope springing into her eyes.

Daniel half-nodded and shrugged.

"But if they can do it, why not us?" Staletta leaned

towards him, pleading with her eyes.

Blinking quickly, Daniel leaned back, shaking his head. "Oh no."

"Oh yes," Staletta sat up straighter. "Maybe it is not so impossible."

Cursing himself for bringing it up, Daniel shook his head. "I am sorry, Star. I know you want to go meet them, but I cannot allow it. It is too dangerous. It is no place for us."

Daniel swallowed hard, trying to remove the bitter taste in his mouth. His chest grew tight as Staletta leaned back against the pillows. The dim light that hope had sparked in her eyes turned to smoke, leaving a cold, black wick sitting vacant in her spot.

Looking away, Daniel choked on the painful lump clutching his throat. "I am so sorry, Star."

8

"Would you like to play your violin? I can fetch it for you."

"I don't think so."

"Would you like to go for a walk? It's a beautiful day outside."

"I don't think so."

"Are you hungry?" Daniel continued. "I can fix you something or we can go out, whatever you'd prefer."

"No, Danny," Staletta replied. "I'm not hungry."

Daniel gave up and stood from the sofa where he had been sitting next to her. "Alright, I'll leave you alone. I'll be downstairs if you need me."

Staletta had been well enough to return home a few short days after the miscarriage, but ever since she had returned home, she had no desire to do anything. The search for her brothers was over. Her baby was gone. There was not much left for her to look forward to.

Daniel knew she needed time, but how much? He was losing his wife to despair. What could he possibly do to get her back?

Staletta breathed a sigh of relief as Daniel left to go downstairs. He had been nice and attentive to her these last few days, but what she needed was time to think. Time to gather her courage. The thought of her brothers would not go away. It pulled at her like a man pulling on a church bell string, the clanging bell not leaving her alone for a second. Now that she knew where they were, how could she not go to them? But knowing where they were, how could she possibly go to such a place?

Say it were possible, she thought to herself. *How different could it be from the rest of your life? How different is it from living in a shack in Ireland? From sailing in a coffin ship? From living on the streets? From working, as a child, in a coal mine? But, I have a life here. I have a husband. I have a baby to think abou – no never mind about that.*

How much more dangerous could it be?

We could hire a guide, her thoughts continued. *Someone who has been there before. We could easily board passage on a ship, couldn't we? But we don't have much money. If only we knew someone who had a ship? Like Bobs – I wonder what ever happened to his ship? What ever happened to him? I could ask around at the ol' pub I played at before; see if anyone will be going to India and wouldn't mind us tagging along? Us? Who am I kidding? Danny will never agree to go. It's impossible.*

Staletta sighed and rubbed her forehead. A headache had creeped in and made a flurry of a nest in her head. *Unless...I have a ship lined up and a solid plan drawn up for how to find them once we reach India...then maybe he'd agree?*

Her mind racing, trying to formulate a semblance of a plan, Staletta lay down on the sofa, quickly falling into a sleep wracked by a dream of traveling across the sea and running through the jungle, running deeper, running farther, looking for her brothers beneath every leaf and every tree.

She twitched in her sleep.

She runs through the jungle, harder as the brush thickens. She knows she is close. She picks up her pace as a flash of blue whips through the trees ahead. There they are. Quick. Run faster. The blue appears once more just beyond the thicket of trees, then disappears. She runs to it, picking up speed, approaching the trees, breaking through the trees, reaching out for the blue...then she's falling, fast, off the edge of the cliff.

She clamps her eyes shut and twitches in her sleep.

She does not hit ground. When she opens her eyes, the Indian jungle is gone. She straightens, looks around. There is a violin in her hands and she is standing on stage at the Theatre Royal, Drury Lane. She hears clapping. The audience wants her to play. She places the violin to her shoulder and starts to play, searching the crowd for the flash of blue she had been chasing.

She's been here before. She knows who will be sitting

in the front row before she even looks. Her mother, her father, her five dead brothers...smiling at her and clapping. Something is different this time. She squints into the darkness of the theatre at two boys sitting just behind her family.

Her heartbeat quickens, the violin falls from her shoulder. Two young boys sit in military uniforms too big for their small frames. Peadar and Pól. They sit watching her, smiling and waving, beckoning her to come join them. Peadar is mouthing something, but she can't make out what. He holds his hand out to her.

She reaches and tries to take a step, but her feet won't move. She pumps her arms as if running, but her feet won't move. She stares at them and they stare back. It's not too far. It's not impossible. There they are. They're right there.

But her feet won't move.

Staletta twitched, coming awake. Slowly, she rose into a sitting position, stretching her arms above her head. She stood; lethargic limbs heavy from disuse this past week. Frowning to herself, she shook her head, clinging to the energy given by the tendril of hope brought to her by the dream. Her brothers were there. They were right there.

"Alright, you can do this," she said aloud, wringing her hands. Her stomach clenched with nervousness as she thought about approaching Daniel, but the thought of finding her brothers tormented her mind. If she did not go to find them, she would regret it the rest of her life.

Biting her lip, she tiptoed down the stairs, partially out of nervousness, partially out of guilt. She realized that she had been curt to him all week. She had sought to avoid him on numerous occasions. She had disregarded that he, too, had lost someone this week and that he, too, grieved.

He was so good to her and she had ignored him in return. He was far too good for her, she resolved, descending the last few steps into the workshop, the guilt almost rising up to choke her. He deserved someone who did not carry death around with them like an old, familiar handbag.

She entered the workshop. Daniel started at the sight of her, dropping his hammer on Henry's toe.

"Watch it, boss." Henry jumped back in alarm, reaching down to inspect his toe.

"Sorry, Henry," Daniel winced, then looked back to Staletta. "Are you alright, Star?"

Nodding and giving him a slight smile, she advanced slowly. "I thought we could go for a short walk," she ventured, twisting her fingers together in front of her. "If you're not too busy."

"Never too busy for you, Star," he ducked his head, turning back to Henry. "Henry, watch the shop for a short while?"

"Yeah, yeah, yeah," Henry replied, tossing the hammer on the workbench, and sitting down on a stool with a disgruntled look on his face.

Staletta passed her arm through Daniel's and he led her outside to the busy street.

"Danny, I want to apologize," Staletta walked along the pavement, studying her shoes instead of looking at him. "I have been distant and unkind to you of late."

"It has been a rough week for us."

Staletta winced at the pain evident in his voice.

"Made rougher by my attitude."

Daniel leaned his head close to hers. "I forgive you, Star." He reached over to rub her chin with his finger.

Relaxing, Staletta lifted her eyes back to him. "Thank you, Danny. You are far too good to me."

"I wish that were true," Daniel pulled her closer. "I wish I could bring your brothers back for you."

Nervousness clenched her stomach and she stiffened. "That was the other thing I wanted to talk to you about."

Daniel guided her around a puddle of water on the sidewalk, but said nothing, giving her a cautious glance.

"I think I have settled on a solution." Staletta drew in a breath. "I think, with some work and planning, we can make it to India and find them. I-I know it sounds crazy. It scares me even, but I can't get it out of my mind."

Staletta grew more nervous as Daniel did not remark upon her solution. "Danny, are you alright?"

"Sorry," Daniel replied, squeezing her arm in turn. He squinted, his brows digging into his forehead, frown lines deepening around his mouth. "I want so badly to agree with you." He paused, shaking his head, "But I cannot."

"I know," Staletta said, a note of anxiety creeping into her voice despite her efforts. "I know, you'd prefer to wait out the Rebellion and for my brothers to return to England, but we both know the chances of survival for a soldier are slim. Daniel, my brothers may never return. If I do not go to them, I will regret it for the rest of my life."

Daniel paused on the sidewalk, pulling her out of the way of the other people, and towards the wall of a building.

"You would willingly go to your death in search of them?"

"I have faced death before and surely will again. I am not afraid of it."

Daniel studied her face, shaking his head in disbelief. "I will not allow it."

He stepped back from her, his features twisted in a grimace of pain? Anger? She could not tell. She stepped forward, looking up to his eyes, her mouth firm. "Don't you understand my need to see them again, Daniel?"

Shaking his head, Daniel held his arms out helplessly. "I do, but...what you're suggesting is suicide."

Staletta crossed her arms, pursing her lips. "That is not fair. If you were separated from your family, I am sure you would do everything you could to see them again. If I were kidnapped one day, wouldn't you throw caution to the wind and try to find me?"

Placing his hands on her shoulders, Daniel sighed. "Of course, I would." He searched her eyes. "But do not ask me to willingly send my wife off to her death. That is something I cannot do."

Dropping her gaze to the street, a tear slipped down her cheek. "I understand." She looked back up at him. "I want to go home now."

9

Moonlight filtered through the sheer curtain on their bedroom window, illuminating Daniel's bare shoulders. Staletta lay on her side, watching them move up and down as he breathed quietly, fast asleep. Resisting the urge to reach out and touch him, she bit her lip, contemplating her next move.

He would be furious if he found out. She knew he did not want any part in it, but she couldn't resist. She propped herself up on her elbow, reaching forward tentatively, brushing her fingertips on his skin. When he did not wake, she slowly slipped out of bed, reached for her gown, and brought it out to the kitchen to dress.

Tiptoeing down the stairs, she left through the door, and paused on the street. The streets looked different than they had a year ago. A year ago, walking down a darkened street in the middle of the night was familiar routine. It was home. Now not so much.

Her heart quickened and she steeled herself. "If you're going to go to India, you'll need more strength than this, girl," she whispered to herself. Throwing her shoulders back and holding her head high, she breathed in the night, letting herself reorient to the unique sounds and shadows of the night. She stepped forward, letting her feet carry her swiftly down to Limehouse, her hand clenched around a knife in her pocket. Upon reaching the docks, she located the nearest pub and slipped inside.

The familiar sounds of raucous laughter, clinking glass, and endless chatter flowed over her. She hunched over, making sure her hood was securely over her head. She didn't need anyone recognizing her tonight. She slipped around the customers, heading towards the barkeep. She stopped in front of the bar and asked quietly, face in shadow. "I'm looking for a sailor by the name of Smitherton Bobs."

The barkeep dried a glass with a rag, but looked at her curiously, eyes narrowed. "Died, a few months back."

Staletta licked her lips. "I know, but I thought maybe you'd heard word of him coming back?"

The barkeep narrowed his eyes to a slit. "You barmy? How many drinks have you had?"

"Never mind," Staletta breathed, turning away disappointedly. Taking a deep breath, she walked to a table crowded with sailors. "I'll buy you a drink if you can tell me the current whereabouts of Smitherton Bobs, Captain of the *Kathryn*."

The sailors laughed, sitting back in their seats. One

took a big swig to empty his glass. Red-faced, he raised his glass, looking at her. "I know where he be."

"You do?" Staletta stepped over to him, eagerly. "Where?"

"Davy Jones Locker." The sailor laughed hysterically, pounding his glass on the table, then thrusting it into her hand. "There ya are, fill her up."

Seething, Staletta pushed the glass back to him and walked away, hearing them mocking her in the background. Disgusted, she left the pub, walking back out into the street in a huff. She breathed in deep and let it back out. She used to be good at handling that sort. She had lost her edge.

Staletta shook it off and ventured down to the next pub, entering, and repeating the routine, only to be laughed at or passed off as crazy. Frustrated, she decided to call it a night and return the next night, and the next, and the next after, searching pub after pub, dock after dock. The overwhelming response: Smitherton Bobs was dead and would never sail again.

10

It was daybreak when she returned home, ascending the stairs as quietly as possible. Defeat weighed heavily on her shoulders and despair made her feet drag like lead anchors. She had gone out each night with nothing to show. Smitherton Bobs was no more and any hope of getting to India had fled her heart.

Opening the bedroom door, she tiptoed inside and started to remove her dress when a rustling sound made her pause and turn around.

"Staletta? Where were you?" Daniel sat up in bed, looking sorely distressed.

Her hands fell away from her bodice. "On a fool's errand."

"Should I be worried?"

She went to sit by his side, looking down at her hands. "I'm sorry, Danny, but I had to."

"What were you doing out there?"

"Looking for Bobs."

Daniel shifted on the bed, breathing out. "Why? Why on Earth would you look for him?"

"I think he'd want to help...if he were still alive," Staletta looked over her shoulder at him. "Everyone says he's dead, but I still don't believe it. But how do I prove it?"

"Help with what?" Daniel protested. "He *is* dead."

"He sent me that paper with my brother's names on it. He couldn't have sent it if he were dead, could he?" Staletta crossed her arms and exhaled.

"He probably sent it before the accident," he said, sitting forward and rubbing her back. "I know you are upset with me. I know you want to find your brothers more than anything else in the world. You were right, it is unfair of me to deny you that. It is selfish for me to want to keep you here. But I have also taken an oath before God to protect you. And I do not take that responsibility lightly."

Nodding, Staletta sighed, turning to face him more evenly. "You are so good to me. And I have been a bad wife, sneaking around behind your back, conspiring against you. I do not know why you put up with me."

Chuckling, he took her hand. "You are passionate and wild. I knew this when I married you and I love you more for it."

As he brought her hand to his lips, she locked eyes with him. "Is there any chance, any hope at all, that you might concede?"

Daniel pulled back, dropping his eyes as he thought it over. "You tempt me so." He chuckled humorlessly. "I make no promises, but I will give it some more consideration."

A glimmer of hope quickened the beat of her heart. Her lips parted in a slight smile and she bent down to kiss him.

Daniel fingered her chin, shaking his head helplessly. "Seeing you smile again might be enough to convince me," he winked, pulling her into bed with him. "You are dangerous."

"How so?" She whispered, settling on top of him.

"You are a tigress that knows what she wants," He flipped her over onto her back, staring down at her longingly, but with a sorrow in his eyes that made her shiver. "And will tear me to pieces to get it."

"Danny," she said to the window, "Danny-boy." She cleared her throat. "I was wondering if you had come to a decision?"

"No, no," She shook her head. "Danny-boy," she paused, clasping her fingers together. "Have you changed your mind yet?"

Wincing, she tapped a tooth with her fingernail. "That's awful. What if I said, 'have you made a decision, or do you still need more time'?"

"I've made my decision."

At the sound of Daniel's voice, Staletta whirled round. Daniel stood at the top of the stairs, smirking at her. Her stomach plummeted to her feet.

"You scared me," she chuckled, placing a hand on her heart. "You heard all of that?"

He smiled, moving around the banister, stepping closer. "I did."

Nodding, Staletta swallowed a lump in her throat. "Well?"

"I have one question to ask before I state my decision," Daniel cocked an eyebrow, placing his hands in his pockets. "If we go, how are we going to get there?"

"I've thought a lot about that," Staletta nervously picked at her fingernail. "If we cannot find Bobs and his ship then I will secure work and save for a passenger vessel."

"But, Star, Bobs is gone, remember? They found his ship wrecked on the reef."

"Did they?" Staletta raised a brow. "Or is that what they want us to think?"

Daniel tisked. "Where did you come up with this conspiracy theory? But..." Daniel paused, tilting his head at her. "I'll humour you. We will go look for Bob's together."

"Problem is, I've already been out and couldn't find him. I'm not sure where else to look."

"*The North Star* might have to come out again, lure him out of hiding. Don't you think?" Daniel playfully nudged her with his elbow.

Smirking, Staletta grasped her skirts in her hands and looked up at him out of the corner of her eye. "Am I to understand that you are saying yes?"

The corners of his mouth twitched as if he were tugging the words out of his mouth. "I am."

A rock dislodged itself in her chest and rolled down

into her stomach uncomfortably. "And you do mean we? As in you and me? As in us together?"

"That is generally what I was thinking, yes," Daniel grinned.

"I never thought you would. I mean your shop, and Henry, and our home..."

Daniel patted her hand. "All will still be here when we get back. You do want to go, don't you?"

Looking at him askance, she shrugged her eyebrows. "Yes," she said after a long pause. "But I admit, it scares me more than anything."

Daniel dropped her arm to hold her hand. He squeezed it tightly, reassuringly. "We'll take every precaution we can. We will plan ahead. We will find a guide. It will not be easy, but we will try."

"What changed your mind?" Staletta asked, stepping closer to him.

Daniel shrugged. "What else can I do?" He paused, his eyes boring into hers so deep it made her knees quiver. "I know you won't rest without at least trying." Placing his thumb on her chin, he leant close. "I love you."

11

A warm summer wind rippled through the night. A figure in a blue taffeta gown floated down the streets, a violin strapped to her back. She moved easily, picking up on her old ways with familiar ease. She stuck to the dark shadows where the lamp light ceased to shine. No one needed to see her before it was time. To keep her footsteps as silent as possible on the hard cobblestones, she stepped lightly on the stones covered in dirt or the hunks of dried manure left from the horses. No one needed to hear her before it was time.

Staletta slipped up to the *Stinking Oyster* in Limehouse, a pub frequented mainly by sailors. If anyone knew of Bobs' whereabouts, it would be one of these crusty men. She and Daniel had posted flyers all over town announcing this event, asking for anyone who knew of Bobs' whereabouts to show up there. They even placed an ad in the newspaper. The whole city had been talking about it. She could tell by the loud noises on the other side of the door, that they had drawn quite a crowd. A spark of hope ignited her heart. Surely at least one person would know what really happened to Bobs.

No one noticed her as she slipped quietly inside and stepped inconspicuously to the back of the room where the piano man played. He looked up from his rowdy tune and spotted her. She smiled and nodded her greeting. His eyes grew wide and he smiled.

The North Star had returned.

By the time the piano tune wound to a close, *The North Star* had her violin out of its box and had readied it beneath her chin. The sound of it mixed harmoniously with the last few notes of the piano. The piano stopped. The violin quivered, a poignant sound cutting right through the uproar of the pub guests, immediately commanding their attention. She sang of the sea and the want of home.

At the end of the song, *The North Star* let the notes fade away. Instead of collecting coin, she raised her voice. "You have all seen the flyers? I am looking for the man called Smitherton Bobs. He sailed away from here several months hence, presumed dead or lost at sea. But I have reason to think differently. Has anyone heard of his whereabouts or caught a glimpse of him at the harbor?"

The guests shuffled around, scratched their necks, shrugged their shoulders, incoherent mumbles, and grunts.

"I don't know where he is," a voice called out, "But I'd sure like to know."

"I don't know neither," another voice echoed from the shadows. "I'm just here to find out."

"I see," said *The North Star*, the flame of hope beginning to diminish. "I would like to hire him for a job. If anyone has information, please let me know before I leave here tonight."

"*The North Star* wants to hire ol' Bobs, eh?" A sailor called out. "Pray tell what for and my memory might be jogged."

The North Star nodded. "Fair enough, sir. I wish to sail to India."

"What business does a pretty gal like you have in India?" The man continued, sticking his pipe in his mouth and taking a draw.

"I am looking for my brothers, sir, they are enlisted in the army, regimented in India."

"*The North Star* has brothers?" the man drawled once more, and the rest of the room exploded in whispers.

"Do you know of Bobs' whereabouts or not, sir?" *The North Star* said impatiently, shifting her feet and tossing her head.

"I might have heard of his shipwreck, but I'm not about to yell out the details for everyone to hear," he said, licking the end of his pipe and staring at her. The gathered crowd moaned at that and disgruntled grunts issued from their mouths. "I'll talk with you somewhere private. Meet me outside?"

The crowd ooohed and slapped the tables, shocked that someone had requested to meet privately with the infamous *North Star*. As far as they knew, she was as the wind, silent, mysterious, invisible, unable to be reached or captured.

The North Star searched the crowd, she knew Daniel was here and when she found him, sitting inconspicuously at a table in the corner, they locked eyes. He nodded in reply.

"Very well, sir," she said. "Lead the way."

The man stood to a bout of applause, his face revealing nothing. He moved around the tables towards the door and *The North Star* followed along behind. No one noticed as a few seconds later, Daniel also slipped out the door.

The sailor led *The North Star* to the alley. She was wary of him and kept her distance. She knew Daniel would be right behind and would be waiting behind the wall, but even so she did not wish to encourage any trouble from this sailor. Sailors were an unpredictable lot, one minute as calm as could be, the next stormy and out of control.

"Where can I find Bobs?" She asked, wishing to get this meeting over as soon as possible.

The man stopped and turned to face her. "As far as you or anyone else is concerned, Smitherton Bobs is dead. Do you understand?"

Her shoulders sagged. "Then why are we having this conversation?"

"I know someone who was close to him. I will take your message to him and if you are someone he wants to work with, he will send notice."

Sighing, *The North Star* conceded. "Bobs knows me. Tell him-I mean, this person-that my brothers are in India, and we need to board passage on a ship in order to get to them. He will know what I am talking about."

"I will give your message to this person and where can he reach you if he is inclined to help?"

"May's Carpentry Shop at 301 Marshalsea Road." *The North Star* replied. She wrung her hands, confused by this twisty conversation. "Sir? When I lost saw Bobs, he was sort of having a breakdown. Is he okay now?"

The man laughed, placing his hands in his pockets, and setting off out of the alley. "Bobs is dead, remember." He stopped at the edge of the alley where Daniel appeared. The sailor tipped his hat at Daniel as if unsurprised he was there. "Good evening."

Daniel nodded to him, moving into the alley.

The North Star's jaw dropped at the sailor's last comment. "Wait a minute...but you said..." she ran after him, but he ignored her, eventually disappearing down a side street. She whirled, returning to Daniel.

"Is he telling the truth? Is Bobs alive or is he dead?"

Daniel ran a hand through his hair, shaking his head helplessly. "I don't know. But if he is still alive, I'll eat my hat."

12

"Express for Mrs. Staletta May," a young boy of fifteen stood at the workshop door, holding out a letter.

Staletta snatched it up quickly, replying "thank you," and absent-mindedly passed him a coin.

"Thank you, ma'am," he said, darting off into the street once more.

Staletta already had the letter open and moved quickly in front of Daniel. "I can't read it, what does it say?"

Daniel looked down at his fingers, brown with wood stain. "Hold it steady and I'll read it to you."

"Okay, how's this?" Staletta said, holding it right in front of his face.

"Just a bit back – yes, that's it, okay," Daniel's eyes scanned the letter quickly, then returned to the top of the letter.

"Well?" Staletta eyed him impatiently. "What does it

say?"

"Star, I need you to get my hat for me."

Wrinkling her nose, Staletta lowered her arms. "What for?"

Daniel shook his head helplessly. "It is to be my lunch today apparently."

Staletta widened her eyes. "It's from Bob's isn't it?"

Shaking his head again, Daniel smiled. "You were right. He's alive."

Leaning back on her heels, Staletta clapped her hands, ever so slightly bouncing up and down. "I knew it." She waved the letter in the air. "What does he say?"

"He says he is delighted to hear you have found your brothers, that he would be honored to take us to India. He says we can depart as early as next week."

"Next week?" Staletta repeated, biting her fingernail. "So soon?"

"We have to go when he can," Daniel returned to the letter. "It says to meet him at St. Saviour's Dock next Saturday at 8:00am for departure."

"Does he say how much payment to bring?"

"The letter contains nothing else, not even a return address." Daniel scanned the letter one last time. "There is a postscript at the bottom that says he wishes to remain secret. I wonder why? Why pretend to be dead? I mean, even his daughter thinks he is dead."

Staletta folded the letter and placed it in her pocket. "Are you worried that we cannot trust him?"

"Yes," Daniel said with no hesitation.

"My one hope is that he is a changed man," Staletta

crossed her arms, thinking back to that moment on the pier when Bobs broke down in surrender.

"Only you spoke to him that day," Daniel shrugged. "All I saw was you tied up in ropes about to be abducted out to sea. That is not an easy thing for me to overlook."

"I understand," Staletta looked down. "Are you still on board? And if so, are we ready to depart so soon?"

He did not hesitate to respond, "I gave you my word."

Nodding, Staletta faked a smile, half turning away from him.

He grabbed her shoulder. "You doubt me?"

"It's not that," Staletta looked up at him, feeling a heaviness in her gut. "I feel awful about making you close the shop. Henry will be out of an apprenticeship. And who know's what danger I will be dragging us into..."

Daniel grabbed a towel to wipe the wood stain off his hands. Stepping closer to her, he wrapped his arms around her in reassurance. "Would India be my first idea for a honeymoon? Heaven's no. But when I pledged myself to you, I promised to always lead you, to always be with you no matter what. A poor husband I would be if I forsook you in your time of need."

Staletta sank into his embrace, burying her face in his chest. She stayed there for a minute, then pulled her head back to look up into his face. "I am asking a lot of you in this instance, and I would understand if you elected to stay behind."

"Never in a million years would I stay behind, Staletta May," he nudged her chin with his fist, grinning broadly. "Don't worry about the shop closing up. I took the liberty of speaking to Mr. Winchelsley. He is going to manage the shop in my absence. Henry will not be losing his apprenticeship. He will continue to learn from Mr. Winchelsley and will do what jobs he is able to do in the meantime, isn't that right, Henry?"

"Yes, boss," Henry replied, emerging from behind a bookcase. "No boss around for months at a time means I can do whatever I want and keep the money for myself, right?" Henry winked at Staletta.

"And that is exactly why Mr. Winchelsley will be supervising," Daniel laughed, turning back to Staletta. "You will need clothing appropriate for sea travel, Indian weather, and cross-country travel."

Staletta nodded. "I think I'll go over to Cynthia and see if she has any clothing that would be appropriate."

Staletta walked the few blocks that separated her from her best friend's shop. Stopping outside the building, she admired the fine gold lettering of the sign above the door that read: 'Cynthia Bobs, Dressmaker'. The shop window was filled up entirely with a mannequin wearing the largest, puffiest, most ruffly, and bow-bestrewn evening gown Star had ever seen. Its extravagance was out of this world, and she was quite sure only the richest of women would be able to afford it.

Pushing the door open, she delighted in the cheerful

sound of the bells ringing, announcing her arrival.

A young girl that was not Cynthia looked up and smiled. "How can I help you, miss?"

"I am looking for Cynthia. Will you tell her Staletta is here to see her?"

The girl nodded and disappeared into the back room. Staletta took a turn about the room, admiring the works in progress and the display models set beautifully around the room. She also had a section where you could purchase matching hats and purses and different sorts of hat pins and hair ornaments. Spotting a hat with a giant pink ostrich feather sticking out of it, Staletta had to try it on. She plucked it from the rack and stuck it on her head. Looking at herself in the mirror on the wall, Staletta laughed, "This is spectacular," she said aloud.

"That does not suit you," Cynthia cried, entering the room quickly.

Staletta whirled around and removed the hat from her head, placing it back primly on the rack. "Especially not where I'm going," she responded, chuckling.

Cynthia cocked her head, but made no reply. "Come on back, Staletta. It is good to see you."

"It is good to see you, too," Staletta followed Cynthia as she led her into the back office where stood Cynthia's desk, littered with sketches of various gowns and fabric swatches. "How are you? Business is good?"

"Business is great," Cynthia smiled, holding out her hands to indicate the entirety of her shop.

"You are where you are meant to be," Staletta noted the contented smile on her features, the satisfied light in her eyes, the ease with which she commanded her business. "And Eleanor? How is she?"

Cynthia waved a hand and rolled her eyes. "You should stop over at the factory sometime. See what she and Blue Ben have done with the place. It's almost unrecognizable."

"Yes, perhaps I will," Staletta looked off to the side, fingering her dress.

"Have a seat and tell me what you've been up to," Cynthia said, indicating a chair next to the desk. "I mean, I haven't seen you since the wedding. Martha, could you bring us some tea?"

The young girl replied yes and hurried away to get the tea things.

Staletta started to explain slowly, "There is bad news, then good news, then somewhat shocking news, I think."

"Start with the bad news," Cynthia said.

Martha returned with the tea things and passed them out to Cynthia and Staletta. Staletta took hers gratefully, but waited until the girl left before launching into her news. She started shakily, "I did write to tell you I was pregnant..."

Cynthia's teacup clattered in the saucer, "Don't tell me..."

"I lost the baby about two weeks ago."

Cynthia's face fell into shadow and her eyes widened. "Staletta—I don't know what to say. I'm so sorry for you."

Staletta stared at her cup, fingering the tiny handle.

"You should have come to me," Cynthia tisked. "I could have helped around the house during that time."

"I would have, but I was not in a right state of mind, I hope you understand."

Cynthia nodded. "Of course, dear."

"Danny was good to me through all of it."

"He's a good man."

"A much better man than the likes of me deserves, that's for sure." Staletta said, sipping her tea.

"Please," Cynthia shifted in her seat, "Tell me what is the good news you have?"

"The good news is," Staletta inhaled, sitting up straighter in her seat, cupping her tea, "I have finally found my brothers."

Cynthia raised an eyebrow. "You found them?"

"Not found them literally, but I know where they are, and I have a way to get to them."

Placing a hand over her heart, Cynthia exclaimed, "Where are they?"

"That's the shocking news. You see, they are in the army, stationed in India, fighting against the Rebellion," Staletta paused as understanding spread over Cynthia's face.

"You are not planning—"

"Planning a trip to India, yes," Staletta exhaled, shrugging her shoulders, and biting her lip. The urge to tell her her father was still alive filled her, but she bit it back. Bobs did not want his daughters to know just yet.

Cynthia's mouth dropped open in shock. "How frightening. You must be terrified?"

Shrugging, Staletta bunched her skirts in her hands

to wipe the sweat from them. "Terrified, excited, exhilarated..."

"Will you be going alone? Surely not! Danny is going? Have you come here to beg me to go with you? I can go with you, but I would need to hire another shop girl, maybe two, which could take some time to arrange..."

"Cynthia, stop," Staletta giggled, "Danny is coming with me. I will not allow you to leave your shop behind. We don't know how long we shall be away. We don't even know if we shall survive."

"Don't say such things as that," Cynthia said, reaching forward and grabbing her hand. "If you need anything, let me know."

"Well, since you ask," Staletta smirked, "I need something to wear. It'll have to be appropriate for cross country trekking, months aboard a ship, hot Indian weather, and who knows what else."

Nodding, Cynthia placed a finger on her chin. "You need something practical. Something light." Cynthia looked up to the ceiling, squishing her lips to the side in thought. "I have an idea," Cynthia looked down again, grinning, "I think that will do nicely."

"What's that?" Staletta asked, her eyes lighting up.

Cynthia turned to her desk, pulled out a fresh parchment, dipped her pen in ink, and quickly began to scratch the pen across the paper in quick succession. "A riding habit. It's a practical outfit. You'll be comfortable and should be able to blend in wherever you are."

Cynthia finished her quick sketch and held it up for Staletta to see. The sketch was of a girl wearing a skirt hitched up to reveal a pair of trousers beneath. A form flattering jacket and a blouse completed the ensemble. Cynthia continued sketching alongside the picture and showed it to Staletta again. "I'll make the jacket, trousers, and skirt out of a matching wool, with a white cotton blouse underneath."

"It's so elegant," Staletta remarked.

"The trousers will certainly help with modesty whilst riding horses or elephants, whichever you should come across," Cynthia smirked. "I think you will be quite comfortable indeed."

"I love it," Staletta shrugged. "Shall we make it blue?"

"That's your signature color, we must."

13

They ate in quiet, their eyes often swinging up to meet the other's as if in mute conversation.

Daniel finally broke the silence after passing a slice of tomato into his mouth. "Are you ready?"

Looking down at the plate of tomatoes, sausage, and eggs she had barely touched, Staletta shrugged. "I think so."

Nodding his agreement, Daniel took a drink of milk. "Better try to eat, I don't know what the food will be like aboard ship."

Staletta agreed half-heartedly, pushing the sausage around her plate with her fork. "Cynthia should be here soon." She remarked, taking a few tentative bites. "Wait 'til you see the outfit she has concocted for me."

Daniel grinned. "I prefer to see you with no outfit." He winked.

Laughing, Staletta grinned back at him.

"At long last," he remarked. "It makes my heart glad

to hear you laugh."

"I'm sorry, Danny-boy. I have not been myself lately, have I?"

"That is alright," he said, rising from the table. "Let's wash up the dishes for the last time."

Staletta quickly finished her breakfast, then, together, they washed and dried their few dishes.

Not long later, Cynthia arrived bearing a garment box in hand. She entered in a great rush. "Sorry I'm late," she said, laying the box on the table. "I still had to press and stitch the hem of the jacket this morning. It's not my best work, but, it's done and that's all that matters."

"Thank you, Cynthia." Staletta said, patting her on the shoulder. "You didn't have much time so I appreciate your efforts. I'm sure it will be stunning. Your work always is. Besides, where we are going, nobody will notice any skipped stitches or uneven lines."

"You think they don't, but they do," she argued, wagging a finger. "And when you tell them where you got this outfit, I don't want my good name soiled by a rotten hem job."

"Of course not," Staletta agreed, smiling broadly. "Thank you, Cynthia. Whatever shall I do without you?"

"Danny will keep you in line for me while you're gone," Cynthia said and nudged Daniel's arm playfully.

"I'll do my best anyway," he laughed.

Cynthia bid them goodbye. "Write to me?"

"If we can, we will," Staletta replied, giving her a hug.

The door closed behind Cynthia. Staletta finished cleaning up breakfast, and they packed the last few items they would need.

Slipping out of her house dress and into a fresh chemise, her fingers itched to see the outfit. She opened the lid of the box and pulled out the first item which she had not ordered: an embroidered summer-weight Symington corset made out of a lightweight mesh. It was a work of art: the bones perfectly aligned and hand-stitched in place, delicate floss embroidery designs in the shape and color of silvery blue stars at the top and bottom of every bone, and two delicate lines of blue insertion lace ran across the top and bottom. Staletta made a mental note to thank Cynthia for the corset. It was an expensive gift and she didn't know how she could ever hope to repay it.

Next, she pulled a matching corset cover out of the box and secured it over her corset, followed by a white cotton blouse.

Staletta pulled out of the box a pair of dark blue breeches, secured at the hip with brass buttons. Daniel helped her fasten the long, wool skirt around her waste, over the breeches. Lastly, Daniel held up the jacket for her to put her arms through the armholes. It was a beautiful blue wool jacket with a flat collar, one row of buttons up the center front, a leather belt synched around the waist, and the whole jacket was outlined in silver binding.

Staletta placed on her head her old blue hat with the ribbon dangling down the back.

Daniel gestured to the door. "It's time."

14

Daniel locked the door behind them. They paused. Daniel reached for her hand, squeezing tightly. Smiling, white teeth flashing in the sunlight, Staletta giggled. "The hard part is over."

"What is that?" Daniel asked, slipping the key into his pocket.

"Walking out the door." Staletta's lips thinned into a line as she let the comforts and security of home fly away on the breeze. "I'm ready."

"Let's go then," Daniel tugged on her arm and they set off down the street, heading towards St. Saviour's Dock, a mere half hour's walk from their home.

Staletta found St. Saviour's Dock to be rather on the small side. She had imagined it as a large dock on the Thames; rather it was an inlet, running between buildings leading out to the river.

"See him anywhere?" Daniel asked, peering out around the docks.

Shaking her head, Staletta crossed her arms. "We wait until he finds us?"

"Suppose so," Daniel walked along the edge, following the walkway until it led out to a more spacious area complete with a sidewalk café and a small crowd of people. "Let's wait here for a bit."

Too anxious to sit, Staletta took to pacing the dock and watching the people at the café. A whistle of music caught her ear. Turning to hear it better, she searched for the source, finding it coming from a boy with bare feet and holed breeches, sitting on a fence by the docks, playing on a wooden flute.

Intrigued, she watched as some passers by dropped a few coins in the slouchy hat lying on the ground in front of him. She stepped over to him, watching him closely, goosebumps forming on her arms. She dropped three pence into the hat, waited for him to finish the song he was playing, and then spoke.

"You play well."

"Thank you, ma'am," he said, grinning up at her.

"What's your name?"

"Archie," he replied, scrunching up his nose.

"Are you playing to bring home money for your family?"

Archie sniffed, wiping his nose with the back of his wrist. "I don't have a family. What's it to you?"

Staletta half-smiled. "I used to do the same thing." She turned her back, showing the violin strapped there.

The boy looked up at her, grinning. "No kidding! You ever went to the workhouse?"

"They tried," she said, nudging his arm, "but I ran away." She winked.

Archie laughed. "I like you, miss. I don't wanna go there. I like playing my music and I can take care of myself."

"I like you too, Archie. How old are you, may I ask?"

"I think I am eight years, ma'am. I usually say my birthday is in August, so I'll be going on nine here in about a month."

"How long have you been playing?"

"Since I could learn to walk, I think," he scratched his head. "Pa taught me."

"I see."

"He taught me a few songs before he died."

Staletta thought for a moment. "Do you like playing by the docks?"

"Yes, ma'am, get lots of different folks coming and going by, boarding ships and the like. Gotta be careful though, men always come by looking to take me off to the workhouse. I've learned to run fast and I learned to hide under the docks."

"I know that well," Staletta grimaced.

"What are you doing here?"

"My husband and I are about to board a ship."

"Where are you heading?" The boy scratched his nose.

"We're going to India."

The boy's eyes lit up. "They got elephants there, don't they?"

"I believe so," Staletta smiled.

"Maybe I could go with you?" The boy asked.

Taken aback, Staletta sputtered, "Why would you want to come with us?"

Archie shrugged, looking down at his hands, suddenly shy. "I don't know."

Staletta sighed. "I'm sorry, but India is no place for a child. It is dangerous there. I think you'd be much better off in a workhouse, as much as I hate to say it."

"Please, ma'am, don't let them send me there. I can't bear it, please ma'am? Please?"

Suddenly regretting her decision to talk with the boy, she turned to leave. "Keep playing your music, young Archie." She smiled and walked away, tossing another coin quickly into his hands.

She walked back to Daniel, where he gazed out at the river. "Look," he said, pointing. "There's a ship out there not too far. I wonder if that's him?"

"Could be," Staletta said, peering at where he had pointed. A rush of fear clenched her gut. "I wonder what he's like now? And what did that sailor mean when he said 'Bobs is dead'? What if it isn't even the real Bobs, just someone masquerading as him?"

Daniel humphed. "I don't know what to think, but I know I'm not looking forward to three months aboard ship with Bobs, even if it is a false Bobs."

Staletta looked around for a place to sit then walked closer to the fence where a row of benches waited. "Wait," she stopped, noticing a man walking towards them.

"Isn't that –" Daniel started.

"The man from the pub? Yes," Staletta finished. She looked up at Daniel. "I guess they are already here."

They picked up their luggage and met the man halfway. The man wore gray trousers and a white shirt. His grayish hair tangled in the wind. His eyes squinted at them through the glare of the sun. "Good, you're early," he said in greeting, stopping in front of them and shaking their hands.

"Where is the ship?" Staletta asked after shaking his hand. "I don't see the *Kathryn* docked here anywhere."

The man frowned, "There is no ship by the name of '*The Kathryn*'. The *Redeemed* sails away yonder."

"We have to wait for it, then?"

The man shook his head. "We'll be taking the dinghy out to meet the ship. If you're ready, you can come along with me."

"That's odd," said Daniel. "Why does he not dock at harbor?"

"Captain Alexander never goes ashore," the man said as he led them over to the dinghy.

Daniel and Staletta exchanged a look as they passed their luggage to the man who had stepped inside the dinghy and held his out hand for their bags.

"Are we sure we have the right ship?" Staletta asked him. "We were hoping for Smitherton Bobs, Captain of the *Kathryn*."

"Aye," the man said. "Though I'll thank you to keep that name to yourself. He goes by Captain Alexander and the ship is called the *Redeemed*."

Daniel finished handing the bags to the man, then helped Staletta into the boat before climbing in himself.

"Last chance to turn back," Staletta said to herself, as the man untied the boat and pushed off, rowing them out to sea.

Staletta and Daniel exchanged nervous glances, but both turned their eyes out to the coastline as they moved farther out into the river.

Smiling at Daniel, she laughed. "Can you believe we're doing this?" She asked.

Daniel shook his head, "Not in the least bit."

"Thank you for doing this for us," Staletta said to the man. "What is your name, by the way?"

The man tipped his head at her. "My name is Malachi."

"Very good to meet you, Malachi. I'm Staletta and this is my husband, Daniel."

"How long have you been a sailor, Malachi?" Daniel asked, shifting on the wood seat.

"I'd say most of my life. Apprenticed to a merchant vessel as a boy and so on and so forth." Malachi spoke as he rowed.

Staletta tore her eyes away from the docks and looked up at the ship as they neared. There on the railing awaiting their arrival, was none other than Smitherton Bobs...or Alexander as he wished to be called. Staletta stared at him in disbelief and even Daniel looked confused at the sight of his face.

Instead of a dark scowl, a joyful smile splayed across his face.

Staletta climbed the ladder up the ship and when she neared the top, Alexander held out a hand to help her up onto the deck. Daniel came next, followed by Malachi.

Staletta stared at the man she once knew, unable to utter a word. His gray streaked hair had grown so long it needed to be tied back with a ribbon. His loose white shirt billowed in the breeze and he wore a pair of tan trousers, with no shoes on his feet. It was such a contrast to the way he used to look: dark suit, close-cropped hair, lumbering, and dark in appearance.

"It is good to see all of you," he said shyly. "Staletta – Star, as beautiful as ever." He turned to Daniel and reached out to shake his hand, pumping it fervently. "Mr. May – er, Daniel."

"Daniel, or Danny, is fine," he replied.

Alexander nodded, wringing his hands. "Congratulations on the wedding."

Staletta smiled. "I see I am not the only one that has changed their name."

He nodded. "A story I am eager to relate to you in time. I can't thank you enough for how you've helped me. I am a – a changed man."

"That's obvious," Staletta laughed.

Alexander turned to help Malachi hoist the dinghy. "Why don't you go below decks and get settled in your cabin while we take care of this. Then we can have tea and I'll tell you about my new life."

"Great," said Staletta, "I can't wait to hear this story."

"Agreed," said Daniel, picking up their bags.

15

"After I talked with you for the last time, that day on my dock," Captain Alexander said as they sat around the table in the dining room, "I knew I had to get away. I realized, like a giant wave crashing down upon me, I had made such a mess of life, I didn't think – I mean, I needed to get away."

"I sailed away to think," Alexander continued, "I did not know where I was going or what I would be doing, but I went." He stopped to take a sip of tea. "It felt good to be free again, to be out on the ocean with no one else around. I could let everything go. I mean, it took a long time. I had so much anger, so much regret, so much hatred for myself, I did think of ending it. I'll be honest, I thought about it a lot. I crashed my beloved ship out on the reef, stranded myself offshore. There I prayed. I'd never prayed before...or so I thought. On my knees in the blaring sun, I cried out to the

Lord, and He delivered me. Years and years of darkness, washed away, just like that," he swept his arm out in front of him.

"That's amazing," Staletta said, truly awed by his testimony.

"I couldn't have done it without you," Alexander said, raising his eyes to hers. "You believed in me."

"On the contrary, I was disgusted with you," Staletta replied defensively. "I don't think any of the credit belongs to me."

Alexander laughed and nodded. "That is fair, but you pushed me; you pushed me over the edge. Nobody had ever pushed me before...and that's exactly what I needed."

"What have you been doing these last few months then?" asked Daniel.

"I'm glad you asked, Danny," Alexander said, turning his gaze on him. "I have started a new business. I help others. Whatever it is they need. Like you two. You need a ride to India, who better to help than me? Or, you need a shipment made to America, but the commercial lines are too expensive. Who better to help than me?"

"You can live on this business?" Daniel asked, interested greatly.

Alexander sat back and templed his fingers. "It's not a great money-making venture, but we aren't necessarily in the business of making money. I have a fantastic crew, all with similar stories to mine, a story of redemption. We believe in the mission and we are determined to keep it going for as long as possible."

"A fascinating story," said Daniel. "I commend you."

He raised his cup to the Captain.

"I still have my days where I struggle…" Alexander twisted his hands, staring fixedly at a spot on the table. He breathed in deep, shaking his head. He looked up to Staletta, eyes smiling once more. "I am glad to hear you found your brothers, well, at least know where to find them."

"Me too," she said.

"It is my fault you are separated," he said, a hauntedness creeping into his eyes. A dark shadow passed over his brow and he looked away.

The guilt was not a hundred percent gone, then, Staletta surmised. His past would forever pain him. He had done many things, things that would not be forgotten or buried, they would always be there lurking in the shadows. That was the nature of sin.

Staletta completed her thought outloud. "The nature of redemption, however, is learning you are forgiven, and you can, in fact, move on."

For the first time, Staletta truly felt those words were true.

16

The Thames began to widen. Daniel looked out beyond the English Channel to the Atlantic Ocean, sucking in his breath. He had never seen the ocean. The sight of it crashed over him, leaving him dizzy and disoriented. There was nothing but blue water and blue sky for as far as the eye could see. What terrifying nothingness lay ahead? No ground for a man to stand on. Nothing to see. Nothing to hear, but one's own terrifying thoughts. Yet, the ocean drew him further in: the beauty, the vastness, the mystery of what lay ahead.

"Star, are you seeing this?" He called over his shoulder, then paused when he noticed her against the stern railing, looking back towards home.

She had removed her jacket and skirt, wearing just the white blouse and the blue trousers, and had put her hair back in a braid. The wind had already tousled her hair, giving her a look of relaxed beauty. She looked wild and it reminded him of the day he had met her, untamed, with little sense of propriety. One of her arms crossed below her chest, the elbow of her other arm resting on the other arm, biting her thumb nail. His eyes narrowed, wondering what she was thinking.

Daniel walked over to her, placing a hand on her shoulder to break her from her reverie. She smiled at him, lowering her arm to cross over the other.

"What are you staring at?" She asked, noticing the attentive look in his eye.

Laughing, he leaned against the railing. "Admiring the beautiful woman I married. But I noticed something..."

"What's that?" She pulled tendrils of hair back behind her ear.

"Your gaze has been fixed on where we have come from, not where we are going."

Shrugging, she sighed. "I am hoping we made the right decision. Back there lies the familiar, the comfortable. Out there..." she turned slowly, leaning her back against the railing and gazing out into the blue "...is the unknown, the frightening."

"Fair enough," said Daniel, chuckling at her wit. "What do you fear the most?"

Drumming her hands on the railing, she looked up at him askance, thinking. "I fear myself."

Daniel breathed out through his nose. "What do you mean by that?"

"I fear my past, the choices I make, the circumstances I get myself into. I fear my purpose in life, my curses in life," she unconsciously dropped a hand to her stomach. "I fear the future; what may or may not happen."

Daniel picked at the wood on the railing. "What you fear most is your fate."

She half-smiled at him, "I never thought of that."

"It makes sense," Daniel shrugged, looking down at her. "Fate is like the wind, you try to catch it in the sails and control it, but sometimes it rages harder than the sails can handle. Yet, sometimes, it barely even ripples the surface."

Staletta smiled broadly. "Daniel the Philosopher."

He chuckled, brushing her cheek with his hand, and winking. "Don't worry, our fates are intertwined. I will always be by your side. I will never leave you nor forsake you."

"Nor will I ever leave you, Danny-boy," she rubbed his arm, then his back. "And what is it you fear the most, husband?"

"Me?" He asked, breathing deeply the fresh sea air. "You...being in pain. I cannot bear the thought of that. Or, for that matter, anyone in my family getting hurt or sick."

Resting her head on his arm, she continued rubbing his back, saying nothing in response.

Captain Alex walked out of the cabin, stopping right outside the door. Staletta watched him take a deep breath and look around. When his eyes landed on them, he patted his stomach, hooked his hands in his pockets and sauntered over.

"Fine weather," he remarked. "Rain for tomorrow, though."

"How do you know, Captain?" Staletta asked.

"You can feel it in the wind."

17

With the sun beginning to set, a bell rang out, and Captain Alex called over to them from the helm. "Dinner time."

Daniel and Staletta had moved over to the bow, still staring out at the sea, watching the English coastline glide past. At Captain Alex's voice, they moved over to join him. He gestured for them to proceed him across the deck and over to the dining room.

A sailor popped out, stopping the captain. "Sir, we have found something below decks you need to see."

"What could you possibly have found that I need to see right this minute?"

The sailor twitched, then threw back his shoulders. "There's a stowaway aboard."

The captain itched his nose. "You found a stowaway? Where?"

"The broom cupboard, Sir."

"Is he dangerous?" the captain pulled back his head, making his hands into fists.

The sailor shook his head, grimacing. "It's a child, Sir."

Surprise lit the captain's face and he inadvertently chuckled. "Very well," he spread out his hands. "Bring him to me."

Staletta's gut clenched when a few moments later, the sailor ushered the boy up onto the deck. "Archie?" She cried.

Captain Alex raised an eyebrow. "You know this boy?"

Dumbfounded, Staletta shook her head. "I met him on the dock when we were waiting for you. Archie, what are you doing here?"

The boy shrugged, smiling sheepishly. "I dunno, ma'am. You were kind to me and a trip to India sounded more fun than sitting on the docks, so I thought I'd—"

"—stowaway aboard a ship heading out to one of the world's most dangerous places with complete strangers?" Staletta glowered down at the boy, an overwhelming surge of protectiveness coming over her.

Archie shrugged again, "Yes."

"How did you get aboard, young man?" Captain Alex knelt beside him, genuine curiosity and not anger splayed on his brow.

"I hid in a sack in the dinghy," Archie shrugged. "I snuck in while that man..." he pointed to Malachi "...was on deck talking to them. Since you thought I was luggage, you just hoisted me right up on board."

"Sneaky," The captain smiled and winked.

Archie beamed, causing Staletta to fold her arms over her chest and shake her head.

"What should we do with him?" asked the captain.

Shaking her head, Staletta sighed. "We'll have to take him back."

Daniel nodded his agreement. "I'm sorry, Archie, but we can't take you along. It's far too dangerous."

The edges of Archie's smile sagged like soggy sandbags. He blinked several times. Licking his lips, he stood tall, squaring back his shoulders. "Begging your pardons," he said, "But if you were alone on the streets like a poor boy like me," here he paused, looking at Staletta with dewy eyes, "wouldn't you seek the help of the nice people that take notice of you?"

"Archie, do not try that with me," Staletta said sternly. Then her voice softened. "I'm sure you understand why you cannot come."

"You'd leave me for dead on the streets, but you won't take me with you?" Archie pouted. "Sure, I understand perfectly."

Staletta turned to Daniel helplessly. Daniel grimaced, his eyes betraying how torn he was. "It would be cruel of us to cast him back to the streets," he conceded after several moments of thought. "We will take him to the orphanage, that's the best place for him."

"I won't go to no orphanage," Archie objected fiercely. "I'd throw myself into the sea before I step foot in one of them."

Daniel rubbed his brow, glancing at Staletta.

Shifting uncomfortably, she shook her head. "I will not take him to an orphanage, nor will I leave him on the streets. Maybe your parents would take him in? Or the Winchelsleys?"

Captain Alex clapped his hands. "Let us eat, then, after prayer and a belly full, the right answer might present itself. Shall we?"

Deciding that was the best course of action, the group gathered in the dining room where plates of venison and boiled vegetables awaited them. At first, Archie hung back as if unsure he was welcome. A gentle push on the shoulder from Captain Alex assured him he was.

"Oh boy," He exclaimed, slipping into a chair next to Staletta, beaming from ear to ear.

"Careful," Staletta warned. "Don't eat too quickly or you'll get a stomach-ache."

"Yes, ma'am," he said, digging into the food with relish.

"Archie," Captain Alex said, "won't you tell us how you came to be orphaned?"

Archie swallowed a lump of potatoes and blinked several times. He shrugged, "a bout of sickness got my family, my parents and my baby sister."

"And how did you end up on the streets?" He continued. "Did you have no other extended family? No family friend willing to take you in?"

"I don't know, Sir," Archie put his fork down, forgetting his food. "Not in London anyway. I wasn't there when they died. I wasn't allowed to see them. They told me they were dead and I didn't want to believe them so I ran away. I've been out on the streets ever since."

"I understand," Staletta spoke to him softly, lowering her fork. His story was so similar to her own, it tugged on her heartstrings. Stifling the urge to hug him, she whispered, "My family is also dead. Except two of my brothers and that is who we are going to find in India."

"I sure do hope we find them, miss," Archie looked up to her, smiling sadly. "Everyone needs a family."

18

After dinner, the captain weighed anchor. The sailors gathered beneath the light of the lanterns and of the stars. Malachi pointed up to the night sky, teaching Archie the constellations and how to navigate by the stars. Captain Alex leaned on the railing, also looking up, a sense of peace surrounding him.

Staletta felt Daniel's weight as he leaned into her shoulder and his hot breath tickled her ear. "You sympathize with the boy."

She nodded, feeling her hair catch on the stubble on Daniel's cheek. "I understand him. I was no different. I cannot blame him for wanting to come along." Turning her face up to Daniel, she locked eyes with him. "But even so, we both know we cannot bring a child into a war."

"Of course not, it would be irresponsible and cruel." Daniel breathed a sigh of relief. "When shall we tell him?

Now or in the morning?"

She hesitated, watching Archie gaze at the stars reflected on the peaceful waters, eyes full of wonder. "The morning."

"I agree, let him have this night of adventure," Daniel wrapped his arm around her, giving her shoulders a soft squeeze.

Captain Alex cleared his throat. "Staletta plays a mighty fine violin. Shall we beg her to play for us?"

The crew perked up, voicing their agreement.

Staletta waved them away, but the crew shouted louder, clapping their hands, and whistling. A sailor named Bobby said, "Come on, then, play us a tune. We don't bite."

"Okay, okay, let me go get it," She stood to retrieve her violin from the cabin and returned, already beginning to play as she walked back. "Any requests?" She asked the crew, still playing a low quiet tune.

"*Come Loose Every Sail to the Breeze,*" Bobby cried out.

"I don't know that one," said Staletta. "You'll have to sing it for me until I get the tune of it."

Bobby put his fingers up as if he were conducting, "Come lads, sing: '*Come, loose every sail to the breeze. The course of my vessel improve; I've done with the toils of the sea, Ye sailors, I am bound to my love.*"

On the chorus everybody started singing:

Ye sailors, I'm bound to my love,

Ye sailors, I'm bound to my love,

I've done with the toils of the seas,

Ye sailors, I'm bound to my love.

Catching the tune quickly, Staletta played the next few stanzas to the accompaniment of Archie's flute and the wild and reckless dancing of the sailors.

"Everybody sing on the last stanza," Captain Alex cheered, "Or you'll walk the plank."

Everyone laughed, clapped, and stomped their feet as they sang the last stanza:

Then hoist every sail to the breeze,

Come, shipmates, and join in the song;

Let's drink while the ship cuts the seas,

To the gale that may drive her along.

Ye sailors, I'm bound to my love,

Ye sailors, I'm bound to my love,

I've done with the toils of the seas,

Ye sailors, I'm bound to my love.

Staletta finished the song, elegantly falling into a curtsy as the sailors whooped and cheered. She then held her arm out towards Archie and he also took a bow as the crowd cheered.

After that, they settled down, gazing out to the sea, thinking their own thoughts. Archie goaded Bobby into teaching him how to tie a knot. When he had accomplished it, he whooped for joy and the sailors around him applauded. Archie turned to Staletta and Daniel, holding up his knot, "I did it. I did it."

"Well, done, Archie," Staletta called and they clapped for him.

Daniel leaned over to Staletta, "You like this boy."

"Yes," she acknowledged, putting her arms around him in a hug. "Yes, I do."

"Not changing your mind, are you?"

She bit her lip. "Of course not."

19

Rain pattered on the roof of the dining room as they gathered for the morning breakfast.

Archie ignored the plate of food in front of him, his eyebrows bunched together giving him a serious expression. "Have you decided to make me part of your group or not? I can make knots for you and carry your bags. I can make a fire and gather wood. And I won't be a bother, I promise, I won't be."

Daniel raised a hand. "Absolutely not, Archie. We are going into a war zone. We cannot, in good conscience, bring you along."

Archies features crumpled as Daniels words pummeled into him.

"It is not that we don't want you, Archie," Staletta paused, searching for words. "We like you, and it's because we like you that we cannot bring you. Does that make sense?"

Folding his arms over his chest, Archie shook his head. "You think I will be a nuisance; I get it."

"It's too dangerous," Daniel clenched his jaw. "We will turn around and take you back to London. We hope to place you in the care of Mr. and Mrs. Winchelsley. They will take good care of you. They have two boys about your age that you can play with."

Taking deep breaths to calm himself, Archie frowned. "You think I am a child."

"You are a child, Archie," Daniel held out his hands. "And we are the adults. This is our decision to make."

Archie pushed back his chair, the legs scraping against the wood floor. He pointed to him and Staletta. "You are not my parents. I don't have parents. I am on my own. I am my own boy. I take care of myself. It's my decision to make."

Daniel passed a glance to Staletta, and she cringed. "I don't know what to say, Danny. On the one hand, I think it a terrible idea. On the other, well, I've been in this boy's shoes. I understand him."

Leaning back, Daniel ran a hand through his hair. "I don't believe this."

Archie brightened, leaning against the table towards Staletta. "If you agree with me, but still don't want me to come along, then I will know in my heart that you don't want me. And if you don't like me and don't want me, then I will go back to the streets."

Staletta placed a hand on her heart. "Oh, Archie…"

"Star, he's manipulating you," Daniel pinched the bridge of his nose.

"Daniel, have some compassion," she shot back. "Archie has gone through hardships a full-grown man could not weather, and he is standing here now, asking to be treated like a man. Are we to refuse him that?"

Sighing deeply, Daniel glanced from Staletta to Archie, then back to Staletta, shaking his head. "A tigress you are." He bit his lip. "You tear me to pieces, and I cannot refute you."

Archie glanced at Staletta. "What is he saying, miss?"

A smile grew on Staletta's lips. "I think he is granting you your own will. Is that right, Danny-boy?"

Daniel took a moment to compose himself, then folded his hands on the tabletop, looking hard at Archie. "You are a child. I know your decision will be clouded by a sense of adventure, so I give you this warning. Adventure is not all starlight and sea shanties. Danger awaits in the heart of the jungle. I want you to look out that window, at those gathering clouds turning blacker by the minute. Those clouds foretell a storm is coming and they promise many more to come. Archie, I am asking you to consider the danger and decide for yourself what you want to do."

Archie looked out at the window, trembling at the blackish clouds as thunder rumbled in the distance. He turned back to them, determination in his eyes. "I want to come with you."

Daniel's shoulders tensed and he breathed in deeply, holding his hands out helplessly. "Why?"

"Because," Archie paused, shifting his weight from one foot to the other. "She was kind to me."

Shoulders relaxing, Daniel ran his tongue along his teeth, raising an eyebrow. "That is a terrible reason." He sighed. "Nevertheless, it is your decision to make. If you want to come with, you shall."

Staletta let out the breath that she had been holding throughout the whole conversation, nervously glancing at Archie, watching the obvious relief pass over his face. For whatever reason, this boy had attached himself to her and Daniel. She worried her lip with her teeth. She liked the boy. She understood him. She would have to be careful, she decided. If she got too close, he would surely go the way of her family and perish. The thought of both Daniel and Archie dying on this trip made her catch her breath. She leaned forward, grasping the edge of the table. She opened her mouth to call it off, to say that she would not allow Archie to come along...

"It is decided then," Captain Alex declared. "Archie, welcome aboard the *Redemption* where new life awaits." He turned to look at Staletta and Daniel, nodding towards the black clouds hovering just beyond the window. "Brace yourselves for the storm. I suggest lashing yourself to your bunks below decks."

He stood then, grabbing his hat. He walked out the door, shouting to his crew, "Man the foredeck, let go the sails."

Staletta and Daniel bolted out of the cabin. Staletta shivered, surprised to find the temperature had dropped.

The rain lashed into her face as she looked around, watching the sailors work with practiced ease, running about deck in response to the commands coming down from the helm. She looked up to see Captain Alex skilfully manning the wheel and surveying the workers below.

For a moment, Staletta had a flashback to the sewing room at Bob's Manufactory. Bobs staring at his workers with hatred and contempt, wanting nothing more than to make their lives as miserable as possible. Coming back to herself, she shook off the memory.

Daniel called up to him, "Captain, is there anything we can do to help?"

Captain Alex looked down at them and chuckled. "Not going to stay below, are you? Well, then, flatten the jib and unhail the rudder."

Staletta and Daniel looked at each other and shrugged.

Captain Alex laughed and pointed at a sailor off to their right, "You there, Tosh, our passengers want to learn the ropes. You want to give them their first lesson?"

Tosh, a young man about Staletta and Daniel's own

age, turned around to them, grinning. He had a rope in each hand and leaned backwards, using his body weight to keep the mizzen mast steady.

"Sure," he called back, "what else have I got to do today." He winked at them. "Alright, you two, grab a rope. It's going to be a wild ride."

Throughout the morning, Stalella and Daniel helped tighten the ropes and followed Tosh's orders. By the end of the afteroon, the storm had finally calmed down. Bobby showed them how to roll out the canvas and then it was smooth sailing once again. The pair plopped down next to the main mast, exhausted and thoroughly soaked. Archie came running out of the cabin, where he had stayed during the storm, freed at last.

"Aww, I missed the fun," he said, his face sour.

"I don't know if I would call that fun," Daniel replied.

Captain Alex walked down the stairs from the helm to join them. "Aye, sometimes a storm is what a person needs. The storm will humble you, force you to remember you are not the most powerful thing in the universe. But they also encourage you, force you to work hard as a team to bring the ship safely through it." He rubbed his hands together, water dripping off his hair. "Aye, it's my favorite time to sail."

"Will it storm much on our journey?" asked Archie.

Captain Alex nodded his head. "That was only a taste of the storms to come."

20

"Where are we?" Staletta asked Captain Alex after scrambling down from the crow's nest for the first time. "I feel lost out here."

Captain Alex chuckled and winked. "Aye, it's easy to lose yourself out here, but sail long enough and you might just find yourself." Captain Alex pointed off to the right. "We are sailing through the English Channel. Over there is England," he switched to pointing to the left, "and over there is France."

"I can't see any land, nor other vessels, it must be terribly far way," Staletta crossed her arms, shivering. Daniel and Archie joined her next to the helm beside the captain.

"Not so far," the captain's lips shrugged. "About thirteen leagues. Tomorrow we'll glimpse the light of the Eddystone Lighthouse, slip out into the Atlantic, and there you'll meet with the true meaning of the word isolation."

Malachi, evidently overhearing their conversation, brought over a map and stretched it out on the top of a barrel. He jabbed a finger at a small dot on the map at the base of England. "That's the lighthouse."

Dragging his finger over, he mapped the course they will take. His finger moved down along the coast of Africa, then tapped his finger at the big open space to the left of the continent. "Nothing but ocean on this side for leagues and leagues and leagues. If we went all the way across, we'd reach the Americas."

Archie raised up on his tiptoes to better see the map. "Which of the spots is India?"

Chuckling, Malachi moved his finger down and around Africa, then went straight up to a spot that resembled a triangle jutting into the water. "That's where we are headed."

"That doesn't seem so bad," Archie declared. "Think we'll be there by next week?"

Malachi's eyes went wide, and he shook his head, glancing at Daniel. "Do you want to tell him or shall I?"

"Archie," Daniel grimaced, putting a hand on his shoulder. "It's a three-month voyage."

Archie relaxed back onto his heels, eyes widening. "Three months?"

"We're going to be a long way from home, unfortunately," he added.

One side of the boy's mouth lifted in a grin. "Aye. I didn't realize that."

Patting his back, Daniel added. "And Lord only

knows how long we'll be in India. Could be a whole year."

Archie cocked his head, nodding. "But I ain't afraid, Sir. I don't have a home to be at otherwise anyway."

"The kids a brick," Malachi lauded. "Sounds like a sailor in the making."

"Can you teach me to be a sailor?" He asked, eyes sparkling.

"Sure, we can," Malachi swept his hand out. "Come along."

Staletta started when Archie turned to her suddenly and asked, "Can I?"

She sputtered. "It's fine by me. Daniel?"

Daniel nodded. "Permission granted. Run along."

When Archie and Malachi had moved down to the main deck, Staletta turned to Daniel. "I thought he was his 'own man', why did he ask for permission?"

"He may seem older than his years, but Archie is still a child."

Staletta thought a moment, struggling to find the right words. Her face scrunched as if it left a bitter aftertaste. "I've never been responsible for a child before. I'm not ready for this."

Daniel nodded in comprehension. "You'll get used to it."

"What if I have to say no to him at some point or punish him?" She bit her lip, fiddling with her hair. "What if he cries?"

Hiding a smile, Daniel turned her to face him directly. "I'll let you in on a well-known secret, children crave instruction. They need it and thrive on it. You'll see.

Besides, Archie is a different sort. Look at him. He is eager to learn. He's a smart boy and not shy of hard work. I don't feel he'll give us much trouble."

"It appears the boy is growing on you, too," She smiled broadly, raising an eyebrow at him.

She received a chuckle in reply.

"Fine weather, we are having," said Captain Alex, making Staletta jump. He had been so quiet, she forgot he was there. "Can't ask for a better start to the voyage."

"Do you expect the fine weather to last?" asked Staletta.

"I doubt it," the captain winked at them. "I'd suggest enjoying it while you can."

"Shall we go see what help we can be amongst the sailors?" Daniel suggested, rubbing his hands together eagerly.

"You're like Archie," she noted. "Eager to learn, eager to work with your hands."

"Mmm," he agreed, making his way to the steps. "Uncomfortable with idleness."

Staletta peered out over the empty ocean. "It's going to be a long voyage."

21

Barely discernable through the rain induced fog, the Eddystone Lighthouse glowed dimly in the distance. Staletta rubbed her arms. The temperature had dropped, the winds had picked up, and the sun had disappeared behind the clouds, leaving the air considerably cooler and the atmosphere far gloomier than the previous days. Staletta ambled around the deck, feeling the ship rock towards starboard, then rock towards the port side, then back to starboard, port, starboard, port, and a rush of acrid bile rose to Staletta's throat. She ran to the rail just in time to release it into the ocean below.

Steadying herself on the railing, she wiped her mouth on the back of her hand, closing her eyes, and wishing for nothing more than solid ground beneath her feet. Rain droplets pattered on her cheeks and she allowed their coolness to calm the dizziness. With eyes still shut, she focused on the feel of the wind as it whipped her clothes about her skin, wisps of hair whipping at her face. She breathed in deep the wet, briny wind, letting it fill her with its freedom.

Opening her eyes, she smiled, feeling much better.

"The wind beckons, does it not?"

Captain Alex's voice drifted down to her from the helm. She looked up and nodded.

"Would you like to sail her?"

"You mean the ship?" Staletta asked, calling through the wind.

Captain Alex waved her up. "Come on."

Staletta hurried up to the helm, fingers trembling at the thought of steering the ship. "Are you sure?"

The captain stepped aside and the wheel started to spin. "Better hold on or we'll fly off course."

Terrified, Staletta grabbed the wheel and steadied it. "What do I do?"

"Hold her steady," he held up his compass. "Stay on a southwesterly course."

The wind pulsed, forcing the wheel hard to the left. Staletta gasped at the force, throwing her weight into it, to pull it back steady. The wind fell as quickly as it had arisen. The wheel jumped to the far right as Staletta overcorrected and the whole ship lurched to the side.

"Sorry," Staletta called out to a few sailors who were up in the rigging. "Sorry about that."

Laughing, Captain Alex steadied himself beside her. "You're doing fine. See how the wind plays with you. To master her, you must anticipate her every whim and her every fury. You must move with her. Understand her."

The wind lurched and Staletta reacted a second too late, causing the ship to rock once more. "It's too powerful."

Reaching a hand up to steady the wheel for her, the captain shook his head. "You'll get it. Notice the sails, how they expand and contract with the movement of the wind. Watch the water. See, right there," he pointed to a spot on the water, "see how it begins to rise, it's coming. Now move the wheel in anticipation, just a hair, that's it, then the wind will hit..."

Staletta watched the sails expand, felt a tug on the wheel, but the captain positioned it so the slightest turn of the wheel brought it under submission. The ship rocked, but it did not lurch.

"See, you can anticipate the wind and instead of fighting it, you move with it," The Captain removed his hand and let her take over again. "That's a lesson I didn't fully understand until after I had met you."

Staletta watched the waves begin to rise, the sails started to puff, and she moved the wheel, catching the wave and riding it out. "I'm proud of you, Captain."

At the feel of her muscles beginning to burn, she released the wheel and stepped away, making room for him to take over. "But you didn't have to run away. You could have stayed; got to know your daughters in a new light."

At the mention of his daughters, the captain froze. "I wasn't sure if they would ever want to see me again."

"Of course, they would," Staletta crossed her arms. "They would at least want to know you are alive."

"I don't quite see what that would accomplish," he

replied, voice a tad frosty.

"I understand the new name, new life picture you have going here, but you should, at the very least, let them know you are still alive, don't you think?" Staletta pressed, but her voice softened at the pained look settling on his features like dust onto an old pot. "Or are you not quite ready for that yet?"

He took an unsteady breath and nodded vigorously. "That is a wind that I am not yet ready to sail."

"Understood," Staletta smiled sadly.

Bobby called down from the crow's nest, "Lighthouse ahead."

As they hadn't seen land for days, this being the ninth day of their journey, the crew and the passengers gathered on deck to watch as the distant specter of rocky cliffs glimmered on the horizon.

"What country is that, Sir?" Archie asked Captain Alex as they gathered on the upper deck to get the best view.

"That is Spain. Cape Finisterre."

After days of rain, the sun had finally come out again, and Staletta squinted through the glare of it. "What are the Spanish like?"

Captain Alex shrugged. "Different."

"It seems foreign to me. So many different worlds I know nothing about."

"Me either," Daniel replied, "although Mr.

Winchelsley did show me many books on Spanish woodworking designs. They are full of color and intricate patterns."

"Can we get any closer?" Archie asked. "I'd sure love to stop and go exploring."

Captain Alex chuckled. "I'm afraid not."

"We're on a mission," Daniel added, smiling down at him. "But maybe on the return journey we could stop."

"Awww," Archie frowned, looking off dreamily at the distant rocks. "Okay."

"You could go up to the crow's nest and look through the telescope," Daniel suggested.

Archie brightened, shouting, "Okay," and sped off up the mast.

Daniel took Staletta by the hand, leading her off to the forecastle deck. "I've been meaning to ask you: since we have free time, would you like for me to teach you how to read and write?"

"I would," she smiled and sat herself down by the foremast. "Where do we start?"

Daniel sat down beside her, pulling out a small Bible and a journal and pen. "We'll start with the alphabet, get you learning what the letters look like and what they sound like, then we'll start reading."

"Sounds easy enough," Staletta rested her head back and listened as Daniel wrote down the alphabet in the journal. She then repeated the sounds back to him multiple times, then scratched out the symbols herself, her tongue sticking out in concentration.

They worked until the temperature started to drop

as the sun began to set, painting the sky in an array of wine-colored storm clouds with smears and swirls of reds, pinks, and blues. Staletta leaned her head against Daniel. "I don't much like being out here on the ocean, but I could get used to the sunsets."

"Even if those storm clouds no doubt mean a sleepless night lies ahead?"

Laughing, Staletta wrinkled her nose and got to her feet, stretching her arms out above her head. "Hmm, maybe not so much."

After dinner, Staletta, Daniel, and Archie retired to their cabin. Staletta could already feel the floor beneath her feet starting to roll, and heard the wind begin to whistle past the ropes. She and Daniel settled into their bunk, Daniel's arm securely tightened around her. As the ship rocked, their bodies bumped into each other, causing their heads to swim with dizziness. More than once, Archie fell out of his bunk and onto the hard floor with a grunt.

"That's it," Archie stated, pulling the blankets off the bed, and smashing them into a corner. He lay down, wedging himself in between the walls and the bunk to keep from rolling around. "Ah, that's better."

Eyes shut, Staletta curled up in a ball, doing the best she could to restrict her stomach muscles, but it was no good. A spasm wracked through her and she reached for the bucket, leaning over the edge of the bunk.

Daniel shifted behind her, then choked, then

shouted, "Hand me that bucket."

Staletta quickly rolled over, passing off the bucket just in time for Daniel to grab it and empty his dinner. He laid back, jamming the pillow over his head. "Make it stop."

Laying her head on his bare chest, she groaned. "I'll get right on that."

The winds rocked the ship the entire night, but ceased with the rising of the sun. The three passengers arrived on deck with grim expressions, lines etched beneath dark eyes, and hair sticking out in odd directions.

Malachi sauntered over, handing them each an apple and a slice of cheese.

At the sight of the food, Staletta's gut clenched. She noticed even Archie, who was the most seaworthy of the three, waved the food away in favor of a large glass of water.

The winds blew for the next few days, leaving them feeling seasick more often than not. Daniel continued his lessons with Staletta and when they felt too sick to even do that, they laid out on the deck playing cards or Spot the Vessel. The sailors had taught them the latter game: the person that spots another vessel first gets an extra ration of salted beef.

Staletta was the first to spot the next landmark as she was taking a turn up in the crow's nest. She gasped as majestic, dewy cliffs suddenly appeared out of the water, their beauty taking her breath away. It took her several minutes of staring at the lush green cliffs before finally calling down, "Land ho."

She scrambled down the mast and over to the captain. "Land ahead, Captain," she reiterated. "Beautiful green cliffs. I've never seen anything like it."

"Ah, the Island of Madeira, off the coast of Morocco. Well done, Staletta," He congratulated.

Bobby came running up, a slab of preserved beef in his hand. He presented it to her ceremonially. "I shall now present to today's winner of Spot the Vessel, one extra ration of salted, preserved beef. Staletta May, you may eat your beef."

Staletta bowed, taking up the beef and nibbling at it while she laughed.

"Enjoy it," Captain Alex warned. "That's the last land we'll see in two, even three weeks."

Staletta laughed at that, but two more weeks passed. He had been right, no land had been spotted, no ships had been spotted, and they had come to being happy at just seeing a bird in the sky or a small fish in the sea. The air had steadily grown hotter with each passing day. The sun scorched down upon them in a way she had never experienced in England.

Staletta and Archie stood together at the rail, looking down at the water.

"I wish I could jump in it and go for a swim," Archie said dreamily, a bead of sweat rolling down his forehead.

"Me too," Staletta nodded her agreement, licking her lips at the thought of a bath.

Daniel walked over, two small glasses in his hands. "Malachi said to drink this." He handed a glass to each one.

"What is it?" Staletta asked, sniffing the clear liquid, and perking up at the citrusy scent.

"Lime juice," Daniel replied. "To ward off scurvy."

Malachi strode up a few minutes later to collect the glasses.

Archie tugged on his arm. "Where are we? Why is it getting so hot?"

"We are running a course off the coast of Africa, heading towards the Equator-the center of the world," Malachi smiled, taking the glasses in his hands.

"Unbelievable," Staletta shook her head, feeling lost. "Malachi, what day is it?"

"It's Sunday, August 15th," he replied. "We've been out to sea over three weeks. How does it feel?"

"Surreal," Staletta said.

As if to accentuate her point, Archie suddenly cried out, "Flying fish, flying fish."

They turned and ran to the rail, peering down to where he pointed at the water. Sure enough, a school of blue fish skimmed over the top of the water, gossamer wings sparkling in the sharp sunlight.

"They're beautiful," Archie gazed lovingly at the flying fish, watching, enraptured, as they dove into the water and then up, taking flight, soaring over the water like birds. Then he wobbled, grabbing at the rail as something large bumped into the hull of the ship, then again, and again.

From the crow's nest came the warning, "Sharks below."

22

"Sharks? Oh boy," Archie leaned over the railing, peering down into the water.

"Careful." Her stomach flip flopping, Staletta hooked a finger through a belt loop on the back of his trousers, eyeing the slick gray skins of the sharks writhing through the water. "You'll fall overboard and become chum."

"Will they take down the ship?" Archie asked, wide-eyed.

Daniel shook his head, chuckling. "The vessel is too big. They are after the fish anyway."

"Awww, bugger."

"What are you staring at?" Captain Alex sidled beside them, peering overboard at the spectacle drawing his sailors to the railing. "Ah, they call that a shiver of sharks." He winked at the boy. "Want to catch one?"

"Oh boy, would I ever," Archie looked up with shining eyes. "But how?"

Taking a step back and twiddling a toothpick in his mouth, Captain Alex addressed his men. "Ready the shark catcher, men. Let's show these city folks how to fish. Quickly, 'afore the sharks start to run."

The men scrambled, running towards a hatch below the mizzen mast. They dove inside, emerging seconds later with a giant net in their arms. They took an edge and fanned it out, having to untangle it in a few spots, then brought it over to the railing.

"Grab an edge there, Archie," said Bobby, grinning widely.

Archie latched on, grasping the edge of the net with trembling hands.

"Heave ho." Captain Alex gave the command, and as one, the sailors heaved the net over the railing where it plopped in the water below.

"How does it work?" Archie asked as Bobby handed him a handle attached to the net hanging in the ocean.

"We wait for a shark to swim into the net, then we pull," Bobby explained.

"How do you know when a shark has swum in the net?" Archie pressed.

"You'll know," Bobby winked.

They didn't have long to wait. After a few moments, the net began to twitch.

"Wow, there, sailors," Captain Alex called. "Heave."

Staletta grasped Daniel's hand and they moved back, giving Archie and the sailors room to work. Together, the men braced themselves and pulled, calling, "Ho."

"Heave."

The sailors took a step back, "Ho."

"Heave."

Then another, "Ho."

"Heave."

After a few more pulls, the sailors stopped as the captain called out, "Halt."

Malachi handed Captain Alex a musket. Positioning himself above where the net hung over the rail, the captain aimed, and a shot rang out across the ocean.

The net kicked and bucked, but a few moments after the shot, it began to still.

The sailors cheered and started hauling the net up and over the railing, until the shark spilled over onto the deck. They moved quickly, extricating the shark fins from the net, exposing its monstrous size, gore encrusted teeth, and coal-black eyes.

"We'll be eating shark tonight, boys," Bobby exclaimed. "And gal," he added, winking up at Staletta.

"I don't think shark sounds good to me," Staletta chuckled, wrinkling her nose at the fishy smell of the beast.

"They're a delicacy in these waters," Captain Alex said. "Once you get past the smell of ammonia, they're not so bad."

"Yuck." Staletta elbowed Daniel. "Are you going to try that?"

Daniel grinned and shrugged. "Of course." Then walked forward to help the sailors move the fish to an appropriate spot for skinning and gutting.

A suffocating odor of fishy urine assailed her nose as the sailors hacked into the shark. Staletta grabbed her stomach and rushed for the rail.

Since the sailors were busying themselves with the shark, Staletta had taken the crow's nest post. Looking through the telescope, she spotted nothing but water in all directions. Sighing, she let the telescope drop to her side, then rested her arm on the rail, watching the clouds gather around the horizon and the lowering sun paint them a firey orange.

Struck by the beauty, she pulled her violin off her back, placing the bow gently across the strings. Softly, she played a few verses from a concerto. The music mixed with the wind and together they clasped hands, dancing across the waves. Smiling, Staletta put her violin away and pulled out the telescope once more.

Peering through it, the same water met her eyes until she pointed it to the south and spotted a lonely sail on the horizon. A figure on the bow waved a white flag in their direction. She lowered the telescope, grinning. "That's an extra ration of beef for me, thank you very much."

She raised the telescope once more, to make sure it wasn't a mirage, then lowered it, making for the ladder. She quickly made it to the bottom.

"There's a vessel ahead, Captain," she said. "To the south. A man on board is waving a white flag."

"They must want to meet. You have a good eye," He grinned. "You're becoming quite the sailor."

Sighing, she shook her head. "The sailor's life is not for me, thank you very much. It's too isolated." Then she shrugged. "But, if you can stand the long bouts of boredom, the rope burns, and survive the torrential storms, you are rewarded with an incomparable beauty and moments of pure wonder."

"Aye," the captain nodded. "I like the wind and the storms the best. Makes a man feel alive."

"The storms can be fun," Staletta acknowledged with a laugh, "after you get over the initial fear of death and embrace the adventure of it, sure."

"Do you fear death, Staletta?" The captain frowned.

Staletta considered that. "Death, no. Dying...yes."

"Ah, you speak of the pain of death."

"Mhm," Staletta crossed her arms, watching the unidentified ship getting closer.

"You speak of the inevitable," the captain continued, also watching the ship grow nearer.

Staletta shivered, knowing he was right.

"Why do we fear the inevitable?" The captain pressed.

"Because," Staletta glanced at him, "we were made to live. Death goes against our nature."

Captain Alex tapped a finger to his chin. "I think we would be much better off if we face it straight on, head held high."

"Have you ever been close to dying?" Staletta turned on him, narrowing her eyes.

"No," he said, swallowing and focusing once more on the nearing ship.

"I have," she said, softening her gaze. "Several times. When you get to that point, there is no strength to hold your head up high."

Cocking an eyebrow, he nodded. "I'm a murderer. Will I have the strength to hold my head up high at the time of my death?" Captain Alex asked in a low voice, as if to himself.

"Only you know the answer to that question." Staletta shrugged, then smiled. "Come on, let's stop philosophizing and go meet this ship."

"Agreed."

They met up with the ship as the sun dipped below the horizon.

"'allo zere," the man aboard called out, throwing the flag aside and waving at them.

"Ahoy," Captain Alex answered. "Whither do you sail and how do you fare?"

"Ve are sailing back to France, Monsieur, and ve do not fair vell. Ve have twelve people aboard, five are sick, and ve do not have provisions left to make it home."

"How long have you been at sea?"

"128 days, Monsieur," the man swept an arm across his brow, licking his lips. "Ve set sail from California. Whither are you going and how do you fare, Monsieur?"

"We are sailing to India," Captain Alex replied, smiling at the crew gathered around them. "Today we caught a shark, and the lad's have been busy preparing it for a feast. Please, join us tonight. We will share our provisions and tend to your sick."

The Frenchman brightened. He called out in French to his crewmen before turning back to Captain Alex. "Ve are grateful, Monsieur. Ve accept."

Since five of the crew from the French vessel were incapacitated from illness, only seven were able to come aboard the *Redemption*. Captain Alex ordered for the plank to be raised across the distance between their ships, and the seven Frenchmen came aboard, seating themselves down around the deck while the crew from the *Redemption* served out plates of shark steak that had marianated all afternoon in a dark, glazed sauce smelling of sweet honey, sugar, salt, and garlicy spices.

The strong smell of ammonia that had emanated from the beast when they had cut into it earlier had caused Staletta no little amount of trepidation at the thought of eating shark, but at the sight and smell of the gooey, brown steaks, her mouth began to water and she grabbed for a plate with relish. After stabbing her fork into the meaty flesh, she moved it to her mouth, savory, exotic flavors tingling on her tongue.

"What is this sauce?" She asked as the cook appeared, handing more plates out to the sailors gathered on deck.

He smiled and winked. "A special recipe from Japan. They call it teriyaki."

"It's divine," Staletta said between mouthfuls, half of her shark steak already gone. "Don't you think, Danny-boy?"

Beside her, Daniel nodded, his mouth similarly stuffed. He swallowed dramatically and clapped. "Well done," he said to the cook.

The cook bowed and finished handing out plates.

After they had eaten their fill, they laid out on the deck, watching the stars sparkling in the sky, listening to the stories of the Frenchmen as Archie questioned them about their time in California.

When Archie's questions slowed and the chatter ceased, Staletta pulled her violin off her back and started to play softly so as not to disturb the musical sound of the water lapping gently against the ship or the fluttering of the sails in the breeze.

The French Captain ceased picking at his teeth and hummed a lilting tune. Staletta picked up the tune and played accordingly. Crossing his arms over his legs, he gazed at the moon and started to sing:

"*Au clair de la lune,*
Mon ami Pierrot,
Prête-moi ta plume
Pour écrire un mot.
Ma chandelle est morte,
Je n'ai plus de feu.
Ouvre-moi ta porte
Pour l'amour de Dieu."

Feeling a pulling sensation on her arm, Staletta looked over to find Archie nudging her. He whispered quietly, "What's he saying?"

She frowned and shook her head in response.

"It sounds...sad," he continued. He leaned over to Daniel. "Do you know what he is saying?"

Daniel leaned over, whispering, "I know little French...something about the moon and a candle dying..."

The captain ended the song, leaned his head back against the mast, gazing at the moon. He breathed in deep, then sprang to his feet, a smile stretched across his features. Bouncing over to Captain Alex, he shook his hand vigorously.

"Zank you, Captain, for your hospitality. Unlike Pierrot from ze song, you have been a kindly neighbor and have opened your door to us. Ve are in your debt."

Waving it away, Captain Alex smiled in return. "The *Redemption* does not loan out kindness, Sir. There is no debt to be paid. Here," the captain gestured to his crew, who sprang up and started loading a few boxes of supplies onto the other ship, "Take these. A few medical supplies, limes, salted meats, and pickled vegetables. It isn't much, but it should get you home."

The French Captain thanked him again, then the crew departed, heading back onto their own ship, and sailing off into the night.

When they had gone and the sailors dispersed to tend to their duties and sleep, Staletta turned to Archie. "Alright, off to bed, young man."

Archie finished a yawn, then nodded his head in agreement. "Goodnight."

He disappeared below decks, leaving she and

Daniel alone. He wrapped an arm around her, feeling her tremble. Even though the night was calm and bright, the breeze held a slight chill.

"You okay?" He asked.

She nodded, leaning into him. "On a night like this, it's hard to imagine anything bad happening. So peaceful, so quiet..."

"Remember it," Daniel kissed the top of her head. "For when times aren't so peaceful."

23

"Brrrr," Staletta huddled in her wool jacket, her hands shoved under her arms in an effort to keep them warm. Staletta stumbled over the deck as heavy winds rammed into the side of the ship.

"Why did it get so cold?" She called to Daniel beside her.

"I don't know," he called back, shrugging.

Staletta struggled against the wind, wanting to reach the helm to ask the captain what was going on. The captain bellowed out orders from his post and though the wind whipped his words away, a faint call reached her ears: "Brace the sheets. Haul home the topsail."

Daniel and Staletta acted on impulse. They had been aboard long enough to recognize the command

and know what to do. Lunging for the ropes, they sprang into action.

The captain noticed them working and shouted angrily, "What are you doing? You should be below decks."

Daniel heaved on a rope and tied it off securely. "We're helping," he shouted up at him.

"Don't you know what's happening?" the captain exclaimed.

"We're in a storm," Staletta chimed in, tying off her rope. She and Daniel then headed towards the helm.

"Aye," Captain Alex nodded, his eyes flashing. "We're in a storm alright. A hurricane."

Staletta's footsteps faltered on the steps leading up to the helm, but they continued making their way over.

"How bad?" Daniel asked as they stepped beside the captain.

"Bad," the captain heaved against the wheel as a gust of wind racked the ship. "This is only the beginning. You'll need to brace yourselves below."

As his words left his mouth, Staletta felt sharp lashes against her face. Blinking rapidly, she grabbed Daniel's arm. "What is it?"

Looking around the deck, slushy white ice started to cover the surface.

"Sleet," Daniel tucked her hair behind her ear, brushing the ice from her forehead.

"Get below decks." Captain Alex pushed at Daniel's back. Daniel grabbed Staletta's hand and together they slid over the icy deck towards the stairs, grasping the railing as they descended.

Right behind them, Alex shouted, "This is where we take our stand. Weigh anchor."

The anchor lowered and the sailors on deck scrambled for cover. Staletta, Daniel, and the captain reached the stairs leading down below decks. Staletta turned as a thumping sound caught her attention. Round balls of ice the size of limes hurtling down onto the ship.

Mesmerized, Staletta watched the hail in fascination, wanting to grab one and hold it in her hands. She made a step towards it, but Daniel held her back. Shaking his head, he said, "Come on, Star."

She nodded and followed him down below decks, where the sound of the hail hitting the roof above them sounded twice as loud. Archie ran over to them, grabbing for Staletta's legs.

"What's happening?"

"We are passing through a hurricane." She patted his head, casting a glance at Captain Alex.

"We've been fortunate, two months at sea and we've weathered each storm fair enough. A hurricane is a different animal. Brace yourselves and don't expect this one to be easy."

Staletta nodded and together with Daniel and Archie, moved to the wall where a series of straps were hooked to the wall. Sitting down on the bench, they strapped themselves in, feeling the ship buck uncontrollably as the wind hit them again.

The hail didn't last long, petering out after a few minutes, but the winds continued, and the rain gushed down in torrents. As soon as the hail had stopped, the captain had gone back up with a handful of sailors, but the rest remained below. Staletta's arms and legs ached from bracing against the wall.

Soon, the winds died down and the rocking ship, tottered to a standstill. Daniel looked around, watching the other sailors relax. "Is that it?"

They chuckled and shook their heads. "For now." The sailors unhitched themselves and hurried above decks.

Daniel shrugged and he and Staletta unstrapped themselves. "Shall we go have a look?"

Staletta agreed and at Archie's persistence, they also allowed him to unstrap. Together they hurried upstairs.

The cold air bit at their exposed faces and the deck was still slick with rain and ice. It was cold enough that the hail remained on deck. Archie ran over and grabbed some, bringing it over to Staletta and Daniel.

Staletta stood transfixed, looking up at the clouds

above them. They were moving fast. The dark clouds had moved off, leaving grayer clouds above them, but even as they watched, the clouds were growing darker.

They watched as the sailors finished rolling up the sails, securing them tightly to the tops of the masts, then repelled down quickly, falling from the sky as quickly as the hail had rained down earlier.

Staletta shivered as the breeze picked up, feeling a slight sense of unease as the ship began to move beneath her feet.

"Here she comes again," Captain Alex called, ushering the passengers below decks once more. "Fiercer than the last."

Staletta, Daniel, and Archie ventured back downstairs just in time to strap themselves in before the ship started hurtling back and forth once more, this time with even greater vengeance.

Grasping her stomach, hair flying in her face, Staletta sucked in her breath, "Ohhh, Danny-boy,"

He reached over, took hold of her hand, and squeezed, chuckling, "Don't even think about it, Star."

She squeezed his hand back and shut her eyes, willing the nausea to leave her, but the ship kept rocking and her vision already began to swim. "Are you okay?" She asked, breathing in and out heavily.

"Fantastic," she heard Daniel respond and knew he was in the same predicament.

"Archie?"

When no response came, Staletta opened her eyes and cast her eyes across Daniel to where Archie sat, face buried in Daniel's arm, one hand firmly clasped to the strap on the wall, the other clenching Daniel's hand.

"He's doing great," Daniel looked down at the top of the boy's head. "He's brave, this one." He smiled up at Staletta even as Archie groaned.

"Archie, it's going to be okay," Staletta sat back in her seat, clutching the straps as the ship bucked back and forth.

Archie groaned again. "Is it almost over?"

"I'm sure it will have to stop soon," Staletta confirmed, even as the wind screamed murder. Over the sound of the wind and the wrecking waves, Captain Alex's voice boomed out one final command: "Let go the sails."

The sea rose, hurtling its great mass into the side of the ship. Her heart beating furiously at the force of the massive concussion, Staletta hollered in shock as the ship pitched to the side...

24

Staletta's head banged into the wall as the ship jarred to a sudden stop. Her stomach lurched as the ship righted itself by swinging back in the opposite direction, then teetered back and forth wildly.

Her gut revolted. Doubling over, a stream of mashed up food and bile spewed from her lips, splattering on the waxed floorboards.

She laid her head back against the wall, dizzy, as the ship ceased cavorting. A hard squeeze on her hand from Daniel re-oriented her to the cabin around them.

"We didn't capsize?" She asked, wiping her mouth with the sleeve of her blouse.

Squeezing her hand twice, Daniel sighed. "Almost, but no."

"I can't take much more of this," Staletta admitted, laughing humorously. "I can't see straight anymore."

Archie groaned. "I don't feel good either."

"Hold on a little longer, kid," Daniel encouraged.

"Okay," he replied, before he retched, emptying his stomach on the floor.

Staletta felt Daniel lean back against the wall, their shoulders brushing. "Are you okay, Danny?"

"I'm fine," he replied, squeezing her hand again and chuckling quietly. "Not quite as sick as you two anyway."

They held on for what seemed like hours, learning to move with the ship as it shook and romped through the wind and waves. Finally, Bobby descended the stairs, a relieved expression on his features. His clothes dripped rain water, and his black hair clung to his forehead.

"Be at peace, the hurricane has passed," he said breathlessly, moving over to help them unstrap from the wall.

Staletta's straps fell off and she sought to rise, but the world had not righted itself in her head. Her legs turned to jelly, and she collapsed in Bobby's arms. He held her until Daniel had unstrapped himself and leant over to grab her. Bobby then moved to unstrap Archie.

"There you are," Daniel spoke to Staletta. "That's it. Get those feet under you."

He helped walk her over to their cot, keeping a firm arm around her waist, taking tentative steps as it seemed the floor kept moving beneath their feet. They made it to the cot and collapsed into it, relief flooding her limbs as she stretched out, delighting in the solid feel of the cot beneath her.

The sailor carried Archie over to the opposite cot and laid him down. "Get some rest, young Archie," he said, tousling the boy's hair. "I'll bring you a bucket, just in case."

Archie was already fast asleep when the sailor returned and placed a bucket beside his cot and one next to Daniel and Staletta. Daniel caught his arm before he turned to leave.

"Why didn't we tip over? We could feel the ship capsizing..."

The sailor nodded. "Aye, the hurricane almost sunk us, but we have a few tricks up our sleeves to best the storms."

"Is there anything I can do to help clean up?"

"Rest," he replied. "We all need rest after a storm like that. We'll begin repairs at mid-morning."

Daniel nodded, laying his head back as the sailor disappeared. Staletta quickly drifted off into sleep.

25

Staletta paced across the deck, fanning herself with a hand. It didn't feel like the end of October. High in the sky, the sun beat down upon her, causing drops of sweat to form on her neck and slip down along her spine. Rolled up sleeves revealed tanned arms and rope-roughened hands. She reached her hand up to her head, scratching a sweaty itch, then let her fingers slide through her hair, noticing how constant exposure to the sun, the wind, and the salt air had given it a rough texture and caused the once straight locks to curl.

Sighing, she placed her hands on her hips, casting her eyes out to sea in hopes of seeing anything other than water. The last time a crew member had spotted a ship was over two weeks prior and it hadn't even come close to them. Sure, they had spotted birds and fish, but three months at sea left a body longing for solid ground and the knowledge that life existed outside of the ship.

Peering up at the sails, Staletta noted that not even a ripple moved across their white expanse. They stood as still as statues in the sky. Curious, she paced to the rail, looking down at the water. Neither a wave nor a ripple licked up against the ship. Looking out at the horizon once more, she clicked her tongue, trying to ignore how much it felt like a wad of wool in her parched mouth.

She turned back around to the deck, her eye catching the sight of Daniel lying strewn out on the deck, hands behind his head, feet crossed, a hat over his eyes, chest bare, and trouser legs rolled up to the calves.

Smiling to herself, she acknowledged how little like an English gentleman he appeared. Like her arms, his chest had tanned and glistened with sweat. The limited diet and physical labor had burned away every ounce of fat on him, accentuating his muscles and providing him with a litheness that hadn't been there before.

Making her way over, she laid down beside him, raising his hat with one finger. He blinked against the sudden onslaught of sunlight, breathed in deep, then yawned, stretching out his arms and legs.

"Star," he acknowledged, after finishing his yawn and settling back into a comfortable position.

"Danny-boy," she smirked, placing a hand on his chest, tracing the muscles with her finger.

He watched her finger, then flicked his eyes up to hers. "What are you thinking?" He asked with a lopsided grin.

She returned the grin and shrugged. "Ohh, nothing in particular," then leaned forward to kiss him.

"I'm sure," he teased.

She laughed, then pulled her head back. "But really I was thinking about how much you've changed these last few months at sea."

"Oh?"

"Mhm, you've grown," she scrunched her face up trying to find the right word, "rugged?"

"Rugged?" He bit his lip, looking down at his chest and his bare feet. Chuckling, he shrugged, "I suppose that's accurate." He flicked his eyes to her. "The same could be said of you. Although for you, the more accurate term might be breezy."

Throwing her head back and laughing throatily she repeated, "Breezy? What is that supposed to mean?"

He laughed and reached for her chin, tracing it with his finger. "You know, you appear loose and wind-tousled... breezy."

"Loose as in baggy?"

"Loose as in free and sprightly."

"I see," Staletta grinned, shaking her head.

"It's been...nice. Getting away from society, I mean." Daniel shifted his hips, wiggled his feet. "You don't have to stand on ceremony, you can go around bare foot, yell at the top of your lungs, and breathe in fresh air, actual, real, fresh air."

"You like it out here?" She looked over to him, raising her brows. "I thought for sure you would be missing your family, missing your shop, missing your craft."

"I do, but that's not to say I don't appreciate the peace that comes with this. I mean, the chance to..." he sighed, grasping for the right words "...be untethered to a certain routine, certain formalities, certain proprieties, and certain responsibilities. A man can discover what it is that truly makes a man. It's refreshing and edifying."

"Hmm," Staletta crossed her hands over her stomach. "I feel impatient. Ready to be on shore. Ready to find my brothers."

Daniel propped himself up on his elbow to look down at her. "There is a big difference between us. You are driven. You have always been driven by survival and a need to belong. Whereas I have never had any of those drives. Everything has been laid out for me, even easy to accomplish, you might say. I have never wanted for food or housing or clothing. I am grateful for that, of course, but that type of lifestyle tends to make a man soft. This voyage…it has given me a new perspective. It will drive me to…" the words escaped him again. He balled a fist "…to be wild at heart. To yield sustenance from the very Earth man was made from. To be courageous and protect my loved ones."

She smirked, pushing her first into his chin playfully. "You grow braver and stronger with each passing day, and I grow more impatient. I should spend more time looking for perspective."

Daniel frowned and shook his head. "I disagree. With each passing day you grow more captivating."

She raised an eyebrow. "How will being captivating help me find my brothers? How will that help us to survive in the wilds of India?"

Shrugging, Daniel shook his head again. "I don't know all things, but I do know your heart matters. The longing you feel to find your brothers makes you even more captivating. It expresses a freedom, a power, a wild beauty that will stop at nothing to accomplish all you were meant to be."

"Wise words from a carpenter," she grinned playfully.

His eyes glittered in the sunlight. "As I said, I like it out here. Gives a man time and space to think. I think it's been good for Archie, too."

Staletta looked over to where Archie sat, playing cards with a group of the sailors. The boy looked at the sailors with admiration, a smile on his face. "He has the blindness of youth. He doesn't know the dangers ahead. He happily goes about and when the dangers hit, he hides his fear of them."

"True," Daniel sighed. "He has an advantage over most boys. Look at the mentors he has aboard this ship. Think of the experiences he will get to have on this voyage that other boys dare only dream about."

"If he survives..."

"Star..." Daniel cast a disapproving eye on her, frowning. "You are a survivor. Where does this cynical talk come from?"

Tightening her lips, she met his gaze. "It is rational. Where I come from, people die."

Daniel sighed, softening his gaze. "But not everyone. Take heart."

She smiled. "I'm sorry, I don't mean to be gloomy. In truth, I love seeing Archie's joy. It is pure and carefree. Why do we lose that as we age?"

Daniel chuckled. "When you've figured that out, let me know."

Bobby passed in front of them, stopping to lean against the mast and wipe his forehead with his arm. "Ah, these doldrums are the worst."

"How far have we moved today?" Staletta asked, sitting up to speak with him better.

"Not much, we are sitting ducks out here until the

wind decides to show up again."

"By the way, how much longer do we have before we reach India?" Staletta rubbed her hands together.

Bobby shrugged, gesturing to Captain Alex who was making his way towards them.

"We're close," The captain replied, "Less than a week out from seeing land."

"A week?" Daniel sat up, rubbing his knees. "I did not realize we were so close."

Staletta breathed out and held her stomach. "Me either. I'm suddenly nervous."

"Don't get too excited," Captain Alex said, holding up a hand. "We'll see how long these doldrums set us back. They have been known to last for days. And when we do finally see land there will be at least another week of coasting along the shoreline until we find your harbor."

Staletta placed a hand on Daniel's shoulder. "Now would be a good time for us to come up with a plan."

Daniel sighed, rubbing the back of his neck. "I think you're right."

26

"We know we have to get to Fort William. As for how to get there, well, we'll have to figure it out as we go along."

Daniel sighed as he rolled up the map of India and tossed it aside on the deck floor. With elbows resting on his crossed legs, he dropped his head into his hands, rubbing tired eyes. He and Staletta had stayed up late into the night, pouring over the map, trying to come up with some semblance of a plan.

"Just so I have this straight," Staletta paused, yawning widely. "Captain Alex will drop us off somewhere along the shoreline at Haldia and from there we will follow the river Hoogly up to the Fort, correct?"

Uncovering his eyes, he nodded and glanced over

to her. "Sounds simple enough, right?"

"It does," she grinned over at him. "I thought for sure we would be traipsing through the jungle trying to outrun the tigers."

"If we can't find anyone to take us up the river, then we might have to," he chuckled, but the thought of that reality tainted the joke and a frown replaced his grin. "Let us pray that doesn't happen. Unfortunately, there aren't just tigers to be wary of in the jungle..."

Daniel watched a shiver pass through her, then she stood from the deck, stretching her arms over her head and yawned once more.

"It's late," Daniel uncurled his legs and pushed himself up to stand beside her. "We should get some sleep. Perhaps these doldrums will pass and we can be on our way tomorrow."

Daniel stepped in the direction of the stairs, but when she didn't follow, he paused to look back. Staletta eyed the sky, pacing along the deck, moving towards the railing.

"Look how bright the stars are tonight."

Daniel glanced up to the sky, squinting at the stars. "Yeah, look at that."

"Daniel, come look."

His eyes shifted from the stars down to her face, veritably glowing in the moonlight. His breath caught at the sight of her natural beauty and a smile twitched the corners of his lips.

"What are you staring at?" She snickered, waving him over with a hurried hand. "You have got to come see this."

Stepping over to her, Daniel peered out to where she pointed, out to the sea.

"It's like there is no sea, like we are hanging suspended in the sky, surrounded by stars. I dare not breath for fear of disturbing it."

No breeze rumpled the water. It appeared as black glass, perfectly reflecting the starscape above. A strange disorientation came over Daniel as he stared, a feeling that there was nothing beneath them, that they hung on nothing. Reaching forward, he touched the rail with his fingertips, needing the grainy, solid feel of wood to feel grounded once more.

"It is just an illusion, yet it feels so real," he said, wrapping an arm around her waist.

Leaning into him, she pointed at a star blazing in the water, then moved her arm up to point to the brightest star in the sky. "There's the north star. My namesake."

"Rèalta," Daniel said in a low voice.

Staletta sighed. "Even as the carriage rolled them away, my brothers yelled back at me to follow the north star and I would find them." She chuckled. "Nonsense, of course, but even so," she held her hand out indicating they were, in fact, sailing north to find them.

Daniel rubbed her back, chuckling softly. "We are sailing north right now, but we also sailed a good way south, and some east…"

"I know it means nothing," Staletta put her arms around him and squeezed. "Just one of those strange things that has stuck in my mind all these years. Now, we are on our way to find them, and there it is."

"Yes, we are on our way, against all odds and circumstances. We are on our way."

Staletta looked at him and smiled, the moonlight reflecting in her eyes so dazzlingly his heart skipped a beat. The urge to kiss her engulfed him, but a question licked at the back of his brain, and he couldn't fathom what her response would be. He had to ask.

Swallowing the urge to kiss her, he cleared his throat. "What will you do when we find them?"

Her brow furrowed and the muscles in her back clenched beneath his arm. Her eyes looked away and it was as if a cloud had passed over the moon.

When she didn't respond, he moved his head lower, trying to catch her eye again. "What happens next?"

She shrugged in response, sighing as she looked back out to the sea of stars. "We have not found them yet. There is no use dwelling on that just yet."

Nodding, Daniel pumped his arm, rubbing her back gently. He tried to resurrect the urge to kiss her, but the moment was lost, and the night was too peaceful, too calm to adventure after it.

27

"Land ho!" Shouted Mizzy from the crow's nest.

Staletta flew out of the cabin quicker than a lightning bolt. She squinted into the distance, spotting green blossoming on the horizon, breaking up the endless blue monotony she had come to know over the last three months.

"I see it," Archie jostled her elbow as he jumped up and down beside her, pointing wildly out to sea.

Staletta craned her neck as Daniel drew up on the other side of her.

"We made it," He grinned broadly, wrapping an arm around Staletta's shoulder.

"Oh boy, think we'll see an elephant? Or a tiger?" Archie asked, pulling on Staletta's arm.

"An elephant would be alright, but I don't think we want to come across any tigers," Daniel replied.

"No, thank you," said Staletta, feeling her gut clench

at the sight of India before her. For Archie this was a vacation, for Daniel, a duty, but for her it was a mission, one she did not think she was strong enough to accomplish. The heat of the sun on board the ship had already gotten to her head a few times, forcing her to go below decks where it was marginally cooler.

"Don't worry," Daniel replied, squeezing her shoulders. "We'll be okay."

"That's easy to say-" Staletta began.

"But hard to control, I know," Daniel finished for her.

Staletta nodded and looked past him as Captain Alex strolled over, holding his arms out wide.

"It's always a jolt seeing land for the first time after months at sea." Captain Alex drew in a deep breath, bringing his arms back down by his sides. "You tend to forget what life smells like, how the trees sound..."

"How the earth feels beneath one's boots," Bobby added as he bustled up beside the captain.

"Is that where we get off?" Archie pointed to a dock on the bay, then craned his neck to look up at the captain.

"That's it," the captain replied in a low voice that made the back of Staletta's neck tingle.

"Oh boy," Archie replied, looking back at the island.

"Are you ready to be on land again, Archie?" Staletta inadvertently rubbed her arms.

He took a few moments to answer, but eventually

replied with, "Yes. I mean, I love sailing, but I want to see the jungle."

"Remember, we are not here for fun," Daniel cautioned. "The jungle is more dangerous than any of us realize."

Archie shrugged. "No more dangerous than weathering a hurricane at sea."

Daniel tensed beside her. "Even so."

"I can handle it, I'm not afraid," Archie replied, crossing his arms and sticking out his chin.

The sentiment resonated with Staletta. When her Pa set her off on a boat headed from Ireland to England, he had told her to be brave, to not be afraid. It was a mantra she had stuck to her entire life, yet she knew it was a lie. Bravery didn't come from not being afraid. It came from being afraid, but doing the thing anyway. What Archie expressed wasn't bravery, it was the carefree nature of youth. That was something, she knew, he would need to outgrow.

As India drew nearer, Staletta could make out the palm trees on the beach and the other ships docked at the harbor. She saw people milling about the docks and caught herself searching the distant faces. Already searching for her brothers.

"Are you ready?"

Malachi's voice broke her eyes away from the shore and she nodded, watching Daniel and Archie nod their agreement.

"It was a pleasure having you all aboard," Malachi removed his hat, held out his hand. "Mrs. May, a fine violin you play. You're all welcome aboard any time, and we'd be happy to have you and Master Archie play us a tune any time you can."

"Thank you, Malachi, we would be delighted." The sentiment warmed Staletta and she held out her hand for him to kiss.

Malachi straightened and replaced his hat with a clearing of his throat. "We won't be docking at harbor. We'll be taking the dinghy ashore. If you're packed, we'll make ready the boat."

"Alright," Staletta wiped her sweaty hands on the legs of her trousers.

Daniel reached down to grab her hand and squeezed it. "I'll get our things ready."

Daniel and Archie went to work getting their things and bringing them out on deck. Staletta said her goodbyes to everyone on board. Lastly, Captain Alex came down from the helm and shook her hand. When Daniel finished with the bags, he also came over and shook hands with the crew, thanking them for everything they had done.

Captain Alex grinned sadly, "Thank you for being our guests these last three months, it's been a delight."

"We should be thanking you," Daniel objected, proffering a handshake.

"Thank you, Captain," Staletta said. "Without your help we would never have gotten here."

"It's the least I could do," Captain Alex replied,

returning Daniel's handshake. "I will pray you find your brothers and no harm shall befall you on your journey. I wish I could be there when you find them so I could sail you back home."

"We will cross that sea when we come to it," chuckled Staletta. "We don't know how long we'll be or if we'll even survive. It would take a miracle."

"I think you will," Captain Alex winked. "Miracles happen to the least of us. Look at me."

"I have an idea," said Malachi. "We could show up here exactly six months from today. If you're on the docks, we'll take you home. If you're not there, we'll come back in another six months to take you home."

Captain Alex brightened. "An excellent idea."

Daniel nodded. "You shouldn't do that for us. It is too grand an offer, but as we have no other plan—"

"It's settled then," Captain Alex shook their hands again. "We'll see you in six months or twelve."

Staletta took a deep breath to steady herself, then descended the ladder into the dinghy, followed by Daniel, Archie, and Malachi. She looked behind to see the captain and the crew waving at them, and she waved back, then turned to face the great unknown looming closer with every stroke of the oars.

28

Staletta watched as Malachi rowed back towards the *Redeemed,* then turned her attention to the new surroundings. Sweat prickling on her lower lip, she wiped it away with the back of her hand. Her eyes scanned the exotic foliage, some with long trunks that wore their leaves at the very top, as if wearing a hat.

She spotted several birds walking along the ground, giant feathers of blue and green fanned out behind them. "Look," she pointed. "They're beautiful."

"Peacocks, I think," Daniel replied, squinting against the bright sun.

Staletta's eyes traveled along the docks, inspecting the natives that hung around the docks, mending nets and tending to boats. Their skin was dark brown and their clothing much more colorful and looser than anything worn in England. The natives sitting around the dock stared at them, chewing a plant that turned their mouths red. Staletta supposed they must appear just as strange and foreign to the natives as the natives did to them.

"Alright, we're here. We need to find a guide or a boat," Daniel looked around as if one would magically appear before them.

"Everyone's staring at us," Archie said, waving at a group of people fishing off the dock.

"Archie," Staletta whispered curtly, "We don't know if they're friendly or not."

"Why wouldn't they be?" He said, slowly lowering his arm.

Staletta looked up at Daniel with an expression that said, 'can you explain?'

Daniel cleared his throat. "The English and the Indians are having a bit of a disagreement at this time. We, as British citizens, might not be welcome in certain parts and places."

"In which parts and places?" Archie asked, eyes going wide.

"We don't know."

Archie crossed his arms, frowning at Daniel.

"But we're civilians," Staletta added. "They won't bother us...we hope."

"That's comforting," Archie rolled his eyes.

Daniel looked at her askance.

"Well," she said in reply, "I did my best."

"Let's move ourselves off the docks and see what lies inland," Daniel suggested.

They picked up their bags and started to walk into

the city of Haldia, Staletta noticing how severely crowded it was. The buildings were close together and there were people everywhere. Flashes of conversation assailed her ears, but the sounds were foreign. Not one English word spoken.

"Daniel," she said, looking around with a sense of dread beginning to form in her gut. "This was a mistake."

"Don't say that, we've only just arrived," he encouraged. "It's going to take some getting used to, but we'll manage."

"Okay," she said in a wavering tone, pulling Archie closer to her.

"What was the first thing you and your brothers did when you arrived in England?"

Staletta thought back to that dreadful day when they, along with hundreds of other immigrants, had stepped off the coffin ship and onto English soil. They had been starving and tired and in shock at the death of their brother. They barely knew what they were doing when they stumbled off the ship. All they had wanted to do was sleep.

"We found a place to lie down and sleep," she answered.

"There you go," Daniel said. "It'll be dark in a few hours. Let's find an inn and tomorrow we can start looking for a guide."

Staletta breathed a sigh of relief, pushing her shoulders back, and tossing her head. "You're right, Danny. I'm letting fear get the best of me."

"You're growing soft," he said as they started moving forward again.

"What?"

"You know, you're not as tough as you used to be when I first met you."

Staletta whacked him on the shoulder. "Are you trying to insult me?"

Daniel winked at her, chuckling softly. "Don't you remember when we first met?"

Archie looked up at them, his eyes widening in curiosity. "I want to hear that story."

"She was tough as nails, Archie," Daniel said. "And stubborn to boot."

"I was not—"

"Don't listen to her, Archie, she was indeed. She was homeless like you. The first time I saw her she was giving away her coin to a sick boy in the alley. The second time I saw her she was fighting for a chance to play her music on the street corner. Then, the night I finally got to meet her; she had been attacked by street thugs."

"They had me beat, Danny, and you rescued me," she drawled. "That's not tough."

"It was, though," Daniel nudged her with his arm. "You were beat up, but you did not quit. You would have kept fighting."

"What happened after that?" Asked Archie, eyes wide.

"There was a mix up. She ended up in jail, and I had to go rescue her again," Daniel winked at her.

"Still, not sounding tough," Staletta smiled, shaking her head.

"Not the point," said Daniel.

"What is the point? That I was miserable and too cowardly to admit it?"

"To remind you of your courage," Daniel replied, stopping suddenly on the street outside of a pale stone building out of which people came and went. "This looks like it could be an inn. Come on, let's go inside and see."

The trio walked inside and stopped at the front desk.

"We'd like a room, please," Daniel spoke slowly, accentuating his words carefully in the hopes that the man spoke English.

"No room here," the man replied quickly, his English thickly accented.

Daniel slumped, but nodded. "Thank you," he said and turned to leave.

As he turned away the man spoke up, "Try across street."

Daniel looked up and thanked him again. They plodded across the street to the next building. "We'd like a room, please?" Daniel asked tentatively.

"Name?"

"Daniel May."

The man behind the desk scratched a pen on paper, shuffled to the wall to take down a set of keys, and motioned for them to follow him.

29

"I sure wish we had spent those three months aboard ship learning Hindi," Staletta slumped into a chair outside a restaurant, her face pink from the exertion of walking around the city in the sticky heat. Wiping her brow, she smoothed back tendrils of hair loosened from her braid.

Archie sat in the chair next to her while Daniel sat down in the one opposite. The boys looked as exhausted and sweaty as she did.

"Three days in India and still we have not found anyone to take us up the river," Staletta's shoulders sagged.

Daniel pulled out the map from his back pocket and spread it out on the table before them. "Look, we know we need to get to Fort William. I estimate it is at least a day's walk, if not two." Daniel studied the map. "But only if we cut cross country."

"But without a guide we could get lost," Staletta said

reasonably.

"Or get eaten," Archie added.

Daniel and Staletta raised their eyes to him humorlessly.

"Sorry," he said. "Guess you're not in the joking mood."

Daniel went back to studying the map, while Staletta gazed out to the people on the street. "Let's order some food and think on it a while."

"Good idea," Daniel said, closing the map, rubbing his eyes, then raising his hand to get a waiter's attention.

As none of them spoke a word of the Hindi language, ordering their food was a challenge. Daniel managed it easily enough by pointing to another guest's plate, then pointing to the three of them. The waiter understood and soon brought them out a platter of rice and chicken and three cups of tea.

After they had eaten, they sat back, avoiding each other's eyes. Daniel leaned forward. "Have we decided?"

Staletta grimaced and shrugged. "I think we try to find a guide for one more day. If by tomorrow morning we have no one to take us, we will walk it alone."

Daniel nodded. "Then that's what we'll do." He laid a few coins on the table to pay for their meal. "Shall we go?"

As he was beginning to rise, the ground rumbled beneath them. The coins on the table jumped and rattled, and the chairs beneath them shook. Daniel grabbed the table to steady it, casting an alarmed expression at Staletta. She returned his look, her eyes wide.

"What was that—" she started to say as a second larger shockwave passed through.

Staletta fell to the ground, covering her head as bits of ceiling crumbled. Over the sound of groaning buildings and the occasional scream, she heard Daniel command Archie to crawl towards her. Archie crawled up next to her and she pulled him close to her side. Daniel crawled over next to her, covering both of their heads to help shield them from the falling debris.

The rumbling finally stopped, but the earth continued to sway beneath her for moments after. It felt much like being aboard ship. When the noises stopped and the dust had settled, Daniel uncovered their heads and they started to rise. Staletta swept at her filthy clothes, choking on the dusty air.

A quick look around told her there had been some damage, but relief flooded her when she saw no buildings had collapsed. The other people were also rising, dusting themselves off, looking around, and chattering excitedly.

Staletta looked down as Archie's trembling hand grasped hers. "What was that?" He asked, trying not to sound half as scared as he was.

"That was an earthquake," Daniel replied, clapping his hands on his pant legs. "Never felt one of those before."

"Me neither," said Staletta. "I hope to never experience that again."

Glancing around nervously, she cast her eyes across the street noticing a man walking out of a building. He looked rather shaken up and the uniform he wore looked oddly familiar to her. "Danny, look. A British officer."

Staletta did not wait for Daniel to look where she pointed, she hurtled after the man like a snake striking for a mouse.

"Sir," she called, running up and grabbing his arm. The man turned in alarm, but steadied himself, straightening his jacket and looking at her oddly.

"Can I help you, Miss?" he asked politely, though he frowned as Daniel and Archie drew up beside her.

"It's good to hear someone else speak English," She said with relief. "You have no idea how long we've been looking for you."

"For me?" The man asked, pointing to himself and scrutinizing them carefully. "Do I know you?"

"No," Staletta replied, waving her hands. "I meant, looking for someone, anyone. You see we are looking for someone to take us to Fort William. My brothers are soldiers and we mean to catch up with them there."

The man scratched his chin and nodded. "I see. Unfortunately, I can't show you the way as I'm going the opposite direction, but I can point you to someone that could help."

"Splendid," Daniel reached out to shake his hand. "Any help is appreciated. We have not found any one to take us up the river yet and were debating walking through the jungle."

"I'd take a boat, if I were you," the man said. "The Hoogly River will take you straight to the fort. Do you have a map with you?"

Daniel took the map out of his pocket and handed it to the man.

The man opened it and studied it for a moment. "Right," he said. "The boating outfit I'd recommend is right about here and there's an English man there that runs it. You'll be able to talk with him and he'll lead you straight and true."

"Perfect," said Staletta, smiling broadly.

"I don't know they'll let you into the fort without authorization though," the man cautioned.

"How do we get authorization?" Daniel asked.

The man stroked his beard. "Well, I suppose I could write you a note. What is the reason you are going there again?"

"Would you please?" Staletta asked, folding her hands beneath her chin. "I need to find my brothers. They are soldiers, as I said. We were separated. I wish to find them again."

The man dropped his hand from his chin in resignation. "And they are at the fort currently?"

Staletta continued to hold her hands under her chin, grimacing slightly. "We don't know."

"How do you plan on finding them if they are not?"

"Well, you see..." Staletta looked at Daniel, helplessly searching for words.

"We were planning on just..." Daniel stopped speaking and looked blankly back at her.

"Just asking around and seeing what we can find out..." Staletta nodded at the officer.

"I see," he looked down at the ground and then back up at them. "Might I suggest joining up as camp followers? You'll get a chance to meet the soldiers and ask around that

168

way."

Staletta glanced at Daniel, then back at the officer when Daniel's eyes revealed nothing but a question back. "Camp followers?"

"Yes, family members of soldiers and officers often travel with the army. We call them camp followers. They help with nursing and setting up and maintaining camp. You'll be put to work helping out with the camp, but it will give you some support and shelter."

Daniel folded his arms and nodded. "That is something to consider. If all goes well, her brother's will be there at the fort, and we won't have to look any further."

Staletta removed her hands from beneath her chin, holding them against her nervous stomach instead. "Will you be able to write us that note?"

The officer nodded slowly. "Have you got a pen?"

Staletta shook her head even as Daniel did the same.

"Alright, let's go inside and see if we can borrow a paper and some ink."

"We appreciate this," Daniel said.

"Countrymen have to stick together in this country, don't we?" He remarked, smirking at them.

"Yes, indeed," Staletta bit her lip and raised her eyebrows excitedly.

"Awful earthquake, that," the man talked as they entered the building, evidently an inn the man had been staying in. He walked up to the front desk and mimed a pen and paper motion. The man at the desk nodded and brought one over, and the officer started scratching out a note.

"Are earthquakes common around here?" Daniel

asked.

He replied without looking up: "I've been here since before the Rebellion started and I've experienced several. This one today was rough, but not the worst I've ever known." He finished up the note, returned the ink to the man, and handed the note to Staletta.

"Take that to the gate when you get to the fort, my signature should get you in. You can say Captain Cranly gave his express permission for you to enter."

Staletta held the paper delicately. "We will."

They ventured outside, but before parting ways, Staletta held the captain back. "Thank you again. We owe you for this."

The man nodded and shook their hands. "Not a problem. I wish you the best of luck in finding your brothers." With a tip of his hat, he turned and disappeared in the crowded street.

Staletta spun on her heel. "Let's go find us a boat."

"Your mood has certainly improved," Archie remarked, smirking at her.

In response, Staletta grabbed him and pulled him close, planting a kiss on his cheek. "That's right, lad," she said.

"Eeeeh, yuck." Archie said and wiped the spot where her lips had left moisture.

30

The next few hours were spent in trying to find the small dockyard to where Captain Cranly had directed them. They first made their way out of the city and moved northwards to where the sea became river. They saw a fair number of docks, but not one with an English gentleman attending it. Once or twice, they had thought they had gone too far and turned back, only to find they were right the first time and had to keep trudging forward.

"We've got to be getting close," Staletta stumbled under the weight of her luggage. She set the bag down and looked up at the sky. "I'm afraid of it getting dark before we ever find the place."

"We'll find it, I'm sure," Daniel shifted the packs on his back and set the one he had been carrying down on the ground. "What did he say the name of this place was?"

"I don't think he said..."

"Wait a minute," Daniel held up a hand, looking ahead to where the trail opened beside the river. They could see the makings of a dock and could hear a few voices, some of which sounded like English. "I think this might be it," Daniel said, relief evident in his voice.

They walked faster and came upon the docks. Sitting in a chair was an Englishman and a woman, having tea and seeming to be in the thralls of conversation. Their conversation stalled as the man caught sight of them emerging from the path like the bedraggled travelers they were.

"Hoy there," the man called, waving.

Staletta waved back and greeted him in turn. "Do you know Captain Cranly?" She asked.

They stopped in front of the couple and shook hands. "We do," the man said. "He's taken our boats a time or two."

Staletta beamed. "He recommended you. We were hoping to rent a boat up the river?"

"Of course," the man replied. "How far are you going?"

"To Fort William," Daniel replied.

"Makes sense, if Captain Cranly sent you," the man replied waving them up. "You got money?"

Daniel shook his coin purse in response.

"Let's get you outfitted then, shall we?" The man grinned. "Have you ever ridden in a boat like these before?"

The man pointed to the boats at the dock. They were native boats unlike anything they had ever seen before in Ireland or England. They looked like hollowed out tree trunks, narrow and only wide enough for one person in a row. Boards stuck out at the front and back as a stabilizer to keep the boats from tipping over.

"Never," said Staletta.

"You are in for a treat then," the man winked, and Staletta couldn't tell if he was being sarcastic or serious. She looked at Daniel, but he shrugged.

"This is a one-way trip, Sir, will we be able to leave the boats at Fort William?" Daniel asked.

"No, no," the man said. "The boats can seat five. We'll send you with two men to paddle for you, they will then come back here with the boat."

"Ah, good," Daniel nodded.

"It's already getting late," Staletta said. "Do we set out right away or in the morning?"

"Whatever you like," the man said. "You'll have to camp out somewhere, it'll take at least two days to get there."

"Ready for a camping trip?" Daniel asked Archie who looked eager to get in the boat.

"Yes!" Archie replied, eyeing the boat eagerly.

"Alright then," said Staletta, watching two native men prepare a boat for them and start loading their luggage. Hands on hips, she smiled into the lowering sun. "Two days until I meet my brothers."

31

The target stared back at him like an angry red eye. Arm back behind his head, Peter placed his thumb against the curved midpoint of his s-shaped jack knife. He struck his arm down, releasing the knife at just the right moment. The knife spun through the air until the blade lodged into the target with a thud.

"Dead center," Jack clapped enthusiastically, walking over to the wall, and plucking out the knife. "Skill that excellent deserves a knife better than this potato peeler."

Peter stepped forward, wresting his knife out of Jack's hand with a frown. "It was a gift from my father before he died. A little respect, please?"

With arms outstretched in surrender Jack backed away. "I meant no offense."

"It may look like nothing to you," Peter examined the knife in his hand. Though he kept the wood handle polished and the blade sharpened, it looked as old and tired as its years. "But this knife is my most prized possession."

"Well, of course, it's a family heirloom…" Jack pulled out a chair and flopped down at the table just outside the barracks.

"It's more than that," Peter sat down next to him, pulling out a stone and running it along the blade affectionately. "It's a reminder of all that I have lost, all of my failures…" Peter gripped the handle in his fist, staring at it. "And a reminder of my duty to find my lost sister."

"Yes, yes, it's a very important knife, we get it," Paul leaned back in his chair, digging in his pocket. He leaned forward, thumping a deck of cards onto the table. "Whist, anyone?"

Jack leaned forward eagerly, removing his cap to reveal dark, slicked back hair. "I'm in."

Peter took one last nostalgic look at his knife, then slipped it into his pocket. "Count me in, too."

"Don't worry, ol' chap," Jack clapped Peter on the back. "Your affections for your knife are," he looked up to the ceiling, waving his hand around in the air. "We'll say noble."

"Impossible is more like it," Paul shuffled the deck,

frustrating Peter by avoiding his eyes. "According to the records, our sister does not exist." He looked up, eyes flicking to the other soldiers gathered outside. "We have room for one more player. Anyone?"

"Sure, I will," Lucas replied, a tall fellow with long fingers and a head full of blonde curls.

"Just because there is no record of a Réalta Burns in any of the orphanages in England does not mean that she does not exist," Peter stared hard at his little brother.

Paul shuffled the cards so fast they were a blur to Peter's eyes. "But it sure doesn't help. I don't want to talk about it anymore. Now that Lucas has joined us, the game is set."

Biting his tongue, Peter sat back watching Paul deal out the cards to each player.

After he had dealt, Paul placed the deck in the middle of the table and flipped over one card. "Spades."

Lucas, seated on Paul's left, played the first trick: a 6 of Spades. Jack threw out a 10, followed by Peter, who threw out a Jack. Paul played a 3 of spades. Peter smiled broadly and swept the cards up into a pile in front of him.

"You may have won that round, Peter," Jack shifted in his chair. "But I will beat all of you this time around."

"We'll see about that," Paul scooped up the cards and pushed them towards Lucas to deal.

"No, Paul will win," Peter winked at his brother. "I may have won the first round, but we all know Paul wins, no matter what."

Lucas dealt out the cards. "It's true. Five years I've known these boys, never won a single game against Paul."

Peter chuckled, watching Paul organize his cards in his hands and contemplate them deeply. As Lucas flipped over the trump card, Paul glanced over the top of his cards.

Paul whistled, "You're all in for it now, bubs."

Peter played a ten, Jack a Queen, Paul, a Jack, and Lucas a five.

"Good ol' Queen of hearts," Jack smugly swooped up the cards, "Better pack it up, boys, you don't stand a chance tonight." Jack chuckled softly to himself at his victory, and he nodded as the crowd around them cheered.

"Alright, alright," said Paul, smiling mischievously. "You may have won that hand, but I've got the rest of them. If any of you chumps feel like surrendering, now would be a good time."

The crowd applauded as Paul won the next round and the next, until all the rounds were his. He sat back, gloating in the praise, gathering up his cards merrily. "Sorry, Jack ol' boy, maybe next time."

Jack laughed merrily and winked, "You're on."

"How you constantly win these games is beyond me," Peter gathered up his cards and pushed them into the center of the table. "Best card shark in all of England, right there."

Paul laughed merrily, "It's all in the wrist, you know," he remarked, flexing his wrist back and forth.

"You've got cards hidden up your sleeve or something?" Lucas playfully grabbed for Paul's wrist, forcing back the sleeve with a grin.

Paul wriggled his bare wrist. "Just that good, my boys. Just that good."

"Somebody has to knock this man down a rung or two," Jack crossed his arms. "Best two out of three?"

"One of us is bound to beat him eventually," Peter rubbed his hands together eagerly.

"Sure, keep telling yourself that, brother," said Paul, winking.

"Now, that's no way to talk to your big brother," Peter flashed him a grin.

"Be careful, Paul, or he won't read you a bedtime story when he tucks you in tonight," Jack burst into laughter before he could finish the sentence.

"Amusing," Paul shrugged his eyebrows and rolled his eyes. He shuffled the cards, performing tricks such as shuffling one handed, holding the cards in one hand and letting them cascade down into the other, and a display where fingers and cards blurred as they cut and wove into each other seamlessly.

Mesmerized, Peter watched the cards shift in his brother's hands. That, coupled with the heat of the day, lulled him into a peaceful state. Inside the walls of the Fort there was no war, no battles to be fought. For a few moments, at least, he could be still. He could enjoy the other's company. He could laugh and not worry about the dangers lurking just beyond.

32

Peter rose from the ground and ran, then slowed to a stop, raising his gun. The gun bucked against his shoulder. He looked up to see the Indian man in front of him keel over to the side, blood oozing out of the gunshot wound. He ran again, stopped, raised the gun, and shot, blasting through the eye of another soldier at the same time a sharp pain swept across his upper arm.

I'm hit. Got to keep moving forward. Don't stop or you'll die.

Glancing over he saw Paul, kneeling on the ground, reloading his musket. A soldier ran up, sword in hand, raising his arm, aiming for the neck...

Peter reached down to his waist, drew his knife and threw it at the soldier, burying the blade deep within the soldier's throat. Blood spurted and the eyes bulged. He shivered, grabbing Paul by the hand, and hauling him to his feet.

"Alright, Paul?"

Paul nodded, swinging his musket up quickly and jabbing it in Peter's direction. Peter flinched and side-stepped, looking behind to see that Paul had skewered a rebel that had been coming up behind him. He caught his breath, nodding his appreciation to his brother.

"Nothing can stop the Burns brothers," Paul reached forward, grasping Peter's hand.

"That's right," Peter clasped his hand, then they released each other. "Let's keep moving."

"Hold on," Paul held up a hand, eyes fixed on a commotion off to the side. "This way."

Peter looked to where Paul indicated, anger growing in his gut as he watched the rebels descend on a group of camp followers. He shouldered his musket and they hurried over, firing as they approached. He took out two rebels, then stopped to reload, but Paul kept moving, firing until his gun was empty. A girl screamed and Paul's head whipped to the side. Peter followed his gaze, spotting a rebel dragging a young woman into a thicket.

Paul squared his jaw.

"I've got a shot," Peter called over, but Paul ignored him, running headlong, tackling the rebel to the ground.

"Stupid," Peter growled, throwing himself to the ground as shots fired past him. He propped himself on his elbows and sighted his musket to cover Paul. Paul and the rebel wrestled, a flurry of punching limbs. Peter held his breath, looking to take the shot at the first opportunity. The rebel scrambled on top of Paul, hands pushing down onto his neck. Peter clenched his teeth, heart pounding against his bones. He could not let Paul die. He tightened his finger on the trigger, the rebels head just in line with the sight...

Paul brought his fists down hard on the man's forearms, releasing the grip on his neck. He flung his hips to the side, rolling the man over, and moving on top. He brought his fists down on the man's face, punching until blood covered his knuckles. When the rebel lay still, Paul reached for his musket, bringing the bayonet down on his chest.

Peter glanced away, feeling bile rise in his throat. But at the sound of voices, he looked back up.

Paul reached down to the girl whose yellow skirts were tangled in the thicket, helping her up. "Are you alright?"

"Yes, I am. Thanks to you."

Paul hauled her to her feet with a powerful pull of his arms, then placed his hand on her back, pushing her gently forwards.

"Stay close, we'll get you somewhere safe, Miss..."

"Lucy." She flinched at the sound of a close by musket shot. "I'm scared."

"Don't worry, it'll be alright," Paul winked at the girl, then pulled her behind him as they approached Peter.

Peter stood from the ground, turning, and facing the battle once more.

"We have to get her to safety, Peter."

Lips pressed tightly together, Peter fired his gun, clearing the path ahead. "Let's go then."

The cries of the other group of camp followers, huddling in the trees pricked his ears. He turned to them, waving them over. "Come, we'll get you to safety."

Relieved, the group of women hitched up their skirts and fell in line behind them.

Keeping his gun at eye level, Peter pushed forwards. The gate into Fort William was not far. Crouching as low as he could, he jogged forward, then stopped, aimed, and fired at two rebels hidden in the brush. The coast cleared, Peter nodded towards the group, beckoning them to keep following.

"We are making a dash for the gate," Peter explained to the group. "Paul, I want you to cover the left and I will take the right. The rest of you, keep close to the ground."

Paul nodded, taking his hand off of Lucy's arm and taking his place next to Peter. Peter grimaced at the looks of panic on the women's faces and knew there was nothing he could say to reassure them. Between this little copse of trees and the gate to the Fort, there was no cover, nothing to hide behind. Just open land with soldiers and rebels at battle.

He dropped his gaze to his musket and quickly reloaded. With a lick of his lips, a loosening of his shoulders, and a reassuring glance to his brother, he hefted his gun. "Here we go. Now!"

Peter took off, ignoring the whimpers coming from behind. Not too far. They could make it. "Get down!" He shouted and the women dropped to the ground as shots fired around them. Peter shot at the rebels, taking out one, two, then a third. He heard Paul shoot twice, then call out "clear!"

"Clear," Peter echoed. "Let's move," he called to the ladies.

They got to their feet and took off once more, gaining

ground quickly. Another shot fired and a woman behind him screamed.

"Down!" He shouted, moving his gun quickly in the direction the shot came from. The rebel aimed right for him...

Peter shot without thinking and the rebel crumpled.

He dropped to his knee, risking a glance back, his gut sinking at the sight of a woman held up by the others, clutching her side where blood spurted.

"Can you help her move?" Peter's voice crackled.

The ladies nodded through their tears.

He nodded his head, tightened his jaw. "Last dash. Ready?"

They all nodded and slower this time, he jumped up and jogged slowly, keeping one eye on the battlefield and the other on the ladies. As they neared the gate, he stopped and ushered the ladies through the gate, and then followed them inside.

Another group of soldiers swarmed up behind, rushing into the gate with their injured in tow.

He located the nearest guard, waving him over. "Get that injured woman to the med cabin immediately." He pointed to the woman that had been shot.

The guard nodded, hefted the woman in his arms and ran off.

Stopping to catch his breath, he looked through the crowd of soldiers and camp followers around him, searching for Paul.

A head of blonde curls peeped out through the crowd. Recognizing that head as belonging to Lucas, he jogged over.

"Have you seen Paul?"

Lucas pointed with his head. "Just saw him. He was with a girl in a yellow dress."

Scoffing, Peter put his hands on his hips and shook his head. "Of course, he is."

"I wasn't expecting a battle today, so close to the Fort," Lucas reached up to scratch the back of his neck, his hand coming away sweaty and filmed with dirt. "Thought it was just going to be a simple matter of escorting the new contingent into the fort."

Peter reached up to his shoulder, inspecting the damage. "Me either." Dropping his arm, he looked back over his shoulder. "We should get back out there."

Curling his lip, Lucas pointed over to the right. "What about Paul?"

Peter glanced over, spotting Paul holding Lucy in his arms, rubbing her back sympathetically. Sighing, he shook his head. "He's too busy. Let's go."

33

"Can we talk?"

Paul sighed, shouldering past Peter blocking the doorway to their barracks. "We were great today, brother. We make a good team."

A vein in Peter's throat throbbed as he clenched his jaw. "Don't do that."

"Do what?" Paul flopped onto his cot, kicking off his boots with his feet.

"Pretend I am not angry with you for what you did today." Peter crossed his arms, glaring.

"I don't know what you're talking about."

"Don't play stupid with me, Paul."

"I saved the life of a lady, yes, shame on me," Paul shifted on the cot, shrugging his shoulders.

"You risked your life needlessly," Peter moved closer, leaning down. "I had a shot."

"It was the heat of the battle, Peter, calm down."

Peter straightened, the vein in his neck pulsing. "You act on impulse. It is foolish."

"Will you relax?" Paul cozied into the cot, holding his arms out wide. "I'm alive, aren't I?"

"You could have died, Paul. You need to be more careful. You need to be more reasonable."

Paul lifted a hand as he talked, touching his fingers to his thumb in the shape of a flapping mouth.

"That's not funny, Paul," Peter turned away in disgust. "You need to grow up."

Paul's face tightened. "Stop it, Peter. I've had enough of you. I don't need you to lecture me."

"Apparently, you do," Peter whirled back around. "You could have died today. It was stupid of you."

"Is that what this is about?"

"What do you mean?"

Paul's cheeks flared. "It's your biggest fear…me dying."

Peter blinked rapidly and said nothing.

"You are afraid of me dying on your watch, that is," Paul continued. "I don't need you mothering me. In case you have not noticed, I am a grown man."

"One that acts like a child," Peter shook his head.

"That is uncalled for." Paul swung his legs off the cot, sitting up straight. "Yes, I took a risk to save a girl today. It was a good thing and you do not get to insult me for it, brother." His Adam's apple bobbed as he swallowed. "Lighten up, Peter."

Peter whirled and advanced on him, grabbing his collar in both hands and pulling him from the cot. "Lighten up? You have no idea the guilt I carry. You have no idea how much I fear losing you."

Suddenly embarrassed by his outburst, Peter let go of his brother, turned away, rubbing his forehead. "I'm sorry, Paul."

Paul snorted, but responded softly, "You won't lose me. We are brothers. We are in this together... until the bitter end."

Peter tossed in his bunk, beads of sweat forming on his brow. The night was hot, lending a feverish heat to the nightmares playing through his mind while he fitfully slept.

First to appear in his thoughts was a vision of Seamus, sick with cholera as they crossed the water separating Ireland from England. *I won't let him die.* Peter thought. *I can't let him die.* But his little brother's face was turning white and his blue eyes were staring at Peter with such pain and such fear. Peter shivered and gagged. Seamus's body quivered and seized, writhing about like a worm on a hook, and all he could do was stand there and watch the life drain from him, the light in his eyes forever going out. Then he was bobbing in the water, dead bodies floating around him, and the sharks were coming for him; their mouths open in gory greed.

Jolting upright, he awoke on the hard-cobbled stones, pushing a holed blanket off his legs, rats squeaking in the corner. His hand brushed against Réalta's soft hair and he brushed it away thinking it was cobwebs. When he realized it was his little sister, he relaxed, remembering they were in Liverpool, camping out in a makeshift hut in the alley, in the slums.

The morning would soon come and together with Réalta and Pól, they would trudge to the coal mines and be lost in darkness, buried beneath the ground like the living dead. He shivered and wiped away a tear, guilt from their miserable fate sticking like a knife in his throat. Placing a hand on Réalta's hair, he combed through it gently. *One day, we'll be free,* he whispered to her.

He felt her move beneath his fingers and in her child's voice she sang, *God bless the moon and God bless me, and God bless that somebody I want to see.* The words started soft, but echoed louder and louder, 'til his head rang. He patted her head. *That's beautiful, óg Réalta,* little star. He smiled, watching her roll to face him.

Gasping, he shrunk back, screaming at the sight of her face. Gnawed by rats there was no nose, no cheek, no lips, and her eyes, her blue eyes, burned into him. He shook his head in disbelief. The ends of her hair caught fire, little sparks flying out before her head was consumed, then he felt her hand in his, and she screamed, *Don't leave me, don't leave me, don't leave me!*

34

"Peter, stop."

His eyes popped open and the flames stopped. He looked over to see Paul staring at him, eyebrows pinched together in concern.

"Peter, you were dreaming something awful," Paul nudged his shoulder, bringing him further awake. "You okay?"

Sighing, Peter nodded, dropping his head in his hands, and rubbing thoroughly. "It was nothing."

"You can't fool me, Peter," Paul moved away and tucked the sheets in around his bunk.

"What?" Peter replied, rising shakily from bed, his movements slow, his brow still sheathed in sweat.

Paul stopped making the bed and stared at him. "You dream about death."

"They are just dreams," Peter shrugged it off,

working to make his own bed.

"It's not your fault, none of it is," Paul clapped him on the back. "Every time we go to battle, you come back with these nightmares."

Peter set his jaw. Standing upright, he shrugged off Paul's hand, pretending like nothing had happened. "Alright, let's roll out for drills." He grabbed his gun and led the way.

Walking out into the open field, Peter took a deep breath, letting the last of his nightmare dissipate in the hot sun. Peter and the other soldiers stripped off their jackets and met in the middle of the field. The Commanding Officer gave the order to start running and they set off, running around the field a few times, until they were liberally soaked in sweat.

This was followed by the soldiers running to the mess hall for a quick drink of water to ward off heat exhaustion. Then back to the field to do more drills involving high knees, shooting stances, and shooting practice. As soon as the morning waned and the heat got to be too much, the drills ended, and the soldiers were dismissed for the noon day meal.

As Peter and Paul walked to the mess hall, a young girl ran to meet them.

"Well, if it isn't Lucy Bright," Paul said striding up to her.

"Well, if it isn't, Paul Burns," she said in return. "How good to see you again."

"Lucy is the daughter of our Lieutenant Colonel Bright." Paul took her hand and kissed it until she giggled flirtatiously.

Peter nodded in greeting, but frowned at the sight of his brother's display.

"How long do you think you will be stationed here at the Fort?" Paul let her hook her arm in his as they continued to walk, Peter glowering beside them.

"Oh, for a while I suspect. How long have you been here?"

"We've been here a year, but there has been talk of us moving on soon."

"I hope I can stay with your regiment," she tilted her head to Paul's shoulder, tightening her grip. "I just met you, my hero. It would be heartbreaking to say goodbye so soon."

"I promise to spend every free moment with you, my lady."

She giggled. "I hear that you are the best card shark in the Fort. I must play with you sometime."

"I'm sure we can manage that," Paul nudged Peter's arm.

Peter glared at him, but added as cheerfully as he could, "Yes, that would be splendid."

"Good, it's settled then. Peter and I have the evening off from our duties. We can plan for a game of Whist and a stroll through the park later."

"Yes, indeed," Lucy said, smoothly pulling her arm out of his. "Well, Mother is waiting for me. I better be off."

Paul watched her saunter off down the lane. "That is a fine woman."

Peter shook his head. "What woman? She's a child, Paul."

"There's only seven years difference between her and I, that's not so bad," he said defensively.

"What do you like about her anyway?" Peter crossed his arms and stalked off.

"I don't need to answer that," Paul followed along behind in his wake. "Why are you always so upset with me? Every time I try to have fun you're always there to bring me down. I find a girl I like and there you are, looking down on me again. I am tired of it, Peter."

Peter's shoulders sagged and he stopped walking. "I don't wish to fight."

"Well, then stop fighting me," Paul glowered, facing him directly.

Peter looked down and sighed. "I'm sorry, alright. I don't understand why I do it."

Scowling, Paul grudgingly forgave him. "I do know," he said, "You're too protective. You're smothering me."

"I know," Peter replied, knowing it was true, but also knowing he would not be able to stop. "I cannot help it."

"We need to find you a girl, then maybe you'll get off my back," Paul cast him a smile and punched his shoulder.

"Maybe someday," Peter looked up to the sky, feeling the hot breeze on his skin. "If we make it out of here alive."

He brought his gaze back down to Paul. Paul nudged his arm and shook his head.

"I forgot to tell Lucy something," he glanced over his shoulder, trying to spot where she had walked. "I'll be right back."

"Mhm," Peter threw his hand up as Paul jogged to catch up with Lucy. He shook his head as Paul leaned close to her, whispering in her ear. She giggled, covering her mouth with her hand.

Peter kicked the ground and turned away. The sight of Paul with the girl made his stomach roil with sickness. He smacked his lips against the bitter taste in his mouth. How could Paul be flirting when their sister was out there, alone, impoverished, or dead? How could he frolic in the field when war surrounded them and every day another person died? It just wasn't right...

The next day at lunch, Peter looked at Paul over his

plate of rice and chicken covered in a curry sauce with a side of figs. Paul bobbed his head to a song only he could hear, chewing contentedly.

"How was your walk with Lucy last night?" Peter took a bite of chicken, chewing it slowly.

"It was magical, Peter," Paul wagged his fork in the air as he spoke. "Do you know that spot in the park with all those trees and the meadow of green grass?"

Peter nodded.

"When the fireflies come out and you've got a beautiful woman by your side..." Paul shook his head, crossed his arms, and stared back at Peter. "...it's the best time to be alive."

"Is that so?" Peter raised an eyebrow, fighting back the urge to lecture him about the consequences of keeping a Commanding Officer's daughter out so late.

"Yes, you should try it some time."

Peter snorted and shook his head vehemently. "No, thank you."

"Why not, Peter?"

Peter pushed his plate forward. "Oh, look." He gestured around to all the soldiers leaving the mess hall like a school of fish. "Lunch is over. It's time for garrison duty." Peter stood quickly. "Come on now, pip pip."

Paul shoveled the last of his meal into his mouth and stood hurriedly. "Don't think this conversation is over, because it isn't."

Shrugging, Peter turned and led the way down to the stairs of the mess hall and out into the bright sunny courtyard. When they had stepped onto the well-traveled footpath leading to the northern wall, Paul suddenly stopped short.

"I forgot my deck of cards in there," he said, nudging Peter's shoulder.

"Okay, I'll wait for you out here," Peter said, adjusting the gun on his shoulder. He watched Paul run up into the dilapidated building. As Paul disappeared into the building, a great shockwave shook the earth. Peter steadied himself and looked around in panic, wondering if they were under cannon fire. The other soldiers walking about also looked around, unsure of what happened.

Peter's legs felt as they did the first few days aboard ship, wobbly as if on water, not solid ground. A few seconds later, a second stronger shockwave passed through. Peter fell to the ground. He heard some people screaming and then a great crack and a rumbling of stone. He looked up to find the mess hall roof split in two, crumbling in upon itself.

Peter watched in horror as the building groaned, creaked, and collapsed to the ground in a cloud of white dust. He screamed, vaulting to his feet, and launching towards the building.

Choking on the dust billowing around, Peter tried to fan it away with his arms, then hauled away chunks of the building and walls. He called out his brother's name, looking around desperately at the debris.

He scrambled on top of the wreckage, searching for some sign of his brother, a hand, a foot, anything. Then he saw it, a pair of boots sticking out motionless from underneath the collapsed wall. Peter's shoulders slumped and he stumbled forward, holding a trembling hand out towards the body. "Paul."

35

Peter fell to his knees on what had been, moments before, the mess hall floor. His hands shook. He didn't think he'd be able to lift the brick wall crushing his brother beneath its weight. "I can't do this," Peter said, bursting into tears.

Placing his hands on the dusty brick, he shoved, successfully hauling the wall a few inches to the right. Feeling snot accumulating beneath his nose, tasting its saltiness on his lips, he lifted his arm, wiping it away, then bent, securing his hands on the brick once more. He heaved once, took a deep breath, and heaved again. Arms burning, he placed his hands on his hips and gulped the air, fighting back the tears, though they burned in his eyes. A tightness in his throat made him choke.

A hand fell on his shoulder. "Hey, you need some help there?"

Peter whirled at the sound of Paul's voice, and

looked up to find him looking down at the boots of the buried man with concern. Peter sputtered for words, then stood, launching himself at his brother, wrapping him in a hug.

"Paul. I thought I'd lost you."

Paul flinched at the sudden hug, then loosely patted Peter on the back as his arms were pinned down, crushed by Peter's arms.

"Nah, you'll never get rid of me that easily," Paul mumbled through squished lips.

Peter released him, turning away as he blinked back tears. "How did you-"

"When I heard the first rumble and the building started to creak, I jumped out the window fast as I could," Paul replied. "This poor bloke must not have got out in time," Paul kicked the man's boots. "Must be the cook. I didn't see anybody else in there."

Peter drew in a deep breath, shaking his head, still standing with his face averted.

Shifting his feet awkwardly, Paul stepped forward, patting Peter on the shoulder. "You alright?"

Peter cleared his throat, nodding slowly. "I'm fine." He pointed to the man still buried under the wall. "Can you help me move this off him?"

"Alright," Paul stepped beside his brother, bending down to lay his hands on the brick.

Together they hauled the brick wall off the man, pushing it over to the side. Though the man's face was torn, covered in blood and mortar dust, Peter confirmed by his uniform that it was the cook. He looked up as a crowd gathered outside the collapsed mess hall.

"Anybody else in there?" One soldier asked, rushing up beside them.

"We don't think so," Paul replied, casting his eyes over the wreck, just in case.

"We must get him out of there," a nurse commanded, sidling up beside them.

Peter and Paul carried him out and handed him to two men with a stretcher.

Lieutenant Colonel Bright appeared at Peter's shoulder. "Are you boys alright?"

Sighing, Peter kneaded his brow with his fingers.

Paul smiled, clapping Peter on the back. "Right as rain, Sir. Had a bit of a scare, but we're all fine here."

"Ah, good," he said. "Had a scare myself. At first, I did not know what was happening, but when I heard the office building creaking, I thought better get out of there as quick as possible and I bolted out of the door."

"Same here," said Paul. "Except I jumped out the window."

"Are you sure you're alright?" The Lieutenant Colonel peered at Peter's face, his eyebrows twitching.

"I'll be fine," he half-smiled, holding his stomach as if he might throw up.

"Get yourself together and report for duty, then."

Wiping the dust off his clothes, Peter turned to his brother. "Come on, Paul."

"Do you want to lie down?" Paul placed his hands on his hips, scrutinizing his face.

Peter turned away. "I'm fine, let's go."

36

Heavy winds shook the barrack walls. Rain beat against the thatched roof making the ceiling sag with the weight of the water. Lightning crackled and thunder rumbled, each percussive blast shaking the soldier's bunks. Paul lay awake listening. Each crack of thunder sounded like walls cracking, each wind gust against the flimsy barrack walls warning of imminent collapse. His thumbs rapping against his breast bone, Paul listened to Peter tossing in his bunk, rolling over, moaning, and mumbling incoherently.

Just another night, another nightmare. Every time something happened to him, Peter had a melt down, would refuse to acknowledge it, and then he'd get angry at him. Paul shook his head in the dark, biting his lower lip. Unbelievable. A tingling of guilt crept up from his gut into his chest and tightened its grip.

Rubbing at his chest, Paul clamped shut his eyes. *It's*

not my fault. The barracks shook as thunder rumbled outside. Blocking out the sounds of Peter tossing in his bunk, Paul brought up an image of Lucy's face, soft blonde hair, pointed chin, tiny nose, pink lips. He smiled in the dark, feeling the tightness in his chest begin to ease. With hands on her waste, she felt so warm, so soft beneath his fingertips. Relaxed now, he began to drift off into sleep, not letting go of her image, the way she felt in his arms. Nothing bad ever happened when he held a woman. No, he'd never let her go.

When the storm broke just before dawn, Paul finally fell fast asleep, but not for long.

The wake-up bell rang just shortly after dawn.

Paul moaned, shuffling out of bed with a curse. Lucy's face still swam before his eyes, but it was fading fast. Above, he heard Peter hurtle upright at the sound of the bell, gasping for breath. They would both be short on sleep this day.

"You getting up or staying in bed all day, soldier?" Lieutenant Colonel Bright patrolled past his bunk, scowling.

"Sorry, Sir," Paul sprang into action, jumping out of his bunk, making his bed, and dressing in his uniform.

"Attention, soldiers," Lieutenant Colonel Bright called out above the noises of the soldiers readying for the day. "Today, we leave for Dinapore. We meet at the train station at 10:00am. Don't be late."

Peter hopped down beside Paul, of course, avoiding his eyes. As Paul fumbled with the buttons on his shirt, he focused on Peter's pale, sweat-strewn face, and the guilt came rushing back all at once, grasping his chest so tight, he almost couldn't breathe. He wanted to reach out and put a hand on his shoulder, pull him aside so they could talk it out. He wanted to help his brother so bad, assure him that everything was going to be okay, that he didn't need to beat himself up for things that were out of his control.

But he watched Peter wipe the sweat away, watch him routinely make his bunk, tuck in his shirt, comb his hair back, and place his hat dead center on his head, and all he could do was nod, as if everything was okay, as if nothing could be amiss. Peter was embarrassed of the nightmares, he knew. Peter didn't want to talk about them. Peter wanted...well, he didn't know what Peter wanted, or what he needed.

"We're finally moving on," Paul said after clearing his throat. "Wonder what we'll be doing in Dinapore?"

"Yes, moving on," Peter replied, straightening his collar.

He managed to catch Peter's eye and the two shared a knowing nod. That was enough. The tightness in his chest began   to   ease   ever   so   slightly.

37

The 19th Foot regiment exited the train at the station outside of Raneegunge. Peter squinted against the sun, smacking his lips at the tormenting heat. Steam rose from the ground where the sun evaporated the rain. The mosquitos swarmed and every second he found himself swatting at another that had landed on his throat.

Lieutenant Colonel Bright stood before the regiment, clearing his throat. "Attention. From here on out we go by foot to Dinapore. We will be required to camp in tents each night. The campsights and trail will be marked out for you by the Quartermaster of the Regiment, who will go before you on a horse. Remember, this forest is overrun with rebels. No one is to wander off alone. Always stick to the company. Always stick to the trail. Understood?"

The company responded in unison. "Yes, Sir."

"Good," Lieutenant Colonel Bright bobbed his head.

"Let us be on our way then."

"Now we're getting some excitement," Paul shifted the pack on his back, taking a deep breath of the hot air.

"Yes, weeks of traveling on foot ahead of us, what could be better?"

"Don't be sour," Paul said. "We have a long journey ahead. Let's try to make the best of it."

38

The clouds accumulated throughout the day. Before sunset, they grew darker, surely threatening rain. Daniel and the natives worked to set up the tent where it would receive the least wind resistance. With large knives, they hacked at fallen sticks, making stakes to push into the ground, then tying ropes to the stakes to lash the tents more securely to the ground.

"We are in for a storm tonight, aren't we?" Staletta rubbed her arms, watching Daniel stretch a rope taught and stake it in the ground. She rifled through her pack, pulling out her wool jacket. Even though it was still hot and humid, the wind was picking up, giving her chills.

Daniel moved to lash down the backside of the tent. "Do you think you could get a fire going before the rain starts?"

Staletta stood from the log she had been sitting on

and bent down over their firepit. Archie returned from gathering wood and piled it up for her. She grabbed the flint and rubbed it until it sparked and caught a few pieces of bark on fire just as a few drops of rain began to fall.

"Daniel, I don't think we are going to make it in time," she squinted up at the darkening sky, feeling the wind pick up at her back. The tops of the trees started rocking back and forth and the wind roared through the branches, making the leaves shake treacherously. Staletta glanced back down at her sparking fire, watching it dwindle down to smoke.

Having finished with the tent, Daniel came over to look down at the firepit. "The tents are ready. I suppose we better hunker down, wait it out. Maybe the storm will pass through quickly."

Staletta called over to Archie, standing looking out at the Hoogly River. "Archie, there's a storm coming. We better get inside the tents."

"Okay, ma'am," he said, tossing a stone into the river to see how far he could throw it.

He scrambled up the bank, then slithered into the tent behind Staletta. Daniel crawled into the tent behind her, secured the opening with rope, and sat back. Heavy drops of rain thumped on the canvas, first slowly, then gradually sped into a downpour.

Archie leaned closer into Staletta as the tent started to shake with the force of the wind. She cast a concerned glance at Daniel.

"It'll be alright," he said, tossing a blanket over top of them. "As long as the tent holds," he frowned, watching the sides of the tent pitch inward with each punch of the wind.

Having to raise her voice over the sound of the wind and rain, Staletta asked, "What do we do if it doesn't?"

Daniel sighed. "We get wet."

Staletta could already feel wetness where she sat, as the rain soaked the ground outside, and started pooling underneath the sides of the tent. Archie noticeably shivered beside her, and she wrapped an arm around him, squeezing his shoulder.

"We've been through worse than this. Remember the storms aboard ship?"

Archie swallowed. "At least on ship we could hide below decks."

"We'll be fine," Staletta said even as a great ripping noise from outside made them jump. There was creaking and groaning and then a large thump that made the ground shake. "Daniel, what was that?"

"Sounded like a tree fell," he replied, paler than usual. The top of the tent bent inwards against the steady deluge of rain. Daniel knelt in the middle of the tent, his knees sinking into the mud. He raised his arms over his head to brace the sagging fabric.

Another gust of wind stampeded the tent and one of the straps tied to a stake came loose. Daniel abandoned his position in the middle of the tent and scrambled outside, grasping hold of the flapping canvas.

"Can you grab that other end?" he called frantically.

Hearing his call, Staletta crawled outside, grabbing the tie end. She pulled, making it as tight as she possibly could against the wind pushing her over and the rain soaking her to the bone. She wiped the water out of her eyes only to have it flood them once more, then bent down and started tying the rope back onto the stake. Her fingers fumbled with the wet rope. After several attempts, the rope looped around the stake. She knotted it, and tightened it as best she could, then stepped on the stake to make sure it was set in the mushy ground. Breathless, she crawled back into the tent, followed closely by Daniel.

Dripping wet, with hair pulled loose from her braid, Staletta wiped her face on the soaked blanket.

Daniel raised one side of his mouth in a lopsided grin. He resumed his place in the middle of the tent, raising his arms towards the fabric. "You're cute when you're wet."

Staletta rolled her eyes and laughed at the same time Archie said, "Eww, yuck."

"If this storm doesn't let up it's going to be a long night," Daniel grimaced, shifting under the weight of the tent.

The storm finally died down in the early morning. Staletta and Daniel had switched spots so she had then been holding up the middle and Daniel went out into the storm to secure two more sides that had come loose during the night. When the rains finally stopped and the wind ceased, they relaxed, falling to the soggy ground in exhaustion.

"Time for bed?" Staletta asked, closing her eyes against the rising sun.

"I've slept in the rain before," said Archie, "But

nothing half as bad as that."

Daniel ruffled his hair. "You did great, kid." Daniel then waved to the natives who were already stoking a fire.

Slapping at a giant mosquito that landed on her arm, Staletta sat up, feeling the humidity glistening on her skin. "Too bad the storm didn't kill these off."

Daniel nodded his agreement. "Will you help me strike the tent?"

The next hour was spent packing up the camp and helping the natives prepare some breakfast. When the camp was cleaned up and their clothes had somewhat dried out, they loaded up the boats and set off up the river once more.

39

The boat drew up outside of Fort William just before sundown. They bid farewell to the natives who started pitching their tents for the night, and then set off for the closest gate. As they neared, Daniel bent to whisper in her ear.

"I read about this fort in the paper once. It's called a star fort, meaning it was built in the shape of a star."

Staletta stopped walking, looking up at him through her eyelashes. "The shape of a star?"

"The design is supposed to be ideal for a defensive position," Daniel explained, "The Italians started it back in medieval times, and it's been adapted over the course of –"

"Follow the star, Réalta, the one you were named after, "We'll find you. Don't be afraid."

Staletta ceased listening to Daniel's story, and the words of her brother crying out to her so long ago, filled her thoughts. Her eyes clouded over and saw not the great fortress in front of her, but the cold blackness of iron bars and the faces of her brothers, white against the dark bars, their hands reaching out towards her, grasping nothing but the wind.

"Follow the Star, Réalta."

"Follow the star, Réalta," she said aloud, grasping Daniel's shoulder.

Already shaking his head, Daniel replied, "Don't even go there, Star. It's coincidence."

Staletta blinked rapidly and the dank streets of Liverpool melted away before her eyes, the world becoming once more colored in green tropical plants, the sun setting in a blaze, illuminating the star fort in orange light. "Yes," she breathed, and laughed. "Yes, of course, you're right. But, even so..." She pointed to the fort, beaming at him.

He shook his head, resuming walking to the gate.

"Don't you see?" She asked, pointing to the fort again. "I followed the star. It's right there. I'm going to find them." She stood up straight, proud, and determined.

"I know, I know," Daniel replied, a smile in his voice. "Star-I'm glad you're excited, and I do think we are on the right track, but it's a coincidence. It's not a sign."

Staletta suddenly jolted forward, grabbing Daniel's shoulder until he turned to face her.

"What is it?" Daniel asked, concern in his voice.

"They could be in there," she nodded to the fort, holding her hands in front of her, fiddling with her fingernails.

"Yes?" Daniel narrowed his eyes at her.

212

"What if-" She sighed and shook her head.

"What if what?" Archie bounced on the balls of his feet.

Staletta scratched her forehead. "What if they don't want to see me?"

His face softening, Daniel reached forward to grab her hand. "Nonsense."

"It's been ten years. What if they have changed?" Staletta licked her lips. "What if they don't remember me?"

Daniel squeezed her hands. "You're having second thoughts when we've come this far?"

"Well," Staletta shrugged shyly. "Yes."

"Come on," Daniel tugged on her arm. "I'll be right beside you."

"Me too," Archie grabbed her other hand and started to pull.

As they approached the gate, a guard on the ramparts caulked his gun. "Who are you and what's your business here?"

Licking her lips, Staletta stepped forward tentatively. "I'm Staletta and this is my husband Daniel, and the lad's name is Archie. We are here to find out the whereabouts of two soldiers named Peter and Paul Burns."

"Peter and Paul Burns?" The guard cocked his head to the side, chewing on his lip. "Never heard of 'em."

Staletta lowered her head under the onslaught of her stomach falling to her feet. She took a shaky breath, then raised her head again, feeling Daniel squeezing her hand. "May we be allowed to enter to see if we can find someone who might know of their whereabouts?"

"I don't know as I should," The guard said, leaning back, eyeing them suspiciously. "You could be part of the mutiny..."

"I promise we aren't. Look, we have a note," Staletta dug in her pack, uncovering a soiled piece of parchment. Daintily holding it by two fingers, Staletta opened it carefully, looking up at the guard sheepishly.

"We got caught out in the storm last night and it seems the note got a bit wet, but..."-peering closely at the note-"...you can still make out the signature of Captain Cranly."

She held up the note proudly and smiled.

The guard scratched his chin. "Captain Cranly, you say?"

"That's right." Staletta confirmed, waving the note in the air like a white handkerchief from the hand of a lady looking for a suitor.

"Very well, then. I'll meet you at the gate and if it is indeed signed by Captain Cranly, you may enter," the guard disappeared and appeared a few moments later at the entrance of the gate.

Staletta rushed forward, handing him the note. He peered at her sceptically, smacked his lips, and then flicked his gaze to the note. His mouth moved soundlessly as he endeavoured to read the badly smudged note but nodded when he saw the partial signature at the bottom.

"The signature looks valid. I shall let you enter, as promised."

"Thank you, kindly," Staletta said, beaming brightly, snatching the note from the guard's hand in case they might need it to enter anywhere else.

"Well done, Star," Daniel said, nudging her with his elbow.

"A real military fort," Archie exclaimed in wonder. "Look at the cannons. And the soldiers."

"It is a different world," Staletta looked around at the buildings, from dilapidated barrack to lavish government house, and the soldiers running through drills or walking along the ramparts, guns at the ready.

"What should we do?" Staletta asked Daniel. "Start asking around?"

"I suppose so," Daniel replied, turning to the nearest building, a plain and shabby looking barrack. He walked up to it and knocked on the door.

A soldier opened the door, scratching his head and looking around confusedly at the sight of the threesome before him.

"Can I help you?" He asked, brows furrowed.

"We are looking for two soldiers, Peter and Paul Burns." Staletta said. "Do you know them?"

"Can't say as I do, Miss," the soldier shrugged.

Staletta nodded. "Do you know who might be able to tell us more?"

"I suppose any of the Commanding Officers could help."

"And where might the Commanding Officers be found?"

"Try that large, white building over there," the soldier replied, pointing to a stately building towering above the rest.

Daniel shook the man's hand. "Thank you, you've been an enormous help."

"Yes, thank you," said Staletta, tipping her hat at him.

The man returned into the depths of the barracks and left the trio standing outside.

"I guess we go to find a general or something?" Archie asked.

"Let's try that building," Daniel turned to gaze at the building the soldier had pointed to. "Certainly, looks like a place where the upper officers would gather."

Staletta nodded, letting him lead the way.

As they walked back out onto the path up to the estate-like building, they passed a soldier lounging at a table outside the barracks. He had his hands behind his head and feet crossed on top of the table. When he caught sight of the trio he whistled to get their attention. "Fancy a game of cards?"

"I'm afraid not, we are on a mission," Daniel replied, nodding politely.

"A mission?" The soldier's eyebrows rose, forehead wrinkling. "Color me intrigued."

Daniel frowned and placed a hand on Staletta's arm. "Excuse us," he said to the soldier. "It's a matter of great importance."

The soldier grinned broadly and held out his hands. "Might I be able to help? You three don't look like you have ever stepped foot on a military base before."

Staletta crossed her arms, pursed her lips. "Are you a commanding officer?"

The man shook his head.

216

"You wouldn't happen to know if one is nearby, would you?" Staletta continued.

"Depends on what you need them for," The soldier replied, turning his attention to picking at something on the top of his hand.

Staletta hesitated. "We are looking for two men in the 19th foot regiment."

The man took his arms out from behind his head and moved his feet down to the ground. "I have friends in the 19th Foot. What are their names?"

"Peter and Paul Burns," she replied.

The man nodded. "Ah yes, good 'ol Burns brothers. Two good friends of mine, I dare say."

Staletta's hand dropped to her flip-flopping stomach. The other hand drifted to her mouth. "Please, where are they? Will you take us to them?"

The man paused to lean forward, his lips downturning. "I'm afraid you missed them. They were dispatched just yesterday."

Blinking rapidly, Staletta's hand tightened around her mouth, then she closed her eyes, half turning away. Daniel's hand quickly warmed the small of her back.

"What is this about?" the soldier asked, crossing his arms. "Who are you and what do you want with the Burns' brothers?"

Unable to answer, Staletta was relieved when Daniel spoke. "She is their sister." He paused. "It's a long story, but the short version is that they have not seen each other in te-"

"Ten years." The man rapidly stood, clapping the cap

off his head as he swung around in a circle, then threw the cap down on the ground. Hands on hips, he shook his head furiously. "One day. You missed them by one miserable day."

"You know?" Staletta quickly turned back to him.

"Of course, I know about Rèalta," the soldier licked his lips, sighing. He glanced down at her. "My name is Jack. Believe me when I say your brothers want nothing more than to see you again."

Feeling a tendril of hope resurfacing, Staletta stood. "They spoke of me?"

"They told me as soon as their contract with the army was up, they were going to go find you, but...here you are."

Smiling, Staletta nodded. "Here I am." Her smile faltered. "And I'm too late."

Daniel grabbed Jack's shoulder "Do you know where they were heading?"

"Dinapore," the man said instantly. "They were headed for Dinapore."

"Thank you," Staletta beamed up at the soldier. "You've no idea how grateful I am. Danny, Archie, let's go. We've got to get to Dinapore as soon as possible. We're only a day behind. If we start now, we can catch up, I'm sure of it."

"Hold up there," Jack held up a hand to steady her. "First you must cross the river, board a train, then it's a month long walk to Dinapore. Besides, it is nearly nightfall, you can't walk outside the fort willy nilly."

Staletta opened her mouth to retort, but the seriousness of the journey held her tongue. A month-long march through the jungle? How would they find their way? Her shoulders slumped.

Daniel turned back to Jack, "Do you know if it is possible to hire a guide or someone to take us there?"

Jack shook his head at Daniel's words. "You're talking about a forest crawling with rebels. You may have not noticed, but we're in the middle of a rebellion here."

"We understand that," Staletta replied. "But what else can we do? I know you understand...I must find my brothers."

"I'll tell you what, I like you and I like your brothers, and I would dearly like to see you reunited once more. My regiment, the 10th foot, will be dispatched to Dinapore in a few days. If you wish to come along, I will personally help you get set up in the army."

"Set up in the army?" Daniel asked, not liking the sound of that.

"Not as soldiers, of course," the man clarified.

"Aww shoot," Archie said, turning away in disappointment.

The man chuckled at the boy's reaction. "As camp followers," he continued. "Is there a job you can do, some skills that might be useful?"

"I'm a carpenter by trade," Daniel supplied.

"Alright, I'm sure we'll find something for you...the baggage train or the animals." Jack replied. He turned his gaze to Staletta and the boy. "And what about you two?"

Staletta cleared her throat. "I play the violin."

"And I play the flute," Archie replied.

"There could be a spot in the army band for you two

then. If not, Staletta, you can help as a nurse. The boy can help with the animals."

Staletta shrugged at Daniel. "What do you think?" She asked. "Should we do it?"

He shifted on his feet, scratching his head. "I don't like the idea of being tied to the army. We might get caught up in a battle. But on the other hand, if we strike out on our own, then there is no protection for us. At least in the army there would be some measure of protection."

"Either way is dangerous for you," Jack shrugged. "You could always stay here, wait for your brother's to someday return...or not. It's up to you."

"It's your decision, Star," Daniel placed a hand on her back. "We are with you, regardless."

Breathing in through her nose, Staletta nodded, knowing she was not just responsible for herself, she was responsible for Daniel and Archie, as well. Was it selfish to want to go? Was it reckless? Should they stay here, hoping her brothers would someday return, *if* they survived? Biting her lip, she steeled herself, breathed in and out deeply, then opened her mouth.

"Start tuning your flute, Archie. We're marching to Dinapore."

Jack glowed like a lantern suddenly struck to light while Archie jumped up and down excitedly. Staletta eyed Daniel, watching him nod in acceptance. The knowledge there was no going back from this decision weighed heavily between their gazes. Though she knew he would never condemn her, the selfishness of her quest was not lost on her. She did not need to find her brothers, she only desired to. If her desire led Daniel or Archie into death, she would have to bear that guilty burden.

"Alright, then," Jack broke the nervous tension with a clap of his hands. "Let's go get you situated."

Daniel took Staletta's hand and smiled. "Do not fear. If all else fails, at least we will still have each other."

40

"Lucas," Paul patted his friend on the shoulder. "I think I've finally got it; you want to test it out with me?"

Lucas shook his head. "I don't think so, mate. I got one hand on my gun and one hand swatting mosquitos. I don't think I can do all that, play cards, and still walk at the same time."

"Come on, give it a try, eh?" Paul stuck the cards out towards him temptingly.

"Sorry, mate," he pushed the cards away.

Paul grimaced, then brightened as he turned to Peter. "Brother, you want to see my new magic trick, do you not?"

Peter flicked his eyes at Paul and shook his head, his mouth turning down in a frown.

"There's Peter, cheerful as always," Paul did a little

skip and winked at his brother.

Peter sighed and squinted up at the sky. "It's going to rain, I warrant."

"Well, aren't we the gloomiest regiment in the Queen's army," Paul said sarcastically. He raised his voice, "Magic tricks, step on up. Anybody want to witness the amazing Paul perform his newest, his grandest, his most mesmerizing trick yet? Hmm?"

When nobody responded, Paul deflated. "Ahh, forget it. I bet Jack would if he were here." He and Jack had become quite close over the year spent stationed at the Fort. It had been refreshing to spend time with someone who didn't take themselves too seriously. A month long march up the Grand Trunk Road would have flown by if he were there.

Peter shot his brother another glare.

"Why are you in such a foul mood?" Paul thrust his cards into his pocket, shifting the weight of his pack.

"Why aren't you? That is a better question," Peter said, wiping his sweaty brow on a sleeve. "The heat is stifling. We have been marching for days. It's going to rain..." He paused as he swatted a mosquito on his cheek. "And these bloody bugs..."

"Because I don't like being a grumpy bum, that's why," Paul spat, crossing his arms over his chest and kicking a rock.

A chuckle caught in Peter's throat. He quickly turned it into a cough, but not soon enough. Paul raised a brow as Peter's lips stretched into a slight smile.

"Aha," Paul pointed a finger in his face. "Made you smile. Mission accomplished. Now, tell me why are you being such a grumpy bum?"

Peter sighed again and shrugged. "I don't know."

"You've been off the entire time we've been in India," Paul threw him a sideways glance. "I mean, it's usual for you to be a bit uptight, but you have taken it to a whole other level here on this continent."

"I know, I know," Peter glanced down. He sighed heavily, then spoke under his breath. "I guess...I guess I am...afraid."

Peter shifted under the weight of his pack and cast Paul another angry glare. "There I said it, are you happy now?"

Clearing his throat, Paul shrugged. "Afraid of what exactly?"

"Forget it," Peter glared at him, then looked back to the road ahead.

"Let me ask you this: if you could be doing anything else right now, what would it be?"

"Finding Réalta, of course."

"But what else would you do?"

Peter glowered, shaking his head. "There is nothing else."

Paul's eyes widened and his limbs reacted, arms flying wide, legs kicking out. "That is exactly your problem." Paul chuckled. "You have no interests, no dreams for your life. You need to relax. Find yourself a woman, or a hobby, anything."

Looking at his brother as if he were speaking a foreign language, Peter shook his head. "We're in the middle of a war. Who has time for hobbies and dreams?"

Paul reached into his pocket, pulled out his deck of cards. "I do. Pick a card."

Rolling his eyes, Peter finally relinquished. "If I play your little game, will you leave me alone?"

"Atleast for a little while, sure."

"Fine."

Paul cheered, throwing his arms up in the air. "We are going to have ourselves a magic show." He fanned the cards out in front of Peter's face. "Are you ready to be astounded?"

"I regret this already," Peter flashed his brother a wicked grin, then plucked a card from his hand.

"Read it, memorize it, but don't say it out loud. Got it?"

"Got it," Peter gazed at the four of diamonds.

"Place it back in the deck."

Peter stuck the card back and Paul shuffled the cards as he often did, in a series of turns and shuffles too quick for the eye to follow. Paul completed the shuffles, then split the deck, holding the middle card up for him to see. "Was that your card, sir?"

"Four of diamonds," Peter swatted at a mosquito as he glimpsed the card. "That's the one."

Holding his arms above his head, Paul applauded himself. "Thank you, everybody. Yes, thank you."

Lucas turned around, walking backwards. "Say, I wouldn't mind seeing that trick again."

"Ah, now that you have seen it in action, you're interested." Paul brought his arms back down, reshuffling the deck.

Lucas snorted as he pulled a card from Paul's hand, examining it. "I should not have dismissed the Amazing Paul so quickly."

"The Amazing Paul, you say," Paul collected the card from Lucas, then started into a display of shuffling that seemed to defy all laws of physics as the cards fell up instead of down. "I like the sound of that, but I like the sound of Paul the Fantastic even better."

"Is that what you will do after the army? Have your own magic show?" Lucas shoved his hands into his pockets, waiting for Paul to reveal his card.

Paul grinned lopsidedly. "Is this your card?"

Lucas's eyes widened and he nodded. "It certainly is, Paul the Fantastic."

Chuckling, Paul shrugged at Lucas's previous question, looking off to the distance. The jungle fell away as they marched, and the land opened up into an expansive, barren coal seam.

"I might," Paul kicked the rocks on the road as his feet suddenly dragged. His jaw tightened as memories of working in a coal mine flashed before his eyes. Nothing but darkness and the chinking of iron tools. Inadvertently, he picked at his fingernails. Back then, they would have been black. "I have thought a lot about what I will do after the army. You Peter?"

"After the army, we are going to find our sister." Peter once again shot him an angry glare. Paul wagged his head with the addition of an eye roll.

"I mean after that," Lucas clarified. "I was thinking of going into teaching."

Brows furrowing, Paul watched the workers scurry in and out of the tunnels. He knew Peter's mind was also flooding with memories of that dark time. He just hoped that this sight would not become nightmares for him that night.

"There is no 'after that.'" Peter replied. "Finding our sister is all there is."

Guilt filled Paul's chest at Peter's words. He wanted to find his sister just as much as Peter, but there was also life to live. There were other people to meet. Other adventures to discover. Should he share Peter's focused determination? Should he let all things go in pursuit of her? Should he cast off all dreams, all hopes, all opportunities for love and happiness? Then he would be just like Peter. Humorless. Ambitionless. A walking shell of a man. No, no he wouldn't do that. And he would do everything in his limited power to keep Peter from falling too far into the darkened pit.

He realized it now. Together they walked a tight line across a deep pit. He needed to be there, right behind Peter, to keep him from falling, and Peter needed to be there in front to keep Paul moving forward, else they both would fall.

Paul drew in a breath only to find it gritty with coal dust. Suppressing the urge to cough from the dust blacking his lungs, he rubbed at his eyes, remembering how gritty they could get, so dirty not even tears could wash it away.

Paul shifted his pack. With the knowledge that he was sacrificing a dream, he let his elbow reach out and clip Peter in the arm. "Together, we will find Réalta."

"Réalta was always such a bright light," Peter chuckled, turning away from the coal seam and rubbing his nose. "Always singing silly songs just to cheer us up. Like you with your magic tricks, Paul. You two were so similar. Then there is me, the serious one. The gloomy one."

Paul shook his head in disagreement. "The responsible one, the leader."

"Some leader."

"Don't go getting gloomy again, Peter, I mean it," Paul warned with a smile. "I worked too hard to get you into a good mood. Don't make me pull out my cards again."

The troops picked up their pace and soon the coal mines were left behind as the road curved off and away.

A soft voice began to sing: "*Why, soldiers, why? Must we be melancholy boys.*"

Paul swatted at his ear, looking around for the source. A nudge on his arm forced him to look in Peter's direction. "Did you hear singing?"

Peter grinned broadly, and Paul, taken aback, shook his head, watching Peter lift his head, open his mouth, and sing over the sound of marching boots: "*Why, soldiers, why? Whose business is to die.*"

Mouth splitting into a grin, Paul threw his arms up, eager to join in: "*What sighing? Fye!*" Paul shouted the song loudly, lifting his arms, beckoning the other soldiers to sing along.

The soldiers joined in, lifting their heads. A cannonade of voices rang out across the Indian plain: "*Damn fear, drink on, be jolly boys. 'Tis he, you, and I; Cold, hot, wet, or dry.*"

41

Peter wrapped his fingers around a mug of hot tea. Closing his eyes against the faint lick of the fire, he listened to the wood crackling, lambs bleating, and cow hooves thumping on the ground. He chuckled as an elephant bellowed, then listened for the insects, but the wind drew his attention away and he listened to it playing in the trees, whispering something to him that he did not understand. He tightened his eyes, listening harder. *Please tell me what to do. Give us strength to carry on, protection from harm...*

"We could slip into the forest, no one would even notice that we are gone."

"Oh, Paul, I just don't feel that well tonight."

Peter opened his eyes, shoulders slumping as he watched Paul escorting Lucy over to the fire.

"We'll just sit here then," Paul groused, settling onto the log opposite Peter.

Lucy sat down next to Paul, giggling as he wound an arm around her, massaging her shoulder, then reaching up to her ear. "Look," he pulled out a card.

Lucy slapped him on the chest. "How did you do that? That's amazing. Your brother is ever so talented, Peter."

Frowning, Peter rubbed his brow. "Yes, he does astound me sometimes." Fixing Paul with a pointed stare, he raised a brow.

Paul grinned widely in response, pulling Lucy closer to him. "Peter's grouchy again."

Lucy giggled. "Peter is always grouchy." She leaned forward. "You need a woman and I know just the one."

"Oh no," Peter shook his head.

"Valerie," Lucy nodded, nudging Paul. "Don't you think they would be absolutely sublime?" She glanced over to another campfire and tossed her head. "Or Julia. Or her sister Irene. Either one of them would be just fabulous, Peter."

Peter glanced over to where she was looking and saw a girl with squash colored hair watching him. He looked away quickly, pinching the bridge of his nose. "Thank you, Lucy, but I really am not interested."

"There is something not quite right about your brother," Lucy tisked, turning to Paul.

"He is a bit uptight," Paul kissed Lucy until she giggled. "Come on, Peter. It's a lot of fun." He flashed him a grin.

Shaking his head, Peter set down his mug of tea in the grass and stood.

"Where are you going?"

"Anywhere, but here." Peter straightened his jacket, then set off across the darkened campsite. He shook his shoulders as he walked through the camp, trying to shake off the grubby feeling with which that encounter had left him.

It was not right. Paul should not be treating Lucy as if she were a bauble. She was a Lieutenant Colonel's daughter. He should be treating her with the respect and dignity due to a young lady in her station. And, as a lady in her station, she should not be encouraging Paul. The urge to tell her father the whole sordid affair welled up in him, but he set his features, pushing the urge away. It was not his place to interfere.

He placed his hands on the makeshift pen that encircled the lambs, watching them calmly munching on the grasses. The horses and elephants that accompanied the army shuffled and snorted nearby.

As he stood just outside the campsite, the voices of the soldiers had distanced, allowing his head to clear.

He took a deep breath of the night air, letting it calm his agitated spirit. Breathing out, he relaxed his shoulders. *I just want things to be right. I want Réalta to come home. I want to go home.* He threw a hand up, shaking his head. *We have no home to go to.*

A growl in the darkness.

Peter stiffened, the hairs on the back of his neck standing straight up as a tiger leaped from a tree above his head, feet landing on the ground inside the lamb pen with elegant grace. The lambs reacted, darting wildly to the sides, bleating bloody murder. The tiger pounced, snatching one by the haunches and pulling it back, jaws crunching down on its neck.

Backstepping, Peter fumbled for his musket, but it was not there. He cast his mind back to where he had left it, leaning against the log at the fire. He cursed himself for not bringing it with. As he stared at the tiger, it whirled around to face him. The tiger's black eye pierced into him, watching him. Frozen, Peter stared back, mouth open as his heart raced.

Lazily, the tiger looked away, leaned back on its legs, and, with lamb firmly clamped in its jaws, pounced over the short wall. Shouts from behind alerted Peter to the presence of soldiers running up, guns at the ready.

"No," Peter pushed down on the barrel of the gun held by the soldier next to him. "Leave him be."

The tiger disappeared into the black forest.

"Are you mad?" The soldier whirled on Peter, pointing into the forest. "You let it get away."

Peter fixed him with a stare. "He was after the lambs, not us. A gun shot would have only alerted the rebels to our presence."

"He is right," Lieutenant Colonel Bright strode up beside them, watching the terrified lambs racing around the pen. "No gun shots in this territory. Nice work, Officer Burns." He turned around, addressing the gathered soldiers. "We'll set up a perimeter and build up the fires, and no harm will come to us this night."

Staring up at the sky, Peter felt his tongue lay like a wool sock in his mouth. He smacked his lips, feeling sweat trickle down both sides of his face, pooling along his collar. Sticking a finger between his throat and shirt, he pulled at the fabric, willing it to loosen. Feet heavy like bricks, he picked up one and set it down, picked up the other and set it down, focusing on the rhythmic march and trying to forget the heat.

Beside him, Paul wiped at his brow and huffed a sigh. "This is insufferable."

"What, no magic tricks today, Paul?" Peter swallowed hard, wishing for nothing more than a cool stream to fall into.

Up ahead, a commotion snagged Peter's attention. He craned his neck to see over the heads of the soldiers marching in front of him. The men in front stopped short. Peter pulled back just in time to avoid running into them. "What is going on?"

Moving slightly to the side, he peered through a gap in the soldier's bodies. A soldier lay face down on the ground, two soldiers bending down to pick him up by the arms.

Peter's ears pricked, picking up the rumblings of conversation going around:

"Heat exhaustion."

"Bloke just collapsed."

Pulling back, Peter stood up straight, swallowing past the dryness in his throat. Taking his place beside Paul, they continued marching.

"No," Paul shook his head. "No magic tricks today."

Peter hunkered under his pack, kept his eyes fixed ahead, and steeled his mind against any thoughts of heat or thirst. All day they marched and as the sun fell, they pulled up to their campsite, collapsing with relief onto the cooling grass.

Kicking his boots off and stretching out his aching legs, Peter rested back his head, looking up at the sky. "Survived another day."

Paul pulled off his boots, sighing in relief. "The day isn't over just yet. There is still time."

234

"Those men," Peter grimaced, closing his eyes against the images in his head. The day had been long and hot, the hottest day they had ever experienced during their year in India. Five men had collapsed during the march. All dead. "Are we going to make it out of here alive?"

Shrugging, Paul looked up as Julia and Irene drew close.

"Water, gentlemen?" Irene poured a small glass from a hip flask and handed it to Paul. "I am surprised at you, Paul."

Julia bent down next to Peter. Dimly aware of her presence, he took the glass. He threw back the small glass of water, feeling like it was not hardly enough, then lifted the glass back to Julia with a low, "Thank you."

She quickly snatched the glass and turned away. Peter winced at her pinched expression. *I've done something wrong, haven't I?* He thought, but brushed it away as Paul's voice took over.

"Why is that?"

"I thought for sure you would be more concerned about Lucy." Irene took Paul's glass and started moving away.

"What do you mean?" Paul stiffened. "Has something happened to her?"

"You do not know?" Irene placed a hand on her

collar bone and fixed him with a stare. "Lucy is ill. She has been with the nurses all day. It does not look good, I am afraid."

"What is it? What is wrong with her?" Paul started to his feet, brushing the grass off his trousers.

Irene looked down at her feet, moving away to the next batch of soldiers. She looked back up at Paul one last time. "Cholera."

Paul looked away as his jaw hardened.

Peter knew the look, knew the memories flooding through him of their brother Seamus. Peter saw it too, the image of Seamus vomiting, spasming, then finally lying still. Peter stood, reaching a hand to him. "I am sorry, Paul. What can I do?"

"I will go see her now. I'm sure everything will be fine," Paul flashed him a false grin and set off into the depths of the campsite.

Peter sat down and waited for Paul's eventual return. He had not been gone more than an hour when he stumbled back to the campsite, eyes glazed over.

"What news?" Peter hurtled to his feet as Paul slumped over, wringing his hands. Peter watched his eyes and mouth twitch in the light of the campfire.

He shrugged his shoulders, shook his head. "Just like that...she is dead."

Nodding, Peter relaxed his shoulders, extended a hand as if to console him. But he drew his hand back, biting his lip.

"She was not the only one dying in there, Peter. I could hear them," he paused, turning to stare at the darkness around them, "screaming. And, I did not see it, but from outside of the tent, I heard her father and mother. Their grief...it was too much."

Putting his hands into his pockets, Peter closed his eyes against the picture that conjured in his mind.

"I might have married her, Peter. Someday. After the war."

Peter sighed, staring at the back of his head. "I know, Paul. I know."

42

Peter struck his musket up into the air, refilling his lungs with air.

"And we're all
(And we're all)
Marching on
(Marching on)
The Grand Trunk Road!

The 19th foot was nearing the end of their second week of marching. Their feet lay heavy in their boots and their spirits hung lower than an elephant's trunk. Peter knew they needed encouragement to make it the last leg of the march. The jungle here was thick, the air hot and saturated with humidity. But the road was wide and as long as there was breath in his lungs, Peter would not let discouragement settle over the troops. He lowered his musket, opened his mouth:

And we're all
(And we're all)
Marching on
(Marching on)
To liberty!

Leaves rustling off to the side caught Peter's attention. He narrowed his eyes, seeing something move in between the branches. Maybe an animal or a bird flitting from branch to branch. He tightened his hold on his musket, waited for the army band, consisting of drums and tuba players, to finish their part in between stanzas, then continued the song, keeping one eye on the jungle.

And we're all
(And we're all)
Marching on
(Marching on)
And we're almost home!

A musket peeked out of the dense foliage.

Stopping in his tracks, Peter reached for his musket, falling to his knee. "Look out!"

Shots fired, taking out the two soldiers beside him. Cursing, Peter fired in retaliation, then dropped to his belly, moving his head to the side to look for Paul. When he did not spot him, he turned back to the jungle, watching a tribe of rebels jump out of the trees, waving their swords in the air and hollering out a battle cry. Peter reloaded his musket as quickly as he could, then scrambled to his feet as the soldiers formed a line of defence and fired at the advancing tribe.

A sharp pain seared into his left shoulder. He bit back a scream, inspecting the damage as another musket ball clipped his right hip. He whirled, scrambling back behind the line of soldiers. Pressing his hand against his bloody hip, he looked around. Where was Paul? His breathing coming in and out heavily, he staggered. The sound of metal alerted him to the other soldiers drawing their swords. The rebels had neared enough that they would have to engage in swordfight. He slung his musket over his shoulder.

He drew his sword, whirling just as a rebel descended on him. Their swords contacted, adding to the sound of clanging metal abounding along the road. The pain in his shoulder and hip irritated him, fueling his ire. He gritted his teeth, slashing his sword against the rebel's. He lifted his foot, kicked him in the gut. As the rebel fell backwards with an "oof", Peter roared and jammed his sword into the rebel's chest, pushing into the pommel with all his might.

Ripping the sword back out, he scanned the melee. *Where is Paul?*

Gritting his teeth again, he shot back into the fray, dispatching any rebel that got in his way. As the fighting began to dwindle, Peter ran amongst the fallen. "Paul?" He called out louder. "Paul!"

Beginning to panic, Peter reached for the nearest soldier. "Have you seen Paul?"

The soldier shook his head, continued on.

Peter reached for the next. "My brother, have you seen him?"

Another shake of the head.

A woman's scream rent the air. Peter's head shot up. It came from farther back in the company where the camp followers travelled. He glanced up, spotting Lieutenant Colonel Bright mounted on his horse. The two nodded to each other. The Lieutenant Colonel took off at a full gallop as Peter turned to the two soldiers he had just spoken to.

"Let's go," he hefted his sword and they bolted in the direction of the scream.

A minute later, they arrived on the scene, hollering out a battle cry. As soon as Peter's eyes landed on the scene, his sword arm lowered.

Lieutenant Colonel Bright, mounted on his horse, drove away the last of the rebels. Laying crumpled at the wheel of a wagon was Paul. Beside him lay a rebel, a sword sticking up out of his belly, dead. Paul was not moving.

Peter raised his arms helplessly, then let them fall. He stumbled forward.

A girl he dimly registered as Irene hopped out of the wagon, bending to inspect Paul.

Falling to his brother's side, he saw a sword had split open his stomach. He covered his mouth with his arm, shutting his eyes.

"He still breathes," Irene stood, calling out towards

the gathered crowd. "Bring a stretcher."

She bent back down, ripped the wide hem of her bell-shaped gown all along its perimeter, wadded up the fabric and pressed it against the wound. "He saved us."

Peter looked at her, no words coming to mind.

"We were defenseless, me and my sister," She pointed up to the wagon. Peter's eyes followed, landed on the sight of Julia peeking out of the wagon.

Frowning, Peter looked back at Irene.

"He jumped in right as the rebels descended on us," she looked down at Paul, grasping his hand. "He's a hero."

Still with no words, Peter grasped his other hand until the stretcher arrived, then followed in its wake until they reached the quickly assembled medic tent. The nurse sutured Paul's wound, then turned to him.

"Sir, we need to bandage your wounds," he tore his eyes away from the sight of Paul lying pale on the ground.

"What?"

"Your shoulder, your hip," she pulled him closer. "They will quickly turn infected if not cleaned and bandaged."

"Oh, right," Peter shook his head, remembering his own wounds. He let the nurse tend to him, then returned to his brother's side, sitting on the floor next to him.

Hours he waited, until the sun had gone down. Then Paul finally moved, a grimace forming on his face.

"Ma, I want to come home now," Paul reached forward, eyes still clamped shut.

Peter grabbed his hand and squeezed, moving his face over Paul's. "Paul, it's me. You are going to be okay."

"Pa?" Paul laughed. "I thought I would never see you again."

"No, it's me. Peter."

"Peter?" Paul's eyes flickered open and after several minutes they settled on Peter. He laughed again, then grimaced in pain.

"You are injured. You need to rest."

His eyes closed and he relaxed back onto the ground. "I did it to save Irene. She has such beautiful brown eyes."

Peter snorted, then rolled his eyes. He pulled Paul's hand to his forehead and squeezed it harder. "Same old Paul."

"I couldn't save Rèalta..."

Peter stared at Paul, watched him grimace in pain and swallow hard.

"...But I saved Irene. Will you forgive me?"

Blinking rapidly, Peter leaned back, but gave Paul's hand a reassuring squeeze. That was it. That was why Paul put himself into danger to save these women. It wasn't bravado, was it? All this time, he thought it was just to get a girl. But no. Paul was looking for absolution for losing their sister. Peter breathed out and ran a hand through his hair, a rush of affection for his brother making his chest hurt.

"Peter?" Paul swallowed and opened his dried-out lips.

"Paul, there is nothing to forgive."

He nodded his head slightly. "Peter, I am ready to go home."

Peter sat back, letting his hand drop back down to his side. "I know, Paul. Me too."

43

The train, sitting motionless at the Serampore train station, shrieked, letting out a great puff of smoke. Staletta paced impatiently in front of it.

"We have been standing here for over an hour. What's taking so long?" Staletta crossed her arms, pacing past Daniel and Archie who were seated on their bags at the base of the train.

Staletta continued to pace for twenty more minutes until the Commanding Officer arrived on the train platform, clearing his throat. "Attention, there has been a change of plans. Instead of heading straight for Dinapore, we are ordered to Jamshedpur. We have received word that a large contingent of rebels have been spotted in that area. We go to eliminate them. Alright, board up."

"What?" Staletta asked, gathering up her violin and her pack as everyone on the platform stood and grabbed up their packs and started to board the train. "Where's Jack when you need him?"

A few moments later, Jack arrived, shrugging helplessly. "Sorry, lot," he said in greeting. "I guess we aren't heading straight for Dinapore after all."

Daniel shouldered his pack. "What does that mean for us? Should we continue with your regiment or go our own way?"

Jack considered the options and raised his arms questioningly. "That's up to you, mate, but I'd stick with us if I were you. We'll make it to Dinapore...eventually. Your chances are still better with the company than on your own out there in the jungle."

"But how long will it take to get to Dinapore now?" Staletta asked.

"As long as it takes."

"And what if my brothers move on from Dinapore in that time?"

Jack rubbed the back of his neck. "I don't know what to tell you about that. All I know is we are boarding this train and heading to Jamshedpor. It is your decision. Will you board or stay behind?"

Staletta crossed her arms, eyes boring into the ground, weighing their options. All she wanted was to go straight to her brothers. But she knew they could be eaten alive out there on their own. Sticking to the company was still their best bet. The decision tore at her heart, but they had to do it. There was no other option.

Her eyes swept up to Daniel's and she nodded. "We must board the train."

*

India flew past the window in a blur of forest, plains, and villages. Staletta stared out the window for hours, biting her fingernails, not seeing any of the glorious scenes before her. The sound of the train speeding along the track drowned out the sounds of the soldiers around them and gave her mind a brief respite from her own fearful thoughts.

There was no use dwelling on thoughts of her brothers. They were speeding further away from them. When they would eventually get to see them was anybody's guess. Instead, Staletta thought about the different times she had to remake herself, readapt to whatever new role in which God had placed her. She had started out a scarecrow in the paddies of Ireland, turned immigrant, to coal mine worker, to orphan, to homeless child, to backstage theatre assistant, to violinist, to homeless woman, to North Star, to prisoner, to factory worker, and, finally, to wife.

Of all the roles, it was the latter that gave her the most peace and yet also allowed for the cruellest of convictions. Daniel sat beside her on the train leading deep into dangerous territory, on a fool's mission, without complaint. He was the picture of self-sacrifice. Would she do the same for him? If the situation had been reversed, would she have given up her new business, said goodbye to her family to go off on a whim of one person's desire?

It was easy to say yes to that, but to do it...she wasn't sure she would have had Daniel's fortitude or his sacrifice.

But say Daniel had stuck with his initial plan and refused to go and she then resigned to stay behind, as well. What would have become of her then? Daniel had his carpentry shop, Cynthia had her dressmaking shop, Eleanor and Blue Ben had the factory. She didn't have a role. She had no further purpose. Say they made it, found her brothers, returned home. What then? What would become of her? Motherhood, possibly, but she'd already lost one baby, who was to say the rest wouldn't follow suit? Was she to become a concert violinist? Or take on some other type of work? Help Daniel and Henry in the shop? What would her purpose be, after all of this was said and done?

Daniel leaned over, whispering loudly over the rumble of the train. "You're quiet today."

Broken out of her reverie, Staletta ceased biting her fingernails, and dropped her hand into her lap. She turned her face to the side to look at him. "Sorry, I was lost in thought."

Before they had boarded the train, Daniel had grabbed a chunk of wood from the ground. He had been whittling on it for hours and out of it, an elephant began to take shape. He scraped his knife along the back ridge.

"Your thoughts are not pleasant ones?" He looked up from the elephant, flicking his eyes at her ruined nails.

Flashing him a fake smile, she crossed her arms, hiding her hands underneath. "I am trying to figure out my place in this world."

"What do you mean by that?" He narrowed his eyes.

"What my purpose is," she leaned her head back. "How I will spend my life."

"What have you thought of so far?"

Sighing, Staletta half-shrugged. "Nothing."

Daniel looked up at her again. "Star, the one certainty in life is knowing how little control you have over your own life. Worrying about your life will not add one minute to it. It would be best to sit back, relax, and do what is required of you."

Staletta frowned. "And what is required of me?"

A smile spread diagonally on his face. "To sit back...relax."

Sighing, Staletta shook her head. "Danny-boy, you do know how to bewilder a girl."

Daniel laughed. "I give you nothing but the truth, as I have experienced it."

"Do you miss home?" Staletta pierced him with her eyes.

He paused his whittling. "I do."

She nodded fervently. "Me too. It feels good to long for a home to be back to."

"Someday we will return. Henry will have taken over the shop. I will have to win it back from him in a dueling match or some such thing. Probably will have squatters living in our apartment we will have to clean out. We'll be busy," he winked.

Staletta laughed at the thought of that fiction, nudging him with her elbow. "You always know how to cheer me up."

"Well, you always know how to get me into dangerous situations, so we're even," Daniel smirked as Staletta playfully punched him in the leg.

"What would I do without you?" Her face scrunched, eyes darting around, thinking back to where she would be if she had not met him that day in the alley.

"You would be fine without me," he nodded. "You're a survivor."

"But I wouldn't be happy. I would not have a family. I would be alone, miserable, cranky..."

Daniel put his whittling down, face growing sour. "And I would be, too...stuck with Claire." He stuck out his tongue, pretending to vomit.

Giggling, Staletta elbowed him in the ribs, remembering the spoiled antics of Daniel's former lover. "That's terrible."

Archie, seated in front of them, popped his head over the seat at the sound of their laughter. "What's terrible?"

"Nothing, Archie," Staletta suppressed her giggles by pressing her lips together and taking a breath. "We were discussing Daniel's old lover."

Archie shivered, screwing up his nose and eyes. "Yuck. Why anyone would want a lover is beyond me."

"I said that once, too," Daniel leaned forward. "But when you are older, you'll think differently. You'll meet a special girl who will completely turn your life on it's head and you'll never look back."

"Hmm," Archie thought about it. "Okay...but she better like shark fishing because I plan to do that a lot and I ain't changing that for her."

Staletta and Daniel shared a look, trying not to laugh.

"Fair enough," Daniel said, looking out the window as the train began to slow down. "I think we've made it to

Jamshedpur."

Peering out of the window, Staletta saw nothing but trees and then the trees thinned out, and town buildings swept past the window, moving slower and slower each time. The train hollered its arrival and, a few moments later, came to a screeching halt.

She stood; her legs sweaty and cramped from sitting for the ten-hour ride. The soldiers began filing out and soon it was their turn to exit the train. Stepping out, they swung their packs onto their backs, following the other camp followers as they followed the soldiers.

"Company halt," Luitenant Morgan shouted above the crowd. "There are no trains through the jungle. From here out we march on foot. Always keep close to the company. There are worse things than rebels lurking in these forests."

"Oh boy," Archie exclaimed as the company started to march. "This is going to be great."

Staletta shared a concerned glance with Daniel. Archie's enthusiasm warmed her heart, but this was no vacation as they had warned him multiple times. Real danger was imminent. A sense of guilt washed over her at the thought of him coming to a disastrous end long before his time.

Her thoughts vanished as they marched up to the top of a hill. As they passed over the top, the view stole her breath away and the vast beauty of the land before her eclipsed all thoughts of danger.

Sprawling out before them was an expanse of rolling green hills on the far side of a misty lake. Dipping their trunks into the lake were a herd of wild elephants. In the shallow water, the calves splashed like children while the adults spewed water across their backs.

Sucking in her breath, Staletta reached over to grab for Daniel's hand. "I've never seen anything so beautiful."

"I have," Daniel locked his eyes on her, smiling. "But it is a close second," he remarked.

She rolled her eyes, hooked her arm in his, and reached for Archie's hand. "This might turn out to be an alright adventure after all."

Together, they made their way down the hill and around the lake, disappearing into the darkened depths of the jungle.

44

Sweat dripped down the back of her neck as she walked outside the nurse's tent, hands on hips. Overhead, the sun mercilessly broke through the jungle canopy. Slumping, Staletta wiped an arm across her brow, then rolled up her sleeves, taking in a deep breath. Little breeze and high humidity made it difficult to breathe. The desire to lay down and sleep weighed heavily upon her.

She shook her head and bent to pick up the bucket of water lying on the ground, then turned, hauling it back to the tent. She stopped at the entrance where a table sat along the wall. She reached for a handful of rags sitting on top of it, then resumed entering the tent.

"It is far too hot for December," she remarked to a lady in an orange skirt and a white top, bent over a man lying on the cot.

"Agreed," the lady looked up, bobbing her head. "I have been here nigh on two years; still have not gotten used to a hot Christmas."

"Two years?" Staletta sat down on a stool on the other side of the cot, dropping the rags into the bucket of water as she did so. Sticking her hand in, she swished the rags around until they were soaked, then plucked out one rag. She squeezed out the excess water, then leaned forward, dabbing the man's face with the cooled cloth. "Where are you from, Eileen?"

"I am from Manchester," Eileen straightened, putting a bottle of medicine on the table next to the cot. "And you?"

"London."

"Aye, it's like to be snowing back home this time of year," Eileen turned, made her way over to a second cot.

Staletta heard a sigh and looked up to find Eileen pulling a sheet over the man's body and face. Her hand froze as it hovered over the sick man's forehead. "Eileen?"

"Will you help me for a moment?" The older woman asked over her shoulder.

"Certainly," Staletta rose immediately, dropping the rag back into the bucket. She dried her hands on her pant legs and went to her side.

Pointing to the next cot over, she mumbled, "Cover him up, please."

Eyes going wide, Staletta stared at Eileen's passive face. "What happened to him?"

Eileen gave her a curt nod and moved back to the previous soldier. "Heat exhaustion. There ain't much you can do about it. The body just gives out. I saw two die from it yesterday, now two again today. Let us try and prevent a third."

Staring down at the dead soldier's face, Staletta pulled the sheet up to his chin, unable to look away from his rigid face. That could easily have been Daniel lying there...or Archie. Mortified at the thought, she stifled a sob and quickly thrust the sheet over the man's face, turning around with a hand to her mouth.

"I didn't take you for a squeamish one," Eileen shot her a glance, then pointed for her to get back to her bucket of rags. "You'll get used to death soon enough. Once you see it everyday and in so many different forms."

Staletta resumed her spot on her stool, looking up at Eileen with a frown. "I am quite used to death, thank you very much."

Raising a brow, Eileen shrugged. "I meant no offense. Who ain't these days, after all? Yes, hard times we live in."

"It's just that-" Staletta bit her lip as she reached

back into the bucket for a rag. She wrung it out, then slowly dabbed at the soldier's face again. "Well, you're married, aren't you? How do you handle knowing that your husband could die here at any moment?"

A knowing gleam passed across Eileen's eyes and she nodded fervently. "There is nothing I can do. The first step is to accept that."

"What if I can't?"

"It's like this: I keep telling my George to stay out of the sun and in the shade if he can help it, but you know how it is with them soldiers, they don't got a choice where they stand. Where they stand is where they stand. And where they walk is where they walk."

Staletta imagined Daniel or Archie collapsing to the ground as they tended to the livestock. She would be left out here alone. Her fool's errand would destroy the lives of too many. The thought sickened her. She swallowed, trying to force down the rising guilt pooling like bile in her throat. "I have made a terrible mistake."

"What's that, girl?"

She looked up to find Eileen peering at her closely. "You have grown pale. Is the heat getting to you, too?"

"Yes," Staletta forced a smile. "Yes, it is."

"Well, go on, get some water," Eileen shooed her away with a flick of her hand. "Nurses are no good to the army if they're dead."

"Yes, ma'am," Staletta lowered her face as she rose

from her stool, then scampered outside. Once again, the open air was a blessed relief from the closeness of the tents, but the direct sun was worse by far. Staletta picked her way through the camp, weaving in between the wild rows of trees and shrubs, heading for the sound of the bleating lambs and the earthy smell of the cattle. As she neared, she looked around, hoping for a glimpse of Daniel and Archie.

She had almost given up when they appeared out of the trees, hauling loads of cut grass in their arms. Staletta hurried over to greet them as they dumped the load over the fence then smacked their hands together to remove the grass clinging to their sweaty skin.

Daniel passed his sleeve over his brow. His face glistened with sweat, drops falling off the end of his nose. His shirt was untucked, and half the buttons undone. His hair was matted with sweat on one side and sticking up on the other. Archie's face was red, and his shoulders drooped low.

"Archie, go get some water," Staletta stopped in front of them, looking at his face with concern. "Now."

Dismally, Archie nodded, then headed for the food tents.

"You should get some, too," she remarked, noting Daniel was still trying to catch his breath. Despite the heat, she wrapped her arms around herself and looked down at her feet, too afraid to look at him.

"I will, in a minute."

"How is it going today?" She looked up at him guiltily.

Shrugging, he frowned. "Same as every day. Couple more loads of grass to do yet. Then, I suppose we will have to tend to the soldier's horses when they return from patrol."

Shifting on her feet, Staletta nodded her head. "This was a mistake, Danny."

He narrowed his eyes, cocked his head. "What is?"

"Coming here," she lowered her face even more. "You, having to do all of this work. Risking your life..."

He only shrugged his shoulders in response, then pointed to the food tent. "Water?"

"Men are already dying." She rubbed her arms, hugged herself tighter.

Hearing his feet shift in the grass, she looked up to find him staring at her. "We knew the realty when we made our decision."

"Yes, but then it didn't feel real," she rubbed her palm across her forehead. "Now, it does."

"It's too late to turn back now," Daniel reached forward, grabbing her waist and turning her around. "Let's go get some water."

Staletta nodded. Together they walked over to where river water boiled in large pots over fires built in the ground. They found Archie next to a pot that had been removed from the fire to cool. They dipped their waterskins inside. They filled them up, drank them thirstily, then filled them back up again.

"Archie, why don't you go on back to our tent and rest. You have worked hard today, lad. A good day's work," Daniel patted him on the back.

Exhausted, Archie nodded his head in agreement. "Feeding cattle isn't as much fun as tending sails. I think I'll stick to the sea."

Staletta worked up a chuckle and patted his shoulder. "I know it doesn't feel like it, but guess what today is?"

Shrugging, Archie shook his head.

"It's Christmas Day," Staletta forced a smile. Archie shrugged carelessly in response, turning to walk back to their tent.

Not feeling festive herself, Staletta didn't blame him for not expressing joy at the idea that it was Christmas. It certainly didn't feel like Christmas. They were exhausted, overheated, and with the sudden outbreak of deaths in the camp, her heart lay heavy in her chest, weighing down any chance of joy.

They were five months in on this journey to find her brothers. The days neither flew by nor dragged, they just sort of blended one day into the next, like a smear. Every chore had become routine, every day just like the last. Every day her feet weighed heavier in her boots, her heart hanging lower in her chest while the guilt piling in her stomach towered higher each day. The hope of finding her brothers, though she stoked it every day, had reduced to softly glowing embers buried in a bed of coal.

They were so close and yet the passing days brought her no closer. If Archie or Daniel were to collapse, fall victim to the heat...if one of them were to die...

Staletta placed a hand to her mouth at the sudden rise of acrid bile in her throat.

"Staletta-"

She swallowed it down. "Maybe we should turn back. Let's go home."

"Staletta," Daniel moved close, grabbing her hand. "There is no going back."

45

February 1859

"Company! Prepare to march." A voice thundered through the encampment, followed by the ringing of bells.

Archie stirred in his bedroll. "What's happening?"

Staletta and Daniel steadily awoke, rubbing their eyes and sitting up. Daniel moved first, going to the tent flap, and peering outside.

"We march at first light." The voice exclaimed, bells ringing.

It was still dark out and Daniel guessed they had an hour or two before first light. He sat back in the tent. "We better pack up."

The three started to pack their belongings and their tent. When they were mostly done, Jack came running up.

"Good day, how are you three?" He asked, out of breath from running across the camp.

"We're fine," Daniel shook his head. "Haven't seen you in a while."

"Nah, I've been out with the rebel hunting parties most days, but I did want to come over and let you know I hadn't forgotten about you."

Staletta helped Daniel stuff the tent cover into a bag. "Do you know where we are heading?"

Jack removed his hat, smoothing his hair down with one hand. "We're going to Bihar. That will be a few days away from where your brothers are stationed."

"What?" Staletta dropped her end of the bag and the tent slid out.

"I thought you would like that," he replaced his hat on top of his head, smiling smugly.

Four months in the jungle and finally the words she had been waiting to hear. It had been a rough four months and there had been times-many times- when she didn't think they would make it. Not but a month ago, sickness had passed through the camp. Archie had been out for several days, but had scraped through where others had not. The heat had gotten so bad there for awhile, they had all suffered some form of heat exhaustion.

Not-so-patiently, she had waited. She had worked in the medic tents. She had done the soldiers laundry.

She had played her violin to cheer the soldiers and keep them going. She had not-so-patiently bit her fingernails, kicked the ground, silently screaming for the camp to move forward and still they stayed, encamped in the same jungle for months.

Now, finally, they could move.

Staletta turned back to Daniel, her expression harried. "We need to pack quickly. I want to get on the road as soon as possible." She bent to pick up the tent once more.

"Steady on, steady on," Jack held up a hand. "We won't be there tomorrow. It's a mighty long march to Bihar. A lot of rivers to forge, forests to tread, and plains to cross. We have more than a fortnight of walking ahead of us. This ain't no country stroll."

"I know, I know," Staletta tightened the strings on the bag and slung it over her shoulder. "I will walk any distance to see my brothers once more."

"And nothing will stop her," Daniel smirked.

Staletta grabbed Archie's pack from the ground and thrust it into his arms. She then grabbed Daniel's and likewise handed it to him. She slung her's over her shoulder along with her violin, and patted Daniel on the arm.

"Come along, boys, we have a long walk ahead."

46

Staletta dropped her pack on the sandy bank of the Falgu river not far from the border separating the districts of Jarkhand and Bihar. Flopping down in the sand, she immediately removed her boots and stockings, revealing swollen feet covered in blisters. Easing them into the water, she felt the throbbing pain cease for a few blissful moments.

Archie was not far behind her, tearing off his shirt and shoes and plunging into the water headfirst. Daniel looked around the bank, then, with hands on hips, he surveyed the area around them.

They had left off following the Grand Trunk Road and forged through the forest until they met with the river. The river was not very wide. It would be easy enough to forge the next day. Moving the animals across would be the biggest challenge.

"I'm not sure my feet are going to last another week of marching," Staletta sucked in her breath as she pulled her feet out of the water, inspecting the damage.

"I'll get a poultice out of your pack," Daniel bent, digging through her pack for a small tin. He also pulled out a cotton shirt from his own pack, then went to sit beside her.

He let the sun dry her feet, then gently spread the white poultice around on her sores. She winced every time he touched a spot.

"I'm sorry," he cringed. "These sores could easily get infected."

"I know," she said, gritting her teeth.

When he was done, he ripped the cotton shirt into strips, then bound them around her feet. "There, is that better?"

She nodded and gingerly put her boots back on her feet, then rested her chin on her knees. "I should go help set up the nurse's tent."

"And I need to go take care of the animals," Daniel reached for her hand and pulled her to her feet.

"We are making good progress," She smiled, testing her weight on her blistered feet. "One more week, Danny. Then I will see my brothers. Just one more week."

He rubbed her back, leaned his head in close to

hers, then...a gun shot rang out, echoing over the river.

"Get down!" Daniel shouted, pulling her back against the sand and throwing his arm over her head.

Staletta tasted sand, gritty against her tongue, but as another shot rang out, she pressed harder against the ground.

"Where's Archie?" Daniel shouted next to her ear.

"In the water." Her heart pounded, wanting to risk a glance to see if he was alright.

Daniel flared his nostrils, turning back around to the water and then waving when he spotted Archie, floating offshore. "Archie, come here, but stay low."

Crawling through the sand, Archie made his way towards them, reaching Daniel's side just as the thundering of the guns rang out anew.

Daniel grasped Staletta in one hand and Archie in the other, sprinting for the cover of the trees. Collapsing at the base of a tree, Daniel pushed Staletta and Archie down, covering them with his body.

The guns cracked and soldiers screamed.

Huddling closer to the ground, Daniel caught site of another camp follower, huddling at the base of the tree next to them.

"Arm yourselves as best you can," the man called over, showcasing a musket with a slight shift of his arms.

"Arm ourselves?" Daniel called over. "With what?"

"With a musket, a'course," the man shouted back.

Staletta turned her head to Daniel. "But we don't have one."

Daniel gaped. "I know. I didn't know camp followers were allowed guns."

Staletta looked around at the faces of the camp followers huddling in the trees around them until she spotted Eileen. She called out her name, and the woman, sporting her own rifle musket, turned to face her. "Where did you get that?" Staletta shouted.

"From the armory supply, of course," she called back. "You don't have one?"

Staletta stared at her blankly and shook her head. Eileen tisked, then after a quick glance at the distant trees to make sure the coast was clear, she stood and ran over to her and Daniel, lying down beside them. "I'll keep you covered. I would advise procuring a rifle when the next opportunity arises."

"But we are civilians, aren't we? Are civilians allowed to carry?" Staletta gazed at her questioningly.

"There are no civilians here, dear."

Staletta swallowed, sharing a glance with Daniel.

Eileen and the rest of the camp followers with rifles fired into the tree line.

Daniel threw an arm over Archie's head. Putting her hands over her ears to stifle the deafening noise, Staletta cowered into the ground, feeling Archie tremble between her and Daniel. She snaked an arm around him and squeezed him tight.

A scream rent the air from just beside them and Staletta squeezed him tighter, wanting to scream, but burrowing her mouth into Daniel's arm instead.

Eileen's gun sounded and ceased as she reloaded.

Then a bullet buried itself in the ground next to Staletta's ear, a burst of dirt splattering her head. A scream tore from her lips and she moved to cover Archie more. Daniel cursed and moved to cover them both.

The gun shots fired repeatedly as screams rang out.

Staletta scrunched up her eyes, whispering desperate prayers through trembling lips.

Then shouts sounded and swords clattered, replacing the gut-wrenching blasts of the guns.

Eileen reached back, shaking them. "They fight with swords now."

She looked up, seeing Eileen lying still, but poised to shoot again if need be. Then she looked beyond, to the sight of swords slashing into men's bodies with desperate abandon. The jungle floor had sprung up with blood-red roses where the bodies of too many lay slaughtered.

As she watched, the British soldiers quickly dispatched the rebels and the fighting died down.

"Thank you, Lord," Eileen declared, getting to her feet ever so slowly.

Daniel rose, then reached down to help Staletta and Archie to their feet.

Staletta drew back at the look on Daniel's face. A mixture of horror set his jaw, and one of wild determination glinted black in his green eyes. "Eileen," Daniel pointed to her rifle. "Teach me to shoot."

With her gun thrown over her shoulder, orange skirt billowing in the breeze, Eileen placed a hand on her hip and nodded her head. "Of course. Find yourself a gun. I'll teach you."

47

Staletta placed the rifle against her shoulder. It weighed heavy in her arms, so heavy it was difficult to hold steady. Looking down the barrel, she aligned the sight to the paper nailed to a tree across the beach. She breathed out in exasperation as the sight wobbled to different points on the paper. Her arms trembled beneath the weight of the rifle. Letting her arms relax, she brought the gun down to her waist, shook out one arm, then the other. She needed to aim and fire quickly for her arms to not tire as easily.

She set her eyes on the target, raised the gun, aimed, and fired. She winced as the rifle kicked back into her shoulder.

Eileen walked down to the target as Staletta lowered her gun. Eileen took one glance and shook her head, heading back towards them. "Missed."

"Awww," Staletta kicked the sand and moved aside, rubbing her shoulder.

"It's okay, just takes practice, dear," Eileen motioned for Daniel to go next.

Daniel raised his rifle, took his time to find the target, then fired.

Eileen moved towards the target and nodded in appreciaton. She pointed to the top corner of the paper. "Not bad for your first shot," she said, moving back towards them.

"Staletta, we need to get you on the target," Eileen planted her feet next to Staletta, showing her how to stand by putting her weight on her back foot and locking the butt of the rifle into her shoulder to brace against the kickback. "Make sure the center of the target is directly in the center of the sight and squeeze the trigger. Don't blink as you squeeze the trigger, or you'll lift the gun off target. You must hold it steady. Do not hold your breath either. You want to be relaxed. Slowly breathe out and squeeze the trigger."

"Got it," Staletta took her place, taking a few moments to get her feet into position. Thinking back, she remembered how difficult it was to learn how to hold a violin under her chin properly. A gun was a far cry from a violin, but if she could learn one, she could learn another. She rolled her shoulders back to loosen them, then hefted the gun, bracing it firmly on her shoulder. She lowered her head until her cheek grazed the wood handle and her eye was level with the sight.

She found the target. She sucked in the air through her nose, then with parted lips, she let the air out, squeezing the trigger at the same time. The gun bucked against her shoulder, but not as painfully as the first time. She lowered it, placing a hand across her brow to shield her vision from the setting sun as she peered at the target. "Did I hit it?"

Eileen quick-stepped to the target, pointing to its far-right side. "You hit it," she called back. "Nicely done."

Staletta rocked back on her heels and leaned into Daniel. "I hit the target."

"I see that," Daniel tilted his head at her. "How about some friendly competition, hmm?"

Shifting her rifle from her right hand to the left, she placed her right on her hip, and raised an eyebrow. "What did you have in mind?"

"Last one to hit the center of the target is a rotten egg," Daniel winked at her.

Her hand dropped from her hip and she placed both hands on the barrel of the gun, rolling her eyes. "Danny-boy, that's so childish." She sniffed, watching him from the corner of her eye.

He chuckled, placing himself into position to shoot.

"Not afraid, are you?"

Her jaw dropped in mock offense. "Never." She lifted her chin. "Alright, you're on."

Archie stood from where he had been sitting and watching them. "I want in on this, too."

Daniel fired, then straightened as he peered at the target. "Sorry, kid, you have to be taller than the gun in order to fire it."

"But I *am* taller than the gun." Archie moved to stand beside Daniel's gun.

Daniel placed the butt of the gun to the ground, then bent to see the difference in height. He sucked air in through clenched teeth, then shook his head. "Sorry, kid, but not quite. About an inch too short."

"Awww," Archie sagged, dragging his feet back to the spot he had been sitting and dropping back to the ground.

"Getting closer," Eileen called, pointing to the newest hole on the paper.

He flashed Staletta a smug grin. She smirked back, then took her place. The competition lasted several rounds until Daniel finally hit the center of the target.

"Sorry, Star," he clenched his teeth, sucking air in through them once more. "Looks like you're the rotten egg this evening."

Sticking her tongue out at him, she crossed her arms, then chuckled. "I might be a rotten egg, but I'm proud of myself."

Chuckling, Daniel walked over to her, wrapping her in a hug. "You did great. Keep practicing. And let us pray we never need to fire them again."

48

"We made it," Staletta's boots crunched on the road in a heavy, slow pattern, but the sight of the city of Bihar coalescing like a blessed mirage in the midst of a desert, quickened her steps. "Danny, I can't believe we made it." She laughed, adding a hop into her step.

Beside her, Daniel sighed heavily. "At last. Can we just take a moment to reflect on the fact that we survived a month-long march across India?"

"And that we are only days, Danny, *days* away from meeting my brothers?" Staletta placed her hands beneath her chin, squealing. "We have come so far, and I have been looking for so long."

Elbowing her gently, Daniel smiled at her, his teeth flashing in the bright sunlight. "It is worth the journey. I was sceptical at first but seeing the joy in your eyes has made it all worth it."

"I never thought I would say this, but I am looking forward to a bath," Archie reached to scratch the back of his neck.

Snickering, Staletta reached to finger her hair, plaited in a braid over her shoulder. It was almost brown from the dust of the road and she wrinkled her nose at the gritty feeling of it between her fingers. "Agreed."

The town of Bihar loomed closer. She could see it appearing out of the trees. Nervousness gripped her stomach at the thought of seeing her brothers again. No, not nervousness, Staletta decided. Giddiness. She balled her fists and gently bounced them on her legs as they neared the town walls.

"What is the plan to meet your brothers?" Archie looked up at Staletta.

"We will stop in town, get cleaned up, then depart from the army. It's only a two day walk to Dinapore. I'm sure we can manage that on our own." Staletta smiled down at him.

Out of the crowd marching around them, Jack pushed his way through and fell in step beside them. "Thought I should come visit you one last time before you go off to meet your brothers."

"Thank you, Jack. Without you, we never would have made it this far." Staletta beamed at him.

"It was my pleasure," Jack stopped walking to take a bow. He then turned to Daniel. "Say, would you mind helping us move the carts into town?"

"I suppose I could help, one last time," Daniel smiled and clapped him on the back. "Star, Archie, stay with the camp followers. I will come find you when I am done."

Placing a hand on Archie's back, Staletta nodded at Daniel. "See you soon, Danny-boy."

49

Staletta walked down the street in the small town of Bihar, her feet weighing heavily at the end of her legs. The sun blazed down, causing sweat to dimple her forehead and trickle down her spine. She smiled as Archie walked beside her, kicking pebbles with every step. On either side of the street were thatched huts and mud-walled bunkers. As this section of Bihar was, after all, a British military encampment, the streets were busy with soldiers and camp followers, settling into their assigned places for the night.

"Come along, Archie," Staletta stopped in the street, turning around to find Archie crouched on the ground, picking at something in the dirt.

He picked it up and straightened, holding it up for her to see. "Look, I found a coin."

"It's very nice, now come along," Staletta waved her hand. "I think our hut is on the other side of town."

A gun shot rang out and Staletta's hand flew to Archie's shoulder. Stopping dead in her tracks, she heard the clap of distant guns and horses screaming.

"Star?" Archie trembled beneath her hand.

A musket ball whizzed past Staletta's head. Squeezing Archie's shoulder, she dropped to the ground, pulling Archie down with her. "Cover your head," She yelled over the sharp sound of gunfire.

Archie wrapped his arms over the back of his head, his face buried in the grass. She covered her own head but peeped out beneath her arms. Shots fired. Rebels poured into the streets, firing at will, grabbing camp followers as they went.

"Archie, we need to get to shelter," she cried. "When I give the word, start crawling. Stay as low to the ground as you can. We are going to move straight ahead to that lean to. Understand?"

"Yes, ma'am," he replied.

"Okay, go." She called and they started to crawl. She held back until Archie had moved in front of her. "Faster, we are almost there."

They reached the lean-to and upon finding a musket laying outside the door, Archie grabbed it and held it close to his chest.

"Stay back in the shadows so they can't see you," she said, although she stood at the doorway, peeking out, and looking down the street.

She looked back out the door and seeing that the area had cleared, turned to look back at Archie.

"Where did they come from?" Archie's voice quivered out of the shadows.

"I don't know," Staletta helplessly shook her head. The rebels had caught them in a surprise attack.

"We need to go find Danny..."

Her words cut off as a rebel appeared in front of her, grabbied her, and she felt her feet lift free from the ground as he hoisted her into the air. She screamed in shock, kicking out violently with her legs. Managing to wrangle out of his arms, she fell to the ground in a tangle of limbs. Untangling herself, she looked up as the man descended on her, sabre in hand. She crawled backwards, searching the ground with her hands, hoping to feel something she could use as a weapon. Nothing.

The man raised the sabre and slashed downwards. Staletta rolled away quickly to the side. The man raised his sabre again, took two steps towards her-she cringed, breathing fast, knowing the sword was but inches away.

The man stiffened, eyes wide, mouth gaping. Staletta shrieked as he collapsed to the ground beside her.

Archie stood behind where the man had been, musket clutched in his hands, bloody bayonet sticking out of the top. Archie dropped the weapon, wide-eyed and staring at the body.

Staletta caught her breath, stood on wobbly legs, and moved over to him. "Archie?" He held his hands up, looking at them as if in terror, his face twisted in a silent scream, tears racing down his cheeks. She dropped to her knees, wrapping him in a hug. "Archie, it's okay."

Frozen in place, his body did not respond to her hug, other than to tremble against hers. He felt small in her arms, fragile, like a paper doll. If she squeezed too hard, he would crumple.

Pulling back, she held his face in her hands. "Archie, look at me." With much effort, he wrenched his eyes away from the corpse and cast them onto her. Staletta recoiled at the horror lurking in the depths of his eyes.

"It's okay," she dropped her hands from his face, and stood. "I need you to come with me. Okay? Can you do that?"

He sniffled, nodding slowly.

"Good." Turning on her heel, she grabbed the musket from the ground with one hand and held Archie's hand with the other. As they neared the doorway, she dropped his hand and held up the musket, peering out the doorway and around to the sides.

"We're going to run for the next building. On the count of three. One...two...three."

Grabbing his hand again, they launched out the door, sprinting for the building next door. They hit the side of the wall, Staletta forcing Archie behind her. She lifted the musket and pointed it around. Her arms trembling beneath its weight.

She moved up the wall to peer around the corner. "Again, on the count of three, we sprint for the next building. One...two...three."

They rushed off, this time making it halfway before a rebel rushed out and fired at them. They stopped, Archie clutching Staletta from behind. Without even thinking, she raised the musket, sighted, and shot. The man collapsed.

"Go!" She cried, pulling Archie along to the next building.

Slamming into the side of the wall again, Staletta took a moment to catch her breath and examine Archie to make sure he was alright. His face had completely drained of color, but he was otherwise unharmed. Smiling at him reassuringly, she inched forward to the edge of the wall.

Sounds of fighting met her ears and peering around the corner confirmed it. The British soldiers were locked in battle with the rebels. Some were shooting from a distance and others were in the throes of a sabre fight. It looked like utter chaos to Staletta. They had been caught unprepared, and it showed.

She turned back to Archie, indicating they should crouch down. "We have to sit tight. We are out of gunpowder. We can't reload this thing," she said laying the musket at her side.

"Wha-what happens if we are attacked again?" Archie asked in a cracked whisper.

"The British soldiers are right on the other side of this wall. We'll be fine," she said, looking around to make sure that statement was still true. "Oh, where's Danny?"

Biting her lip, she refused to think about the possibility of him laying on the ground, forgotten and trampled, dead eyes accusing her of dragging him there so he could die. That tendril of thought creeped into her mind and she snarled, brushing it away.

Growing antsy quickly she did not think she could wait there any longer. She bit her lip again and looked at

Archie.

"What?" He asked, noticing her intent gaze.

"I have to find Danny." She licked her lips. "You should stay here."

Archie grabbed her arm. "I'm not staying here alone."

"You'll be safe here."

"You know that's not true," Archie's fingernails dug into her flesh.

At the sound of a woman screaming, Staletta looked out around the wall. The rebels were grabbing women, dragging them across the ground, hauling them into buildings to do things Staletta sickened at the thought of. They slaughtered the men on sight.

Staletta blinked rapidly. He was right. There were no safe places here. "We'll go together. Let's go around the back," she pointed, and they moved along the wall towards the back. "Jack said they were going to the carts. We're going to make our way over there." She looked around the corner and turned back. "We're not far from them. We are going to make another break for it. Sprint as fast as you can."

"Are there rebels back there?" He asked in terror.

Staletta hesitated then responded truthfully. "They are everywhere. Are you with me?"

Archie gulped, but nodded his head.

"Brave lad," Staletta smiled sadly at him.

She readied herself, held onto Archie's hand, and stepped out from behind the wall. Musket still in hand, they sprinted. They could hear gunfire around them, the cries of men who had been shot rising even louder, and still they ran. Musket balls whizzed past her head. They kept running, tripping occasionally over the uneven ground, until they were almost upon the carts. A glimpse of Daniel's white shirt slowed her to a stop.

His plain white shirt made him stick out against the line of blue jacketed soldiers crouched behind the stacks of hay and feed for the bullocks, cows, and horses with which they travelled, but Daniel crouched beside them, firing his musket, no less a soldier than they. A warmth of pride swelled in her chest. Squeezing Archie's hand, she pulled him back into a run, making their way down to Daniel.

The thunder of a musket froze her in her steps, and a lightning pain burned across her shoulder. Crying out, she dropped her musket, her hand moving to her bloody shoulder. She bit her lip, putting pressure on the wound.

"Staletta!" Archie screamed.

"I'm okay, Archie," she whirled to look at him, but Archie was gone.

"Archie!" She cried. Spinning on her heel, she came face to face with a group of rebels. She gasped and backpedalled, but one of them reached forward, grabbing her and holding a knife to her ribcage. Groaning, she caught sight of Archie squirming in the arms of another rebel.

"Let him go," She cried, sucking in her breath as the knife stuck in her side sharply.

She could not understand their language, but the leader spoke, pointed to the cart over his shoulder. The rebel holding her moved the knife to her throat while a second rebel roughly tied her hands together behind her back, then lashed a rope around her ankles. In an effortless movement, a rebel lifted her in his arms, tossing her into the back of the cart. She landed with a thud, wincing as her shoulder rammed into the hard, wood floor. They tossed Archie in beside her and she wiggled over to his side, struggling to sit upright.

The rebels tossed more camp followers into the cart, and then jumped in themselves. Staletta peered over the edge of the cart, searching desperately for Daniel. Panic flooded her as she caught sight of him, gun to his shoulder, firing into a line of rebels, unaware that they had been captured.

"Danny!" She screamed, at the top of her lungs. "Danny, help us!"

Daniel's head swivelled to her and she could see him mouth the word 'no' as he saw what was happening. She watched him raise the musket to fire...then her vision went black.

50

Daniel watched as the rebel he shot toppled over the edge of the cart at the same moment one of them struck Staletta over the head with the butt of his gun. She crumpled lifelessly and Daniel's stomach turned into a sour pool of despair. Anger tearing at his heart, he raised his gun and fired a second shot. The man driving the cart urged the horses into a run. Out of ammunition, Daniel dropped the gun, sprinting after the cart. But the cart was getting further away and his legs faltered as the cart disappeared around a corner.

He forgot about the fighting and the other rebels, fixating on the spot where the cart had disappeared. He looked around for something, anything, to ride. Spotting a horse in the paddock, Daniel ran for it.

Jack came running up to Daniel, shaking his head furiously. "What do you think you're doing?"

"Star and Archie...they've been taken. I'm going after them," he said, tightening the straps beneath the horse's belly.

"Don't be a fool," Jack shouted. "You can't ride after them by yourself. They'll kill you on sight."

"What else am I supposed to do?" Daniel shouted, wild-eyed.

"Think about it," Jack replied. "They have *taken* them. They haven't *killed* them."

"Who is to say they won't?" Daniel said, strapping the reins to the horse and mounting up without a saddle.

Jack grabbed the bridle and held the horse from moving. "If they were not killed on sight, they won't kill them now. They are hostages. They will use them for information and probably keep them as prisoners of war."

"That's comforting," Daniel said sarcastically, trying to kick the horse into moving. Jack held tighter to the bridle. "Or they'll torture them for information and kill them after they've gotten it."

"Danny, you're not thinking clearly." Jack cried. "You cannot go after them."

Stifling a sob, Daniel breathed heavily. Though he did not want to admit it, Jack's reasoning was sound. Daniel could not hope to ride into a rebel camp by himself and expect to come out of it alive. "Then what am I supposed to do?" Daniel's voice cracked.

Jack breathed heavily, trying to keep his own voice calm. "Wait. Wait until we have regathered our troops. We can plan an ambush, follow their trail, and overtake them."

"They took my wife, Jack," Daniel shook the reins,

gripping them until his fingers turned white. "I know what they do to women." Eyes turning red, he stared hard at Jack, clenched his jaw. "I have heard the stories. And, Archie, he is just a boy, Jack."

"I know," Jack lowered his head. "I know, but I cannot let you go. Your death will not save them. We have to wait for the proper time."

Daniel choked back a sob. "How can I sit by and do nothing?"

Jack looked back at him, helplessly shrugging. "I don't know. But for their sakes and your own, you have to."

Daniel breathed out heavily, and finally, with a slump of his shoulders, he allowed the tears to fall. "Alright...I'll wait."

Jack looked away, letting go of the horse's reins. "I'm sorry, Daniel," he said, coming around the horse and waiting for Daniel to dismount.

His legs as heavy as cannons, Daniel slipped sluggishly out of the saddle. The cannonball precariously lodged in the pit of his stomach rolled into place, just waiting to be lit.

51

Firm hands pulled her to her feet, shaking the bleariness from her eyes. A dull ache in her skull clouded her thoughts. The sudden onslaught of unfamiliar voices shouting and speaking incoherently jumbled her thoughts even more. Her eyes groggily opened as she was yanked forward. The bright sunlight pierced her eyes, causing her head to hurt all the more. Blinking back the pain, the face of an Indian man came into view.

Captured. Stricken over the head. Daniel's face fading into black. It all came rushing back.

As the Indian man pulled her from the cart, a sudden panic gripped her gut. Fighting against the ropes tied around her wrists, she whipped her head from side to side. "Archie! Archie!"

A backhanded slap across her cheek greeted her cry. Head whipping to the side, she gasped and slowly brought her head back around to her captor, shooting him a glare.

In response, the man pushed her forward into the group of women unloading from the coat. There must have been at least ten women in all. Staletta recognized them all from the camp. The women exchanged knowing glances, but too afraid to speak, said not a word. Staletta pierced them with her eyes.

"Archie?"

A weight hurtled against her legs and clung there. Craning her neck around, relief flooded her.

"Archie." She swallowed, relaxing her shoulders. "Are you alright?"

Nodding his head against her hip, he mumbled an indecipherable response.

"It's okay, Archie," She breathed in deep and bit her lip, watching their captors wrangle the prisoners together. "We will get out of here. Somehow."

Staletta bit her lip as the Indian soldier caught her speaking. He began to near and she stiffened, cringing as his hand lifted, but did not fall.

She straightened as he walked away, and heeding his warning, said not a word. The ladies behind her shifted and a figure drew up beside her. Turning her head to look, her eyes met with the woman beside her.

Staletta's heart sank with dread, yet lifted at the thought that she was not alone.

It was Eileen. Eileen nodded ever-so-slightly, and even with their hands firmly tied behind their backs, she reached over and grasped Staletta's hand in a reassuring squeeze.

Jostled, Staletta shuffled her feet as the rebel soldiers herded the last of the prisoners into the group. Flicking her eyes from side-to-side, she noted the number of soldiers surrounding them, her eyes landing on a bayonet pointed straight at her. She pulled Archie closer and shrank back.

A man speaking rapidly in the native tongue emerged out of the crowd of soldiers, wearing a hat festooned with a large feather and robes of loosely folded red linen. He pointed to the soldiers, shouting out commands.

Staletta stiffened at the sight of him, not liking his quick steps, his deeply lined face, his abrupt and sharp tone-of-voice.

Stopping in front of the crowd of prisoners, the man surveyed them as if surveying a new herd of cattle, eyes roving, assessing. Staletta imagined him picking out the weakest, identifying the strongest.

"Welcome," the man purred in a heavily accented voice. "As of right now, you are one of us." He held his arms out, extending to the group of rebels standing around them. "You are no longer loyal to the British army. You serve us now. Understand?"

Staletta felt the prisoners around her shifting, not daring to say a word. Her gut clenched and her mind reeled, trying to understand the implications of his words. Was he asking them to turn traitor?

When the prisoners failed to respond, the honey in his voice hardened and cracked. "You do or you die. Now, do you understand?"

A hushed murmur surrounded Staletta as the prisoners acquiesced. Their voices tickled her ears like flyaway hairs tossed by the wind. She involuntarily tossed her head from side to side, narrowing her eyes at the other prisoners who looked down at their shoes, trying not to make eye contact with the threatening man. Turning her gaze back onto the man, she squared her soldiers, stiffened her neck, glaring at him.

Biting her lip, she fidgeted as his eyes landed on her, swiping up and down her figure, then up and down again.

He paused, stepped back, and smiled casually. Then in his native tongue, rambled off a quick sentence, which was followed by laughter from the soldiers.

Staletta narrowed her eyes and frowned, flicking her head from soldier to soldier as they looked at her and laughed. The taunts reminded her of nights spent playing at the local pubs, where the men and waitresses would laugh and jeer at her. She smirked to herself, remembering how she had learned to quickly turn their jeers back onto themselves with an unexpected retort...or a slight jab in the throat with the end of her violin bow.

Shrugging, she tossed her head and laughed along with the soldiers until they stopped. She raised her brows and set her gaze back onto the man in the red robes. With his thumbs hooked into his belt and a lazy smile on his lips, he jerked his head at her.

"What shall I do with you? If you refuse to help me, I have no choice but to kill you."

"That is a problem, indeed, Sir." Staletta's grip tightened on Archie's shirt, but she made her features relax, not wanting to betray how her legs were trembling.

The man tossed his head back, chuckling deep in his throat, then took a step closer. "You are very different from the rest," he nodded at the other women, his eyes looking her up and down again.

"I'm sure I don't know what you mean, Sir." Staletta swallowed lightly, trying to keep her head held as high as possible.

"What role did you play in the British army?" He asked, the lazy smile crumbling from his lips.

Swallowing quickly, then licking her lips, she thought dimly of her violin. With a sinking heart, she realized it had been on her back before she blacked out. Now, it was gone. Pushing the stray thought away, she replied, "I am a medic and play in the band."

"Ah, yes," the man nodded, looking her up and down again, causing her to frown. "Musician explains it."

Thinking that was a rather odd thing to say, Staletta shifted her feet, casting her mind around for something to say, something that would get them, all of them, out of this situation. "I demand you release us," she spouted, squaring her shoulders and firming her voice. "We are civilians, we want no part in your rebellion."

The man chuckled and looked at his men, encouraging them to laugh along with him.

"I'm afraid you are in no position to be making demands," the man stepped closer and Staletta unconsciously stepped back.

"You were with the British army and as such you are privy to certain information I would very much like to know."

"We are only camp followers, Sir," she sputtered. "We have no information. If anything, at least let this boy go. He is just a child. He knows nothing."

The man tucked his arms behind his back, settling in front of her. "If you have no information to give me, then there is no use in keeping you around." The commander flicked his eyes lazily towards the guard. "Kill the boy."

Gasping, Staletta pushed Archie behind her with her

hip and leg. She heard him whimper and press his face into her back. "No," Staletta shook her head at the man, and set her jaw. "What is it you want to know?"

The commander flicked his eyes back towards her. "I want to know where your regiment is planning to go next. I want to know their routines. I want to know their weaknesses, their strengths. I want to know everything."

"Sir, we are just camp followers," she reiterated, wracking her mind again for something, anything to say. "We don't know the army's weaknesses and strengths." A risky thought entered her mind. She tried to push it away, but it came quickly back, spouting out of her mouth. "And do you really think the British officers tell any of us their plans?" She scoffed. "You should have taken hostage a Commanding Officer if you wanted that kind of information. That was poor planning on your part."

The commander snarled. Raising his hand, he brought it stinging across her face.

Head whipping to the side, she screwed up her eyes, fighting back the tears threatening to come. When the stinging lessened, she turned her gaze back to him, wanting to stop the words from coming, but it was too late. "Oh, I see, you aren't capable of capturing the trained officers. You only have the skill to capture the women and children."

The man moved forward, grasping her chin in his hands. He peered deeply into her eyes. "I don't think you understand who you are insulting. Tell me, are you prepared to die?"

Staletta pulled back her head, trying to release her chin from his grasp, but he squeezed harder and shook her head until she stilled.

"Answer me."

She looked back into his eyes as determinedly as he did hers. "Yes."

The man stepped back and opened his arms wide. He indicated for the guards to grab Archie. "That leaves you with two options. You can either tell me everything you know or watch the boy's guts spill out before your eyes."

The guards encroached on her. She squared herself between them and Archie, but a guard easily grabbed her, and pulled her aside, while a second guard grabbed for Archie, and pulled him out in front of the red-robed man.

Enraged, Staletta bit back an angry retort and pulled against the guard holding her tightly in his clutches. Her mind raced to think of anything to say, to scream that she did not know anything, but she knew this man would not care. There was no way of escaping. She looked at Archie, saw the fear in his eyes, saw the child within him shrinking out of existence.

"Alright," she breathed out, and glowered at the man. "I'll tell you anything, anything you want to know."

52

"What are you going to tell them?" Archie whispered as the rebels pushed him and Staletta towards a large tent in the middle of the rebel encampment.

"I don't know, but I'll think of something," she whispered back.

Staletta fell to her knees as the guard pushed her into the tent. A rug sprawled on the ground softened the fall, but not enough to keep it from jarring her bones. She winced in pain as the man bent, grabbing the front of her blouse, and hefted her to her feet in one powerful movement.

"I am done playing games with you, Strange One. Answer my questions, else the boy dies."

He reached down, grabbing Archie by the neck.

"What do you know?" the man growled at her, holding a sabre to Archie's throat.

"What do you want to know?" Staletta stammered, unable to look away from Archie.

"What are they planning?" He spoke through gritted teeth, giving Archie a shake.

"You can't be any more specific?" Staletta pleaded with the commander, searching her mind for some useful information to give him.

"Will they follow us, or do they have other orders?"

Staletta licked her lips, panic gripping her heart. Would the army rescue them? What would Daniel do? Surely, he would come. But how? She swallowed, setting her jaw to appear braver than she felt. "Yes, they will come after you. You have captured important medics, myself and one other. They will come for us."

The man leaned back, eyeing her warily. He humphed. "How do we outrun them?"

Staletta broke, looking at him in disbelief. "I am a camp follower, not a-a-a military strategist. How can you even ask that of me?"

Archie squealed as the sabre knicked the skin under his chin.

"I will ask whatever I wish to ask," the commander barked. "You have travelled with the army; you know their routines. You know what they do. Tell me what you know."

Staletta pulled against the guard that held her, but he was the stronger.

"Alright, alright," Staletta breathed out. "They are efficient, well-disciplined. Everything from the time they wake to the time they depart is strict routine. I suppose all you would need to do is stay one step ahead of their routine and you can outrun them."

"Ahh," the man released Archie, pushing him back towards Staletta. "Now, we are getting somewhere." He smiled, indicating stools located in the middle of the tent. "Have a seat. Guards, remove their bonds."

The guards cut the ropes around her hands and Staletta sat down tentatively, keeping a firm grasp on Archie's hand. The man seated himself opposite.

"I'm afraid we haven't been properly introduced. My name is Commander Khaneesh. And yours?"

Hesitating, Staletta narrowed her eyes at him.

"I assume your husband is an officer and that is why you are following the camp?"

Not taking her eyes from him, she tilted her head. "I don't need to answer that."

"You expect your dear husband to come looking for you, don't you, Strange One?"

Staletta met his gaze. "Of course, he will. And you better be prepared when he does."

Commander Khaneesh smiled broadly, revealing a row of surprisingly white teeth. "I see doubt in your eyes."

"And I see fear in yours," Staletta shot back. "You are afraid to be overrun. You have already betrayed that to me."

Commander Khaneesh laughed. "You are a strange one. I don't believe you are a British officer's wife. The question is, who are you?"

"I am no one."

"That may be, but you are the only one of the captives that dared to speak and that tells me something about you."

Staletta pursed her lips.

"Bravado."

"Never heard of it."

Khaneesh tisked. "You push back. You take risks. You are a musician. But better yet, a performer."

Frowning, Staletta looked away from his gaze, focusing on Archie instead.

"That is all the answer I need."

Staletta looked back to watch him grin and settle back comfortably in his chair.

"I'd say you have an hour maybe two before the British come for you," Staletta glanced away, looking back at Archie instead, her heart racing. "You should release us all now before they slaughter you. If you do, I promise I won't tell them where you are."

Khaneesh chuckled. He rose suddenly, rambling off

orders to the soldiers in his native tongue, then he turned back to them, clapping his hands. "Ever been to Delhi?"

Her heart sinking even further, she said: "Never heard of it."

"A grand city, about 700 kilometers to the west."

Staletta felt a punch to her gut. Her brothers were so close. Dinapore was only a few days walk from where they now were. If they were taken to Delhi, it'd be weeks, even a month out and back again. No, she was not going to be taken farther away. Not again. She had waited too long. This was her only chance to get to them. No, she would not do it. "You can't make it. The British will certainly outrun you. You can't make it!"

"But you said if we stay one step ahead, we can outrun them," Commander Khaneesh smirked. "Am I to understand you are lying? Because that would mean the boy gets a sabre through his chest."

Staletta pushed to her feet and snarled. "We're not going to Delhi!"

Commander Khaneesh laughed, calling for the guards to grab her. The world went red as she struggled against them, but they were too strong. Her gut exploded in pain as a fist concussed into her stomach. She doubled over, gasping for breath. The soldiers knee rose rapidly, aiming straight for her face. Gasping, she curled into a tight ball, pushing her face into the dirt.

"Enough," Khaneesh's command stilled the guards knee seconds before it connected with her head. "This one is too much of a nuisance, take them out and kill them both."

Staletta panicked at Khaneesh's command, grunting as the soldier hauled her to her feet by yanking on her arm.

The guard's nails dug into her skin and she grimaced in pain. "Please don't do this," she wailed, watching Archie struggle against the guard's grasp.

Relentless, he pushed them forward until Archie stumbled over the uneven ground and fell. The guard grunted, releasing Staletta to reach down and haul the boy to his feet. Quickly, Staletta looked around for a weapon, cursing when nothing showed itself. Turning back to the guard, she saw him reach for her. She backstepped, shaking her head.

The guard growled, reaching for her again.

She took another step back and wobbled as her foot landed on a rock. Her gaze tore from the guard and glanced to the side as she righted herself. Her eyes landed on the sight of a violin. A tendril of a thought filtered into her thoughts, but she didn't take the time to decipher it. She lunged for the violin, grabbed it, and quickly thrust it under her chin.

She played as the guard descended. He paused

mid-step, looking back towards Commander Khaneesh and shrugging helplessly.

Taking a firm step forward, she played the violin, brandishing the music as if it were a weapon. The guard took a step back.

"*Thee haughty tyrants ne'er shall tame,*" Staletta sang out, frowning at the Commander, "*all their attempts to bend thee down will but arouse thy generous flame.*" Then she shrugged. "*And work their woe and thy renown.*"

Staletta stepped forward again, then marched towards the Commander. "*Rule, Britannia. Britannia rule the waves. Britons never, never, never shall be slaves.*"

Thrusting out with her violin bow, Staletta fell into a deep, theatrical bow, and rose, fixing him with a scowl.

Khaneesh clapped, a grin growing on his face. "My, my," he said, his clapping. "Daring."

Staletta smirked, nodding her head gratefully, taking that as a compliment.

"Fortunately for you, I find it amusing rather than threatening," The Commander's cheeks quirked as he smiled. "Well, I cannot kill you now." The Commander's cheeks quirked as he smiled. "Oh yes, I have a good use for you. You shall be my personal entertainer."

Staletta gritted her teeth. In some ways, this man reminded her of Bobs, but she figured, if she could handle Bobs, she could handle this man, too. Peering down at Archie, she gave him a reassuring smile as relief flooded through her. Archie was not going to be killed, and that was all that mattered.

"You are my slaves, you understand?" The commander stated. "As prisoners of war you will never be free; you will never be paid for your work. You might, at the end of the day, wish I had killed you."

Staletta heard Archie swallow hard and felt him tremble. She nudged him gently with her elbow. "Is that so?" She said in a steady voice. "To me it sounds like a fairly good deal. Free food, free lodging, a chance to play the music I love whenever I want. How could a girl go wrong with that?"

Commander Khaneesh chuckled and walked over to sit before them. "I cannot decide if I like you or despise you." He smacked his lips. "You are, as the British say, cheeky. That's not something you see in a lot of intelligent women. Nevertheless, you amuse me."

Staletta nodded her head, acknowledging the thinly veiled insult, but letting it slide.

The guards grabbed for her and Archie, this time retying their hands behind their backs. As they stumbled back towards Eileen and the other prisoners, Archie whispered towards her, "Star, why did you sing *that* song? I mean, didn't you think it would make him even angrier?"

Staletta chuckled humorlessly, "I meant to. I learned this lesson awhile ago: in order to stay alive you either have to be useful or intriguing." Staletta cast him a shadowed gaze. "We have no usefulness here, Archie. Intrigue is the only option we have."

Archie's mouth opened in an O shape as her words sunk in. "I understand."

"Don't worry, Archie," she said. "I promised I would never let anything happen to you, and I meant it."

Roughly, the soldier threw her and Archie back into the huddle of women prisoners as Khaneesh followed along behind.

"Form a line," Khaneesh yelled, waving his arms at them. "We march for Delhi."

53

Long after the sun had set and the jungle had darkened to an impenetrable gloom, Khaneesh, riding on the back of a great elephant, called for them to halt. Exhausted, Staletta stumbled to a standstill, wincing as her swollen feet pulsed in her boots. She looked over to find Archie standing still, head tottering on his neck as if he would fall asleep standing up. On her other side, Eileen glanced her way, lending her the smallest of reassuring smiles. Staletta nodded back and sighed.

The soldiers surrounded them and pushed them to a cleared spot beneath the trees that would serve as their campsite. The soldiers knife sliced through the ropes on Staletta's wrists, and a rush of relief passed over her. She brought her arms around to the front, rubbing her wrists where the ropes had cut into the skin. Rolling her shoulders, she winced with pain as the muscles released from their cramped position.

Soon a soldier came up, dropping a small bundle of cloth in front of each prisoner.

"What is this?" Staletta bent, picking up the bundle in front of her.

"Our bedrolls, I presume," Eileen sighed and bent to pick up her own.

Staletta untied the string wrapped around her bundle, and sure enough, a length of cloth unrolled. It was a long, single sheet of thin cotton. Laying it down on the ground in front of her, she smoothed out the edges, and collapsed onto it. Reaching over, she helped Archie to straighten out his sheet and watched as he fell onto it.

"I'm sorry, Archie," Staletta whispered to him, reaching out to take his hand. "This is all my fault."

Archie blinked at her and raised a corner of his mouth, trying to give her a reassuring smile. "I'm okay."

"Are you?" She widened her eyes, looking at him hard. "You have had many trials this day. If-if you want to talk, I'm here."

He nodded slowly.

Lowering her head, she hardened her eyes, pursed her lips. "Danny will come for us and we will be free again. I promise you that."

Archie's eyes fluttered closed and he was asleep in seconds. He wasn't a boy anymore, Staletta thought as a tear leaked from her eye, slipped down her cheek. He had killed a man and been taken prisoner all in one day. He would never be the same. With shaking fingers, she wiped away the trail of tears.

"Star."

Staletta turned to find Eileen sitting on her sheet beside them. "Eileen, how did I let this happen? How did we get captured? How did we get dragged so far away from our husbands? How could I let this child be taken prisoner? How could we have so easily turned traitor to our country?"

"Shhh," Eileen leaned forward and took her hands. "No sense in dwelling on that now. Many innocent folks turn traitor. Captured soldiers, camp followers, even members of the band. When your options are death or turn traitor, I think there are few who would choose the former. Now, we need to focus on staying alive. Keeping that boy alive."

Nodding, Staletta sniffed and took a deep breath. "What happens to those who turn traitor?"

"Oh, if they are soldiers, definitely a court martial. Prison."

Her gut clenching, Staletta looked at her hard. "Do you mean to say that if we get out of here, we will be imprisoned by our own country?"

Eileen sighed and shook her head. "No, I am sure that in our contingent, nothing would be reported, as long as no one does anything too traitorus."

"Such as what?"

"Such as fighting against the troops...really siding with the rebels in their rebellion against British rule."

"I see," Staletta nodded, her gut unclenching ever-so-slightly. "I gave him information, that makes me a traitor. I hope that they can forgive me. Maybe it wouldn't have happened if I hadn't drawn attention to myself."

"Why did you draw attention to yourself?" Eileen

tisked and shook her head, smiling slightly.

Shoulders drooping, Staletta shook her head. "I don't know, Eileen." She cast her eyes around the camp, spotting Khaneesh sitting in his already constructed tent. He smoked a pipe, the smoke lazily drifting up and around his face in front of his dark eyes that were watching her with interest. Staletta turned her gaze back to Eileen. "He watches me "

Eileen flicked her eyes up to see who she referred to, then brought them back to Staletta. "What you did earlier was dangerous. I don't want you taking any more risks. You must be careful with that man."

"He is the one that singled me out," Staletta shrugged.

Softly chuckling, Eileen squeezed her hands, then lifted her finger to wipe dirt from Staletta's cheek. "I don't blame you for trying to save the boy, but you are different. You see, you never had a mother growing up, and, I think, that makes all the difference."

"What on Earth does that mean?" Staletta cocked her head, scoffing.

Breaking into a smile, Eileen shook her head. "It's something in your mannerisms." She stopped speaking, searching for the right words. "You lack a certain decorum, a propriety that your mother would have certainly instilled in you, had she had the chance of it."

"You say I am not proper?" Staletta's eyes widened as her back stiffened.

At that moment, a soldier walked by, dropping chunks of bread in their laps before quickly moving on.

"Nay," Eileen shook her head hurriedly. "Only that

you are more forthright and daring than is proper. I know you have had to fight for your own protection, for your own survival. Where most of us women had a more domesticated upbringing, you have had a wild one. And yet, you are not entirely unsophisticated. You are pretty and small, you sing beautifully and dance so gracefully." Eileen nodded at that. "You are a wild and graceful thing. That is why you always attract attention."

Staletta shook her head, nibbling on her bread. "Oh, Eileen, you do say such strange things." Her eyes inadvertently strayed back to Khaneesh. Finding that he still watched her, she quickly dropped her gaze, feeling an uneasy twinge in her gut. She lowered her mouth to her bread, hoping that he would soon leave her alone.

As she finished chewing her bread, she stiffened at the sound of Khaneesh's voice floating over towards her. "Come here, Performer."

She raised her eyes to Eileen, thinking she would just ignore him, pretend like she had not heard, but Eileen tilted her head, indicating she should go.

"Whatever you do, don't make him mad," Eileen whispered as Staletta rose to her feet, her legs feeling weak from the long day's trek.

She picked her way slowly to his tent, stopping just outside of it.

"I am bored," he said, waving his hand. "Perform something for me."

Picking at her fingernail, Staletta shrugged. "I don't have my violin, sir."

He stared at her for a few seconds, then snapped his

fingers. A guard appeared beside her. "Get her violin," Khaneesh leaned back in his chair. "What do they call you, Performer?"

Opening her mouth to reply with her name, she paused, changing her mind at the last second. "They call me the North Star."

"The North Star?" He puffed on his pipe, the smoke rising quickly. "Well, North Star, let's hope that you play well, otherwise, there will be no use for you."

The soldier appeared again, this time with her violin. A surge of joy rose in her heart at the sight of it, but she squashed the emotion, wanting to appear calm in front of this dangerous man. Tipping her head at his comment, she flashed him a coy smile as she fell into a theatrical bow, rising and bringing the bow down to the violin strings in one fluid movement.

As she did in past times, she began with a rousing tune, one that could make even the surliest rebel soldier tap his finger with the tune. Hopping and whirling as she played, Staletta let the music fuel her strength and quiet her roiling stomach. She flashed her theatrical smiles and tipped her head at the soldiers, making the shyer one's blush and look away.

She finished the tune and started again, playing until the crowd began to grow sleepy and worn out from the day.

Her mind raced to think of a tune to finish off the night, one so different from the others, one so different than anything the rebels would ever want to hear. Something that would make a lasting impression. The one that came to mind was a quiet hymn, full of emotion and longing, *Abide with*

Me.

Letting the violin sing the song for itself, the notes rose and fell in a lilting constant stream. There was no need for dancing. The song commanded stillness, focusing all the attention on the trek of the notes as they wandered over hills and valleys and swept out like the wind towards the wild plains, and the listeners were all caught up in it, all swept up into its depths and cast free to the winds.

Staletta held the last note of the song, letting it quiver out to a trickling tune and she quietly sang a few lyrics in a softened tone. *"Fast falls the eventide. The darkness deepens, Lord with me abide. I fear no foe, with Thee at hand to bless. Ills have no weight and tears no bitterness. Where is death's sting? Where, grave, thy victory? I triumph still, if Thou abide with me."*

Keeping her eyes fixed on Khaneesh, she lowered slowly into her customary bow and rose.

Khaneesh lowered his pipe, letting it carelessly dangle from his fingers. He cleared his throat, dark brown eyes still staring at her. "That is all for tonight."

Lowering her head, Staletta nodded and picked her way back to the bedroll beside Eileen, keeping her violin tucked close to her side.

Eileen laid down on her bedroll as Staletta did the same.

"A beautiful choice," Eileen said, closing her eyes. "A dangerous choice."

Nodding in the darkness, Staletta peered up at the starry sky. "In life, in death, O lord, abide with me."

54

The guard appeared at her feet while the moon was still up. A crust of bread smacked into her face, jolting her awake.

Bleary eyed, Staletta sat up, slowly putting the bread to her teeth and nibbling.

"How early is it?" Archie moaned, laying back down on the ground.

"Get up," the guard roared, causing Archie to jump. "The woman said the British army departs at first light. That means we must depart before first light to stay ahead."

"Come on, Archie," Staletta pulled him back up into a sitting position and pushed the bread into his hand. "Eat. You'll need your strength today."

The guard pointed to a cart loaded with hay. "The

elephant keeper died by the hands of your fellow British officers. You will take his place."

Staletta blanched. "I don't know how to take care of an elephant."

"You will feed the elephants that hay and get them ready for the march." The guard turned on his heel and quick walked a few paces before turning around. Pointing at Archie, he said, "Boy, you will help load the baggage carts. Come."

Archie stood, wiping the crumbs from his clothes. He followed the guard as Staletta swallowed the last of her bread and moved toward the elephant paddock standing beyond where the prisoner's tents had been. There were two elephants in the hurried, makeshift paddock: the Commander's elephant and one other.

She moved toward the commander's elephant first, and it ruffled its ears as she slowly approached, hand held out in front of her.

"Hello, there," she cooed to it, smiling. "That's it."

The elephant sniffed her fingers with his trunk.

"Aww, you're a sweet thing," Staletta gingerly reached up as high as she could and petted the trunk. It felt dusty beneath her fingers as they travelled over the wrinkles and pits carved into the flesh. It wasn't hairy in the way most animals were, but it did have spurts of wiry hairs coming out of the wrinkles in random bursts.

The elephants trunk curled up and rubbed against her cheek, the snout tickling her chin as it felt around her face. She laughed and the elephant breathed out, shifting its feet, and waving its ears.

"You must be hungry," she said, stepping back and moving towards the hay wagon. She hauled arm fulls of hay over to the two elephants in the pen.

"You might be the only good part about being a hostage," she whispered to the elephants as they gratefully accepted the hay. "You are prisoners just as much as I, aren't you?"

Staletta sighed, patting the Commander's elephants neck as it bent to scoop the hay into its trunk, then up into its mouth.

Moments later, Commander Khaneesh stormed over, pulling her out of the way. "It's time to leave. Is my elephant ready?"

"He is eating now, it might be a few minutes yet," Staletta frowned, watching him pull out a stick with a hooked end.

"Why didn't you feed him earlier?" Khaneesh glowered. "Never mind, get out of my way. Guard."

The guard appeared by her side, grabbing her arms, pulling them behind her back, and tying her hands with rope. Archie followed along behind him.

"We don't need this," Staletta whined but allowed him to tie up her hands. "It's hard enough to march, but to have our hands tied, too..."

"An extra precaution in case you get any...ideas," Khaneesh replied.

The guard moved to do to the same to Archie, then started walking them towards the rest of the prisoners lined up, ready to march.

Behind them she heard the elephant trumpet and snort. Looking over her shoulder she watched as Khaneesh scrambled on top of the elephant then smacked it with the sharp end of the stick several times to get it to move.

She gritted her teeth. "You could try being nice to it, you know."

"Shut up, woman," came the reply. "Or I'll use the bullhook on you."

55

They marched for a week until Staletta was sure the British army was too far behind to catch up with them and all hope of finding her brothers had vanished. Exhausted, they rolled into camp and Staletta collapsed on the ground, too tired to rise. Beside her, Archie did the same.

The guard tossed them a handful of dried fruit and nuts, then untied their hands.

"You know what to do," he said, before stalking off.

Archie leaned his head against her shoulder as he munched on the scant meal. "I want to go home."

Taking a shaky breath, Staletta lay her head on top of Archie's. "I know, me too."

She leaned her head further down. Her mouth close to his ear. "We're going to escape. We must come up with a plan and then wait for the right moment. Okay?"

She could feel Archie's head nod against her side.

"Good lad."

The guard appeared out of the trees. "What are you doing? I told you to get to work."

Staletta flinched at his sudden appearance, then frowned at the guard. "We're going, we're going."

Her feet throbbed and her blisters smarted, but she got to her feet, helping Archie to his. Archie moved to the baggage carts and she watched him scramble up the side as if he were running up the sails on the *Redemption.* The knots holding the canvas sheets over the baggage were no match for his fingers. He untied them, ran to the other side, untied it, then moved out of the way as the rebel troops grabbed for their baggage.

She located the hay wagon, grabbed an arm full, and hauled it over to the Commander's elephant. She then went to get another arm full and deposited it in front of the second elephant. She patted each of their trunks and scratched behind their ears.

"We need to get out of here," she whispered to the Commander's elephant as she scratched him. "Will you help us? Me and the boy? Will you take us far away from here?"

The elephant finished his hay and turned his black eye upon her, begging for more.

"I'm sorry," she said, petting its trunk. "Supplies are limited. We all have to ration."

The elephant bucked her gently with his head, then twined his trunk down and around her waist. Before she could do anything, the trunk tightened as thousands of muscles contracted. She sucked in her breath as her feet lifted from the ground.

Her heart beat fast, thinking the elephant meant to squeeze her to death. But, no, he raised her up, depositing her easily on his back. Scrambling into a more comfortable position, she caught her breath, and scratched the top of his head.

"You little minx," she said. "Haven't you ever heard of asking a ladies permission before you go and lift her onto your back? No? Well, it's high time you learned." She giggled, looking around at the camp below, then gazing out into the black forest.

"We're far from home, aren't we?" She leaned back, feeling tears start in her eyes. "I miss Dailily. I miss home. I miss my brothers."

She sucked in her breath as the tears burst, falling on the top of the elephant's head. "I'm sorry, elephant," she said, wiping them up with the torn sleeve of her once white blouse.

The elephant whimpered, waving its ears to comfort her.

"You don't have a name, do you?" The thought struck her. Commander Khaneesh never called him anything. "I can't think of a name suitable for an elephant, but I'll think on it. I'll think of something grand for you."

"Get down from there."

Staletta jumped as the guard's voice assaulted her. She stilled her heart, wiped away the tears remaining in her eyes, and started to dismount from the elephant.

"Hurry it up."

"Hold on, I'm getting down," she swung her legs over the side and dropped to the ground, wincing as pain emanated from her feet and up into her ankles.

"The Commander wants to see you in his tent." The guard grabbed her arm, pushing her through the camp to Commander Khaneesh's tent, stopping on the way to collect Archie.

The guard pushed them into Khaneesh's tent, and they stumbled on the lavish rug spread on the floor. When they entered, Khaneesh turned, indicating for them both to sit on the stools in the middle of the tent. "Have a seat." He finished preparing a drink in the corner, then turned back to face them.

"We have lost the British army," Commander Khaneesh smiled. "Our scouts say they have stopped following us, moved on to a different target." He stepped near, running the back of his hand along her cheek.

Staletta flicked her head back and away, frowning at him in disdain, while her stomach clenched in horror. "You are lying," she said through gritted teeth.

"I'm afraid not," He sipped his drink, then paced in front of her. "Now you understand how fickle the British are, how little their loyalty to their own really is. They are not coming for you, my dear. Your dear husband has abandoned you."

Shaking her head, Staletta refused to believe his words. Heart pounding in her chest, she swallowed back panicked gasps and cast her mind out for something to say, for anything to prove that he was wrong, and that Daniel was still coming. But there was nothing, only a dim fluttering as of a bird with a broken wing, flapping wildly and yet, getting nowhere.

"No matter," Khaneesh continued in a reverent tone as low as a whisper. "I have a grand use for you. You see, North Star, you will be my personal slave for the rest of your life."

A tear escaped down Staletta's cheek. "And if I refuse?"

Khaneesh cocked his head at her, half rolling his eyes, and nodding at Archie. "You already know the answer to that question."

As another tear slipped down her cheek, Staletta fixed her gaze on Archie and nodded solemnly. "If that's what you want, then I'll do it."

"That's what I want," he said, licking his lips. He smiled knowingly and waved for the guard to remove them.

When they arrived back at their campsite and the guard disappeared, the two collapsed onto the ground, holding each other tightly.

"Star?" Archie said through sniffles. "Danny will still come for us, won't he? He wouldn't abandon us?"

Unable to restrain her tears, she let them fall freely on top of his brown locks and squeezed him tighter. How could he come for them? One man against an army of rebels. It was unthinkable. Her body shook with suppressed sobs and she buried her face in his hair trying to regain her composure, to remain strong for him. If anything, she couldn't let him know there was no hope.

She breathed in deep, pulling back. Placing a hand on his cheek, she rubbed it with her thumb and gave him a smile. "He will come."

56

The sound of clanging pots jolted Daniel out of a deep and dreamless sleep. Every nerve in his body jumped as he sat up, reaching to shield Staletta with his arm...but she was not there. As reality washed over him, Daniel's gut clenched and he scrunched his legs up, resting his elbows on his knees. Dropping his head into his hands, he rubbed his face vigorously.

It had been two weeks to the day since she and Archie had been taken. Two weeks since they had even seen the rebels. It was likely they had lost them for good.

Daniel rose from his bedroll and slunk over to the wash bucket. He splashed his face with the warm water, then held his hands over his eyes. Sighing, he rubbed as hard as he could. He slowly pushed his hands up into his hair, gripping it with clenched fingers. Growling, he threw his hands down, backhanding the bucket. It clattered loudly to the ground, water flying.

He whirled, hands on hips, shaking his head. He had never felt such rage. It was primal. It was burning, turning the soft edges of his heart into hardened scales, and there was no one to blame but himself. He should have said no to this voyage, this suicide mission. Even if it broke his wife's heart, he should have forbidden her from going. At least she would still be alive.

He snarled, whirling on his heel, passing his hand through his hair again. "She's not dead until we find a body."

The sentiment reassured him, re-oriented him, and he took a deep breath to ease his pounding heart. He bent, digging through his pack for a mirror and comb. He pulled out the mirror, examining the wild hair upon his head. He hadn't had a hair cut since they left England. It had grown curly in the front and down around his ears. The backs and sides were so thick, it gave his head a voluminous appearance. He pulled out the comb and tamed the swirling vortex to some degree, though without pomade it would still look wild. Months of no shaving had given him a thick carpet of brown hair on his chin.

Dimly, he wished the beard would grow taller, like a vine, to cover the dark circles hanging beneath his eyes. The dark circles had stolen away the cheerfulness of his eyes, left them cold and determined. He did not recognize the man looking back at him. In a cruel twist of fate, he had gone from a man that had everything, to a man that had nothing.

Disgusted with himself, he shoved the mirror back into his pack and stepped out of his tent. It was still dark, and normally they would not depart until morning light, but for the last week they had tried changing up their routine to try and make headway against the rebels. It did no good. Daniel bent to pack up his tent, stopping when he heard footsteps, and the solitary figure of Jack approached.

"Daniel," Jack greeted, nodding, and giving him a quick smile that faltered at the edges.

Daniel continued packing, eyeing him warily. "What is it, Jack?"

Jack reached to scratch the back of his neck. "There's been a slight change of plan and I'm pretty sure you aren't going to like it."

Daniel's hands slipped off the tent and he turned to face Jack squarely. "Tell me."

"We have received new orders," Jack paused to swallow. "We have been ordered to cease our pursuit of this rebel contingent. There are other rebels escaping into lower Bengal and we've been ordered to go after them instead. We leave for Dinapore immediately."

A punch to his gut would not have left Daniel more out of breath. Clenching his teeth together, he tried to catch his breath and keep from screaming. "What about my wife? What about the boy? We are to abandon them to their fate?"

"Look, I know you're upset..."

"Upset?" Daniel thundered, letting go of the slim rope holding his resolve together. "Of course, I'm upset. We are abandoning them. And what am I supposed to do?"

Jack took a step back defensively and held up his arms. "Don't shout at me, mate, I don't give the orders."

Bending to rest his hands on his knees, Daniel

groaned, then stood, crunching a fist to his forehead. "I can't leave her."

Hands in his pockets, Jack shrugged, looking back at him helplessly. "Orders are orders, we have to move on."

Breathing in deep, Daniel ran his tongue over his teeth, nodding his head. He bent to the ground, picking up the tent pegs. He thrust them into Jack's arms. "Finish this up, would you?"

"Daniel, what are you doing?"

As Daniel stalked off angrily, he could hear Jack fumbling with the tent pegs.

Daniel marched up to the commanding officer's tent which was in the process of being struck. There were three officers outside of it, drinking coffee and swapping stories. Unreserved, Daniel marched up to them, fire in his eyes.

"I protest this change in orders," he declared, breathing heavily, and standing up as straight as he could.

The Lieutenant Colonel glanced up at him, taking a bite of biscuit. "So what?"

"I am here to ask you to reconsider. If we could have one more day, I think we can catch them this time."

"Boy," the Lieutenant Colonel chewed on his biscuit. Daniel twinged at the insult, but he said nothing. "You are a camp follower. An extra mouth to feed. A drain on our reserves. Why should we ignore our orders in pursuit of a couple of civilians that were irresponsible enough to get themselves kidnapped? No doubt they have already turned rebel themselves..."

Feeling slapped, Daniel turned white, and a feeling of humiliation came over him. "What do you mean by that?"

"They were taken hostage, correct? Wouldn't you swear fealty to them in exchange for your life?" The Lieutenant Colonel sat back, chewing. "It is no wonder we haven't captured them yet. Your wife gave them inside information."

"Speculation. You don't know my wife gave them any information. You cannot prove it."

The Lieutenant Colonel wiped crumbs from his beard and shifted his feet. "Even so, we have our orders and those come from a higher power than me, so there's no use protesting. We move for Dinapore in less than an hour. I suggest you go finish packing or get out of here."

Taking a moment to calm himself, Daniel realized he was treading on thin ground. This was the army. If he stepped too far out of line, he could be kicked out of the encampment and left to die in the jungle.

Grudgingly, he apologized. "Forgive me," he said. "It was wrong of me to question the orders. I will not do so again."

The Lieutenant Colonel nodded curtly and dismissed him with a paltry wave of his hand. His ears burned as he walked away, hearing the officers mocking him. They thought he was a fool. They thought he was nothing.

Deeply disturbed, Daniel marched back to Jack who had finished striking the tent and was finishing packing it away.

"What are you going to do?"

Avoiding his eyes, Daniel packed up the last of his things, and slung his pack over his back. "The 19th Foot is still in Dinapore, as far as you know?"

"As far as I know, yes," Jack replied.

"Good," Daniel said, his mind whirling in the semblance of a plan. It was not much. It was not anything to go on. But he was desperate.

"You are coming with, then?" Jack asked, surprised. "I half thought you'd ride off and invade the rebel camp yourself."

"That'd be a suicide mission," Daniel chided, but cast a glance over at Jack. "Unless you'd be willing to betray your orders and come with me?"

Jack snorted, "Never."

"Didn't think so," Daniel smirked. "That's why I need to find someone who will."

Narrowing his eyes, Jack shrugged. "Who?"

"Star's brothers, of course."

"You think Peter and Paul will turn rogue?" Jack raised his eyebrows, scoffing. "Not a chance. I mean, Paul might, but Peter? He is a stickler for the rules. It would be entirely outside of his character."

"Maybe." Daniel hoisted his musket over his shoulder and stalked off. "But I have to try."

57

Peter stood on the bank of the Ganges River looking out over the regiment preparing to cross. There were hundreds of soldiers in their blue uniforms waiting to board the barge, alongwith a whole host of camp followers, four hundred bulls, two hundred horses pulling two hundred carts loaded with ammunition, food, camping supplies, and fifty elephants.

"Have you ever seen anything so stunning?" Paul shook his head, turning up one side of his mouth in a grin.

"Not your average garden party, that's for sure," Peter confirmed, squinting into the sun. Of everything, he was most intrigued by the sight of the elephants. Of course, he had seen plenty of elephants since arriving in India, but never so many in one spot. They were marvellous creatures, large, blubbery, wrinkled, and smart. "I would like to ride an elephant," he remarked to Paul.

Paul swatted him on the shoulder with the back of

his hand. "Do it, then."

Peter shot him a jeering look. "I cannot ride an elephant."

"Why not?" Paul laughed. "I would."

"I'm the responsible one, remember," Peter drawled. "The elephants are for the commanding officers, not the soldiers."

"I do remember, and I think it's high time that changed," Paul stood and grabbed his brother's shoulder. "You are riding that elephant today, if it's the last thing I do." Paul thrust a finger in the direction of an elephant filling up its trunk with water from the river and spurting it out across its back.

Looking at his brother, Peter said. "You're bonkers. I can't do that."

"Why not?" Paul reiterated.

Peter opened his mouth to retort, then closed it, not having any good excuse.

"Think about it," Paul continued. "This will be your first opportunity to prove you're not such a – a-"

"A what, Paul?" Peter's expression darkened as he crossed his arms, raised an eyebrow.

"A goosy sop, that's what," Paul drew himself up, looking down his nose.

"I am not a goosy sop."

"Maybe not when you're sleeping..."

"Paul."

"Like it or not, you're not most people's definition of the word 'fun'."

Peter furrowed his brow but uncrossed his arms and

relaxed his shoulders. "I know how to have fun. But now is not the time."

Paul shook his head in disagreement, "With all due respect, brother, you don't. When was the last time you did something so wild you felt as free as the wind, like nothing could ever bring you down?"

Shifting uncomfortably, Peter blinked several times, and frowned. "Not since I was a child. A very long time."

Holding a hand towards the elephant, Paul raised his eyebrows twice quickly. "Now's your chance."

"Ludicrous," Peter rolled his eyes, adjusting his feet and flicking his eyes from Paul to the elephant, then back to Paul. The corner of his mouth twitched as he gazed at the elephant, imagining himself splashing in the water like a child in a puddle. It was ludicrous. It was stupid. It was below his station in life. But Paul's accusations nagged at him.

As boys they had run free through the paddies of Ireland with not a care in the world. That was eons ago, it seemed. Childhood had ended for Peter the day the famine hit. It had been so long since he had felt that wild, free running spirit pulsing in his veins. He felt it, now; the urge to run. The urge to holler. The urge to let it all go.

It was ludicrous. It was stupid.

A small smile seeped onto his stoic face.

The smile mirrored on Paul's face. "Race you?"

"You're on." Peter dashed off, Paul not far behind. Splashing into the river the brothers each met an elephant, petting their long snouts and feeling the big, floppy ears. Mimicking the native elephant handlers, Peter patted the foreleg of his elephant and was pleased when the animal responded by kneeling in front of him, allowing him to step up on the leg and hoist himself onto its back.

"Woo hoo!" Peter called as the elephant lifted itself to stand. He reached down to the elephants neck to steady himself as the animal heaved to one side and then the next. It stepped deeper into the lake until the water deepened in the middle, forcing the elephants to swim rather than walk. It was a bit like being in a boat, but, as Peter thought, ridiculously more fun.

"How's your elephant, dear brother?" Paul called over, waving his hat.

"She smells, but she's a right good swimmer. And yours?"

"A peach, an absolute peach." He called back, bending down, and kissing the top of his elephant's head.

It took the whole day to move the regiment across the river. By the time they were done, it was dark, and they were forced to set up camp for the night. Where Paul had gotten off too, Peter did not know. But he had gathered some logs for the soldiers to sit on around their campsite, and he started a fire. The camp followers were passing out brandy to the soldiers as they sat round the fires, joking, and laughing.

When Paul finally emerged out of the darkness with Irene and Julia hanging on his arms, Peter rolled his eyes. Paul had survived his heroic attempt to save Irene. He would forever have a scar scratched across his stomach, but he healed quickly and seemed his old self again.

"Brother, I've brought you something," Paul beamed, nodding his head towards Julia on his left.

"Paul..." Peter pinched the bridge of his nose, shaking his head.

"What?" Paul brought her over to him and she sat down happily beside him on the log. Paul and Irene sat on the other side of the fire.

"Paul told us you rode the elephants today. How exciting," Julia commented to Peter, pulling out a canister of brandy and filling a cup for him.

Peter took the cup, somewhat annoyed with Paul for bringing her. Peter cleared his throat. "Paul, could I talk to you for a moment?"

Ignoring Peter's request, Paul raised his glass. "I think some congratulations are in order. Cheers!" He cried and the camp around also shouted "Cheers" and took another drink.

Paul dropped his empty glass and pulled Irene close, kissing her fervently. Peter threw up a hand in defeat, then sipped his brandy, looking away out into the night.

At the sound of Julia clearing her throat, he turned back to her. Guilt nagged at his thoughts. He should be friendlier to her and not so cold.

"Paul says you are a troubled man, uptight and apprehensive," she ducked her head, looking up at him through her lashes. "Is that true?"

Grinding his teeth, Peter replied, "Paul talks too much. And what does he know anyway, he never grew up.

He's still just a silly boy."

Julia giggled and leant in closer. "He was certainly wrong about you not being funny," she said, batting her lashes.

Peter considered her brown eyes, the spot of pink in her cheeks, her full lips. His breath caught in his throat and the sudden inclination to kiss her passed through his mind. Disturbed by that sudden thought, he cleared his throat and blinked his eyes, breaking the connection. Casting his eyes down at his glass of brandy, he took another sip, then sighed.

"You carry the weight of the world on your shoulders, don't you?" Julia leaned against his arm. "You look as serious and stern as an old man."

"Then why are you here?" Peter drew in a breath, throwing his shoulders back in exasperation. "The soldiers over there," he pointed off to their left, "would be far more entertaining for you."

She looked over at the soldiers and nodded. One had finished a story, leaving the two other men incoherent with laughter. "I like you better."

Peter snorted, taking another sip. His body felt lighter and a tinge of heat tickled his cheeks. "You lost a bet, is that it?"

Giggling, Julia drew even closer, shaking her head, peering up at him through her long lashes. "A lady never places a bet. It is as I said, I like you."

"We've never met," Peter narrowed his eyes. "How could you like someone you have never met?"

"We have never met, but we have seen each other."

Peter nodded, remembering seeing her a few times, mostly just because of Paul. "I am sorry. I never paid much attention."

"I know," Julia shrugged.

"You are hurt by that?"

"Well," Julia shrugged. "A little. But I have noticed that it isn't just me. You never look at any of the girls. You are unlike your brother. Unlike all the other unattached men here."

"Why is that of such concern to you?" Peter gritted his teeth, knowing Paul had similar thoughts.

Julia leaned into his arm. He could feel the rigidity of her corset pressing against him.

"I find it intriguing. I want to know why."

"Do you?" He craned his neck away, trying to think of anything besides the feel of her chest against his arm.

"Mhm," she leaned her head on his shoulder. "A handsome man like you deserves a good woman by his side. Will you ever marry?"

Peter scratched his forehead, feeling his cheeks burn. "This is niether the time nor the place for romantics. There are battles going on. People are dying."

"And you carry the weight of the world on your shoulders," Julia nodded, her cheek brushing his shoulder. She lifted her head, ran her hand up his arm, massaging his shoulder. "Just relax." She flashed him a smile, her eyes locking onto his. "For one night, can't you just let yourself relax."

Peter tensed as she leaned forward. He swallowed, helplessly watching her face draw near.

"For a few minutes you could forget the world, hmm?" Her lips glistened in the light of the fire, her eyes drawing him ever closer.

At first, he tried to resist, but then he remembered the feeling of breaking loose, carelessly splashing towards an elephant in a river, hooting like a child at the top of his lungs. The same feeling tickled his gut as she leaned close.

Like a river loosed from a dam, he reached for her face, drawing her into a kiss. She kissed him back eagerly and he was sunk, unable to stop or pull away. He kissed her with a desperate thirst he did not know he had. He lost track of time and space, and all that remained was her lips and his unquenchable thirst.

Then, suddenly...

"Julia!" the Field Marshall's voice rebuked.

"Irene!" Came a womans.

Julia broke away from him and it felt like he'd been pulled out of the river, gasping for breath, the trees and the noises of the people returning to him in full blast as he remembered where he was.

"Father," Julia said as she got to her feet.

"Mother," Irene followed suit.

"The impropriety," their mother cried, covering her mouth with her hand.

"This is unacceptable behaviour, young ladies," the Field Marshal reprimanded. Peter's stomach dropped to his feet. The Field Marshal was the highest-ranking officer. He didn't know Julia was *his* daughter.

"To go around throwing yourself at the soldiers. It is a disgrace on your honour, a disgrace to this family. I pray you have the goodness to repent of this outrage."

The Field Marshal and his wife dragged the daughters away. Peter and Paul looked at each other through the flames of the fire. Paul pointed at him, smiling, mouthing the word, "You?"

Peter's stomach bobbed back up to the surface as the Field Marshal walked away. He couldn't help but feel giddy at the look of satisfaction in Paul's eyes and at the realization that kissing Julia had been fun. He nodded his head, then snorted, and then they were both holding their sides, erupting with laughter.

58

A week later, the 19th Foot entered the Tirhut district. They passed through miles of jungle and came upon a village called Moteeharee. Upon finding a bare location amid the trees, the regiment set up their tents, readying for their next orders to come. A week passed and nothing came. Another week passed and nothing came.

"No rebels," Peter said, returning to the tent he shared with Paul and Lucas.

Paul lay on the ground, whistling, his foot bobbing to the tune. Lucas sucked in his saliva, then spat onto his shoe, rubbing the spot vigorously with a cloth.

"I've been to see the Quarter Master." Peter continued. "There was a report that some of the rebels were moving close, but it seems another regiment coming down from the north east scared them off."

"Bloody beggars stole our rebels," Paul said, sitting up on his elbows.

"I think we are the bloody beggars," Lucas said, "begging for something to do, that is. We're dying of boredom here."

"Boredom, fever, heat..." Peter said, eyeing the river outside of their encampment. A few men of the regiment had already fallen ill, most likely due to the river. One death and a couple others not far behind.

"Maybe they won't make us stay here long," Paul said, lying back down. "Maybe we'll be on the march again soon."

"Maybe," Peter said, sitting down on a log and putting his face in his hands. He pulled on his cheeks, then sat up, pulling his jack knife out of his pocket, and beginning to strike it on a sharpening stone.

Peter looked over his shoulder at the sound of feet marching on the ground. A new regiment moved down the lane, complete with elephants, cows, horses, soldiers, carts, and camp followers.

"Look at that," Peter said nudging Paul's foot. "At least we'll have some new company. Maybe they have met with some rebels and we can hear some stories, eh?"

Paul sat up, eyeing the regiment. "Some of those fellows look familiar. Have we stayed with that regiment before?"

"Hmm," Peter looked more closely into the crowd. "I can't tell from here."

"Oh well," said Paul, starting to lay back down.

"Wait a minute," Peter said, and Paul paused, looking over to where he was looking. "I think that might be Jack."

"Jack of the 10th Foot?" Paul said, sitting up fully.

"Yes, it's him. I'd recognize that swaggering gait anywhere," said Lucas, standing up. "So sure of himself."

Peter watched as Jack stopped to talk to a soldier and the soldier pointed up to where they were. Peter waved until Jack caught sight of him and started picking through the rows of tents towards him. Another man he did not recognize and who has not in military garb walked determinedly at Jack's side.

"Jack ol' boy, you're still alive," Paul reached forward, extending his hand toward Jack.

"Indeed, I am, Paul," he grasped Pauls hand and shook it fervently, then also shook Peters. "I have a surprise for you two," unable to keep a smile from passing across his face, Jack beamed. "Mind you, it's a good surprise and a bad surprise. Either way, you are going to be gobsmacked. Do you understand me? Gobsmacked."

"Yes, yes," said Paul. "We are fully prepared to be gobsmacked, now what is it?"

"I have brought with me a man," Jack indicated the brown-haired, non-military man standing next to him. "A man who is, in fact, the husband of your –" Jack paused and took a breath.

The stranger stepped forward. "Your long-lost sister."

59

Peter's face twitched. He rocked back on his heels, then glanced at Paul. Wide-eyed, Paul shrugged in response. Peter swung his eyes back to the stranger. "Our sister?"

The stranger nodded, a quick jerk of his head.

Swallowing nervously, Peter reached into his pocket, running his thumb along the butt of his jack knife. It couldn't be? Could it? Gut clenching, he cast his eyes around the camp, looking for her. Embarrassed by the tears threatening at the corners of his eyes, he kept searching the camp, refusing to look at the man. "Where is she?" His voice came out almost as a whisper.

"Ahhh, that's the rather bad portion of the news," Jack interjected, clapping the stranger on the back. "Do you want to tell them or shall I?"

Peter forced himself to look back at the man.

"I will tell them."

Peter watched as a deep-set pain flickered in the stranger's eyes. Sensing something terrible, he lifted his head, narrowing his eyes at the stranger, a nervous worm beginning to writhe in his already clenched stomach. "What have you done to her?"

The stranger's eyes flashed to his in anger, but the anger quickly faded, replaced with grief. "She was taken hostage by the rebels."

Peter's face twitched and he snorted out a disbelieving laugh. Turning to Paul, he watched his features go through the same confused emotion.

"How do we know any of this is true?" Paul asked, narrowing his eyes on the stranger. "This could be some ploy by the rebels." He turned to Jack. "Are you sure this man is no traitorous mutineer?"

"I'd like to know that, as well," Peter added. "What's your name? How do you know our sister? Why are you even in India? And how did she get captured by the rebels?"

Impatiently, the man scrunched up his face. "I am no traitor."

Jack nodded beside him. "He tells the truth."

"Tell us more, then, and start with your name," Peter demanded, frowning at the stranger.

"My name is Daniel May," He said, taking an impatient breath. "I met your sister in London about two years ago. We were married just last summer. It is her greatest hope to find you, her long-lost brothers. Recently, with the help of a friend, we discovered you had enlisted in the army. With some research, we were able to find you had been dispatched here to India. Knowing where you were after all these years, she could not resist. She had to come find you. We joined up with the 10th Foot and were going to be on our way here to meet you when we were attacked by the rebels. They took her captive along with a young boy that has accompanied us on this trip."

"Réalta is here. She is a hostage in the enemy camp," Peter stated as his hand rubbed his forehead, trying to make sense of the words. He turned to Jack, eyes widening in fear. "Your regiment didn't go after them?"

Jack shook his head slowly. "We tried, but they kept slipping away. Then when we got our orders to come to Tirhut—"

"I am going after them," Daniel interjected without hesitation. "But I cannot go alone. That is why I have come to you. Will you help me rescue your sister from the rebel camp?"

Peter turned, searching for his gun. "Let's go."

"But Peter," Paul grabbed his arm and swung him back. "We can't leave. We have our orders here."

"Look who's being all sensible now," Peter frowned. "When it really matters, you clam up and get scared."

"Peter," Paul clamped his lips together, his hands balling into fists. "Orders are orders."

"I can't believe you, Paul," Peter said, his voice rising and his face heating up. "Réalta is in mortal danger and you're worried about your little orders?"

"I'm not looking forward to receiving-," Paul paused and spoke his next words slowly and distinctly, "-a court martial."

"I don't care," Peter spat. "They can hang me on the gallows for all I care. I will save our sister."

"Peter," Paul said, his voice lowering, shoulders bending back. He stood tall and lifted his head. "You never listen to me. But on this I think you should. We need to go to the commanding officer and ask for leave. Think about it, we have not seen or heard a report of a rebel in this area since we got here. There is nothing else for us to do. It is quite possible they will let us leave on this one mission."

Peter's shoulders sagged and he raised a hand to the back of his neck and rubbed. He thought about it and the more he thought about it, the more sense it started to make. Peter shook his head, breathing out sharply, then chortled. Lips thinning, he turned back to Paul, and looked on him with new eyes. "You're right. Please forgive me."

Paul sniffed, hooking his thumbs in his belt loops. "Alright, then."

"Maybe you are growing up," Peter said, holding his arms out defensively.

Jack nudged Daniel's arm, "Nah, you can't tell they are brothers, can you? Although, I am surprised." He paused, turning back to Peter. "Peter, I never thought in a million years you would ever suggest going against orders. And you, Paul, the voice of reason? What has happened since we parted ways?"

Peter fidgeted as Paul slapped him on the shoulder. "I convinced him to steal a ride on one of the commander's elephants."

Cheeks burning, Peter finally found his gun and hefted it to his shoulder. "Let's go."

"Then he..."

"Paul, they don't need to know." He rubbed his forehead.

"...kissed a Field Marshal's daughter."

Behind him, Jack chortled. "I missed out on all the good stuff."

60

Daniel had the strangest feeling about meeting Peter and Paul. It wasn't right that he got to meet them before Staletta, and he felt awkward approaching them. Besides that, it did not seem quite believable. These men were like characters from an old, forgotten story. They did not exist except for in the memory of one solitary person. Discovering them, meeting them, did not feel quite real.

Although, he could see how the brothers were related to his wife. They had the same face shape, slim ovals; the same fair skin tanned by the Indian sun; the same exact demeanours, sharp and resilient, honed by years of hardship. On the other hand, the brothers had kept their Irish accents while he had never known Staletta to have one.

The five of them ventured over to the commander's tent, where the Quarter Master and two Commanding Officers were having their afternoon tea and biscuits. They gave Daniel a passing glance upon their approach, but settled their eyes on Peter as he took the lead.

Peter cleared his throat, "Good day," he said somewhat nervous.

"Good day, Mr. Burns," The Quarter Master replied. "Fine weather we are having."

"Much improved indeed, Sir," Peter nodded.

"What brings you to my tent, Mr. Burns?" Lieutenant Colonel Bright asked.

"We have received notice that our sister," he paused and nodded towards Paul, "has been taken captive by the rebels. With your permission, Sir, we request to be dispatched to run down that rebel encampment and rescue the hostages."

Lieutenant Colonel Bright sipped his tea, eyes shifting from one Burns brother to the next. Daniel flicked his eyes to Lieutenant Colonel Cartwright. It took every ounce of self-control, but Daniel kept his face stoically passive. Cartwright had been the same man who denied him earlier.

"Request denied," Cartwright cut in.

Peter's face dropped, but he composed himself. "Sir, may I ask why?"

"We've already been after that detachment and they are long gone. You do not know where they are or how many are left to fight. It would be a fool's mission."

"With utmost respect, Sir," Peter licked his lips and continued. "We have nothing to do here. We have been here two weeks getting fat and bored. Far better would it be for a small contingent to go after the rebels, then waiting passively for them to come here."

The Lieutenant Colonel bit into a biscuit and crumbs fell into his beard. Calmly, he brushed them away, then pierced Peter with his gaze. "Son, we don't move hundreds of soldiers and animals at the word of one soldier. We have our orders here and that's final."

Peter looked down and drew a deep breath, trying one last tactic. "Sir, I'm not asking for the entire encampment to move, only a small contingent."

The Lieutenant Colonel eyed him closely, and shared looks with the other officers. "Lieutenant Colonel Bright, these soldiers are in your contingent after all. What do you say?"

Bright steepled his fingers, eyeing Peter casually. "Mr. Burns, I have noticed you. You are a responsible soldier, never cause any trouble. I'm half tempted to let you take a contingent on a rescue mission to see how you would do in commanding it."

"Thank you, Sir," Peter brightened, feeling the tension release, and a tendril of hope to arise.

"You show great initiative, and I think if you were to plan and execute this mission with success there could be a promotion in it for you," Bright nodded and sniffed. "Same for you, Officer Burns," he turned to Paul. "I have witnessed your heroics. You have a penchant for protecting the ladies, as I understand it, including once having saved the life of my daughter, Lucy, may she rest in peace."

A sadness passed over Bright's face, but he lifted his head and breathed in deep. "I would be willing to agree to your request, however, I would need to send word to the

Government House asking for permission to grant you leave. That might take longer than you would expect. I do not see how that could be possible under the circumstances."

For the second time, Peter deflated, but nodded his head. "I understand, Sir."

Cartwright sat back, a smug look passing over his features. Daniel looked at him in distaste as the man reached for another biscuit. He took a bite, chewed, swallowed. "You heard the man. You are dismissed."

As the group slowly turned and walked away, Daniel spoke through gritted teeth, a headache pounding in his temples. "What are we going to do now? That was our one chance to save her."

They drew up outside the Burn's brothers' tent. Daniel put his hands on his hips, angrily staring at the fire.

"Oh, we are going after her," Peter clapped him on the shoulder. "Let's pack our things."

Daniel's eyes shot up. "You are serious?"

"Peter, what are you on about?" Paul stepped closer.

"Well, you heard the Commanding Officer, same as I," Peter held out his arms defensively.

Paul nodded, hooking his thumbs in his pockets, and pursing his lips. "Yes, I heard him say no."

Shaking his head, Peter bent to rummage around, packing the few items that he had scattered around. "No, no, he made it quite clear that he wanted us to go."

Cocking his head, Paul narrowed his eyes. "I do not think he meant for us to go off without permission, Peter."

"But he did," Peter smiled, his eyebrows lifting. "Did you not hear him say how much he would love for us to go,

347

and, how much he would love to promote us if we were to return successful." He paused, holding his brother's gaze. "Sounded an awful lot like encouragement to me."

Daniel nodded his head. "That's good enough for me."

"You're barmy," Paul shook his head, then straightened, and fixed Peter with a serious look. "Permission or not, let's go get her."

Peter placed a hand on Daniel's shoulder. "You must tell us. What is she like?"

"She's beautiful," Daniel shot them a smile, his eyes clouding over as he imagined her face, her voice, her close presence at his side.

"And mysterious," he continued. "She's like the wind. One second you think you know her, you think you have got her pinned down, then in a flash, she's different and you don't know her at all. You're always having to re-learn her and after a while you give up trying because you've discovered you'll never be able to pin her down, but it's okay because you've also discovered that, like the constant wind, she'll never leave you. No matter what, she will never stop looking for you nor ever leave your side."

"We're going to find her," Peter reached forward, grasping Paul's forearm.

Paul grasped his in return, "After 10 years, we're going to see Réalta again."

"I want her back," Daniel's throat constricted. "If we get there and discover she is dead—"

"She is not dead," Peter pointed at Daniel, his lips pursed. "That I will not allow."

348

61

"I want a small contingent," Peter seated himself on a log round the campfire in front of his and Paul's tent.

"We've already got five," Lucas, seated on Peter's left, held up five fingers. "Me, you, Paul, Jack, and Daniel."

"We need a few more," Peter rested his elbows on his knees, steepling his fingers under his chin. "Any thoughts?"

Jack, also seated on a log, legs outstretched and crossed at the ankle, raised a hand. "I have one. Daniel, you and Staletta grew close to the camp follower, Eileen, correct? I'm sure her husband, George, would volunteer."

Daniel nodded his head, chewing the side of his

cheek. "Yes, his wife was also taken prisoner. He will come, no doubt of that."

Peter glanced at Paul, seated on his right. "Any suggestions from our contingent?"

Paul clasped his hands in his lap, his thumbs tapping a rhythm he alone could hear. "I was thinking Sam and Aldridge. They have been beside us in many battles."

Peter nodded. Sam and Aldridge were good soldiers, and as Paul had noted, they had fought well together for years.

Daniel rubbed his hands together, leaning forward. "Who else do we need?"

"We need a tracker. A camp follower would also be nice," Peter cast his eyes over the scattering of soldiers around the campsite. "The best tracker I can think of is Hamish. I can ask him."

"Good, it's settled. I'll find a recruit amongst the camp followers." Daniel sprang to his feet, setting his jaw. "Let's go recruit and after that we'll leave right away."

"Hold on," Peter also stood. "You forget, I am in charge of this contingent. I give the orders here."

Daniel turned to him, narrowing his eyes, and crossing his arms. "What are your orders then, *Sir*?"

"We must approach the recruits with delicacy. We do not want anyone else overhearing or knowing of our mission. Approach them quietly. Make sure no one else is around. Ask them after swearing them to secrecy. Got it?"

Paul and Jack readily agreed. Paul stood, rubbing his

hands together. "I will go recruit Sam and Aldridge."

"And I'll go for Hamish," Peter nodded. "We'll meet back here, make our plan, ready supplies, and head out later tonight."

"Later tonight?" Daniel blanched. "We should not delay any longer than necessary."

Peter's jaw tightened. "If we rush out right away, the soldiers will get suspicious. We have to take our time with this."

"My wife is out there...your sister...and you think we should wait?"

Peter rubbed his forehead, then held his arms out defensively. "We have to do this right. If you have a problem with that, you are welcome to stay behind."

"Stay behind?" Daniel took a step forward. "Are you mad?"

"This is personal for you, I know," Peter lowered his eyes. "Your emotions are already clouding your decisions and that will no doubt get you—and us by extension—into trouble. The more I think about it, the more sense it makes. You should stay behind."

Scoffing, Daniel shook his head. "I will not."

"I'm sorry, but you are not trained for this, you are not military." Peter stepped back, shaking his head. "Face it, Daniel, you are a carpenter. A city boy. Not a soldier. I doubt you even know how to handle that rifle."

Face rigid, Daniel bent to pick up the musket lying at his feet. He checked it was loaded with powder. He reached into his breast pocket for the spare amo he kept there, then shoved the minot balls into their slots. He raised the musket, pointed it across the camp towards a bottle of brandy left forgotten on a log. He fired and the glass shattered into oblivion.

Daniel shoved the gun into Peter's hands and stalked off.

Jack slowly got to his feet, stepped to Peter, and patted him on the shoulder. "I am no expert on these matters, but I believe that was the wrong thing to say."

Four hours later, Peter's contingent sat mounted on horses on the outskirts of camp. Hamish, Sam, Aldridge, and George had agreed to accompany them, alongwith a camp follower named Bonnie, one of Eileen's dearest friends and one with knowledge to attend to their wounds and care for the horses. Daniel loaded his pack on the saddle, then mounted up on his own steed.

"Alright, let's move out," Peter commanded, squeezing the sides of his horse.

They ambled out of sight at a leisurely pace until the campsite was far behind and the Grand Trunk Road came into view. As they set off, Peter turned to Daniel.

"I'm sorry about what I said earlier. There was no cause for it. It was an insult born of fear. I have a lot riding on this mission. The life of my sister, the respect of my Commander, my own life and that of my troops..."

"I get it," Daniel shrugged. "And you are right. I am no soldier."

"Yet you shoot better than most," Peter grinned.

"Steady hands and attention to detail," Jack chimed in. "Carpenters are a skilled bunch."

"Thank you," Daniel nodded in his direction, then turned back to Peter. "What say you, Commander? Shall we ride?"

"One last thing," Peter held his hand out towards Daniel. "We should acknowledge the fact that we are brothers now. As Paul will testify, we may argue occasionally, but that will serve to make our bond stronger. Right, Paul?"

Paul scoffed. "Occasionally? Daniel, beware. He will argue with you all the time, in any place, for any reason." He flashed a grin. "But, we are brothers. Nothing will ever break that bond."

Daniel finally took Peter's proffered hand, then shook that of Paul's. He had not considered the idea of them as his brothers. The idea was new and strange, but not unwelcome. "Brothers. As the eldest of eight children, I have never had the pleasure of an older brother."

"They are insufferable," Paul lamented with a grin and a wink. "Get ready for constant mothering. And do not even think about trying to take the lead. The elder brother always has to be in charge."

Peter flashed a grin, shrugging his agreement of that. "Alright, gentleman. We ride."

They each kicked their horses into a run, setting off down the Grand Truck Road with all haste, dust billowing in their wake.

62

"This is it," Daniel's horse trotted around a clearing in the jungle. "The last place we tracked the rebels before we were called off the hunt."

"How far ahead are they, do you wager?" Peter rested his forearm on the pommel of his saddle as he leaned forward, inspecting the camp.

"At least a fortnight, maybe three." Daniel shook his head, dropping his chin into his hand, trying to force down the churning of his stomach at the thought that they were too far behind.

A scrap of white lying buried in the mud, moved in the slight breeze. Moving quickly, he dismounted, moving towards it, noting it was a scrap of white cloth indented in the large footprint of an elephant. He bent, plucking the white scrap from the ground.

It was badly stained with mud and other unidentifiable substances, but Daniel knew he had seen this scrap of fabric before. He had torn it from one of his own shirts, tied it around Staletta's blistered foot.

"She's been here," he said, casting his gaze up to Peter.

Peter nodded. "Hamish, which direction did they go?"

Hamish inspected the ground. Luckily, it had rained the night before the rebels set out, causing the elephant tracks to stand out in relief. He easily deciphered the direction. "They headed that way," he said, pointing west.

"That seems to be the pattern," Jack trotted up to Peter's side. "Due west."

"They haven't deviated much from that direction," Hamish agreed.

"West it is," Peter shifted in his saddle. "I'd say the most the rebel contingent can do is fifteen miles a day, tops. Ten, is more likely. On horseback, we can do almost thirty miles a day. We can catch them."

Daniel swung back up into his saddle, letting the white scrap of fabric fall back towards the ground.

They left forest far behind. They tracked the rebels across the plains for a week, grateful no rain had fallen to cover the tracks. They were in hard pursuit a full two weeks. The horses were tired, the men were tired, and the enemy was still not in sight.

"We are far from the 19th foot," Paul twisted in his saddle, looking back from where they had come.

Peter chewed on that idea as he had for the last week. He certainly had not thought the rebels would travel this far without stopping for more than a night. "They have to stop sometime."

Daniel drew up next to them, peering intently at the horizon. "There are hills ahead."

"Look at that," Jack whistled from behind. "Never thought I would look forward to being in the jungle again, but after these dreadfully boring plains, variety will be nice."

"Hamish," Peter called ahead, waiting for the man to answer.

"Yeah?"

"Do you think they went through the jungle or around?"

Up ahead, Hamish shook his head and shrugged. "Hard to tell."

Peter sighed. "I was hoping to meet them on the plains. There are more places for them to hide in the jungle."

"I will track them, Sir," Hamish replied. "You have no need to worry about that."

"Let's pick up our pace," Peter leant forward to pat his horse's neck. "I want to reach those hills by nightfall."

63

Daniel dismounted from his horse, hips and legs buckling underneath him. He shook them out, feeling the life come back into them. He stretched his arms up over his head, vertebrae popping. With a sigh, he lowered his arms, then rubbed the back of his neck, moving to collect the reins of his horse and lead it to the small stream running through the jungle.

As the horse drank, he walked a short distance, breathing in the warm night air, peering around at the dark woods around them. The wind was silent, except for the occasional breeze wafting through the upper canopy, making the leaves swish together. The sound of crickets and cicadas filled the night as well as the rustling of some critter in the bushes.

Behind him, the others started making camp and it

wasn't long before they had fed themselves on dried beef and the berries they had collected as they passed into the forest. He set up his tent and crawled inside, easing into his bedroll with a sigh. If only he could see her again. He closed his eyes, remembering her soft white hair and blue eyes rimmed in dark lashes. He remembered the dent in her chin, the feel of her lips, the warmth of her forehead when their faces touched.

The image disappeared as he opened his eyes, throat constricting. The absence of her body in his arms, her voice singing in his ear, left him as empty as an old cicada skin. He rolled over and sighed, trying to recall the sound of her playing her violin.

He smiled, remembering the first time he had heard her play, that icy cold day on the street. She had been filthy, her clothes stained and worn. Hair disheveled. Skin smeared brown with grime. Yet the most beautiful music came from her. She had captured him with the sound of her voice, the music of her violin, juxtaposed with her destitute existence, juxtaposed with her charity, juxtaposed with the desolation evident in her eyes, and the life and hope bursting from her when she danced. A paradox of the senses. If only he could hear her play again.

He rolled onto his back, rubbing his face, hoping exhaustion and the music of the insects would lull him into sleep. Instead, the slightest hint of wind whistled, and his ears locked onto the sound. It lilted high and dropped low. *It sounds like a violin.* Daniel chuckled softly to himself, rolling onto his side, trying to push the sound away and focus on the insects.

The sound repeated, becoming rhythmic in nature. Daniel's eyes popped open and he propped himself on his elbow, staring at the side of the tent. *It cannot be a violin.* He narrowed his eyes as the sound of the wind rose high and skipped a few notes down, then back up, then held, quivering out of existence. Daniel breathed out. "But that is most definitely a violin."

Throwing the blanket aside, he swung his legs underneath him and pushed out of the tent at the same time Peter and Paul emerged from their tents.

"You heard it too?" He asked in a whisper.

Peter nodded his head. "What is it?"

"A violin," Daniel pulled himself out of his tent and stood. "Star plays violin. I'd recognize the sound of it anywhere."

"Are you saying that's her?" Peter shot up, making his way over to Daniel, eyes wide.

Daniel shrugged. "I don't know."

Paul drew up beside him. "Is it the rebels?"

The others had also emerged from their tents and moved to stand with them in front of Daniel's tent.

"There's only one way to find out," Jack chimed in, hefting his gun onto his shoulder.

"Could be other travelers?" Paul shrugged, scratching his forehead.

"Let's sneak in and take a peek," Jack shifted his feet, pointing towards the forest.

"My curiosity is peaked," Daniel bent to retrieve the gun from his tent, then swung it over his shoulder. "Peter, you're the boss. Shall we check it out or not?"

Hesitating, Peter scrunched his lips to the side, and breathed in deep, reluctantly nodding his head. "Let's go." He bent into his tent to collect his gun, then emerged. "But we will go silently. We will not make our presence known to whoever it is."

"What if it is the rebels?" Paul swung his gun over his shoulder and tightened the belt of his trousers.

"If it is, we will reconnoiter and then return back here to plan our attack." Peter eyed each of them individually, lingering on Daniel for the longest span. "Understand?"

Daniel shrugged and nodded. "Understood, Sir."

"We better go before the music stops," Jack started walking towards the sound of the music.

Peter quick-stepped, moving to head up the line. "Follow me."

They followed the music through the trees, until they started to hear the dim sounds of a campground and the violin music sounded louder. The men started to move slower, placing their feet carefully to avoid snapping a fallen branch. At the first sight of the campers, Peter motioned with two fingers, pointing to the trees. Each man moved to hide behind a tree or a bramble.

Daniel peered out around his tree, spotting the campers. His heartbeat quickened at the sight of guns and swords belted at their waists. He waved his hand to get Peter's attention two trees down. "Rebels," he mouthed, only a slight sound emerging from his throat.

Peter nodded that he understood and cast him a hardened look that screamed for him to stand down.

Licking his lips, Daniel breathed in, trying to steady his racing heart. He had to stay still. No matter what he saw. He had to stay still. There was no way he could defeat the rebels on his own. It would be difficult, nigh impossible enough with only the few of them. He breathed out. *What if Star is here? What if she's hurt?*

He shook his head, blinking rapidly, then peered back around the trunk of the tree. The violin music still played.

A voice speaking English punctuated the music, as if giving instruction. *That's odd.* Daniel thought, craning his head to see the violinist and the speaker. They had to be close, but just out of sight. *What if it is her?*

Daniel looked back to Peter, waiting for instruction. Peter looked around the campsight and nodded, then turned back to his men. Using two fingers again he pointed in the direction of their camp, then drew back his hand, putting one finger to his lips in a shooshing motion.

As quietly as they had come, they moved back from the camp, staying low behind the brush to keep from being seen. When they were a few paces back and sure the darkness would hide them, they relaxed, standing up straight and letting their footfalls ease back into normal steps.

A growl, a sudden scream, followed by a gun shot, cracked through the silence of the night. Daniel whirled on his heel, gazing down the line to where Sam stood, gun pointing down at the body of a dead leopard, his chest heaving.

Shouts coming from behind forced Daniel to swivel his head back to the rebel camp, then over to Peter.

Peter opened his mouth to say something, but it was too late. A rebel appeared at the edge of the trees and raised his musket. Peter raised his faster, shooting the rebel straight in the gut.

"Fire." Peter yelled as the rebels descended.

Taking cover behind the trees, the men aimed and shot at the line of rebels. Daniel killed one, stopped to reload, and hefted his gun to shoulder once again. Then a spot of blue caught his eye. The bark of the tree exploded as a musket ball flew past, inches from his face. He pulled his head back, then took a deep breath, and leaned back out, firing. He stopped and looked again for a glimpse of blue, his heart racing up his throat.

There. Just beyond the line of rebels.

Yelling Staletta's name as loud as he could, Daniel watched as she stiffened, then whipped her head out to where he was still hidden in the trees. She had a violin in hand and a man was pulling on her arm, leading her into the forest.

He yelled her name again, then plunged out behind the tree, raising his musket, shooting at the line of rebels.

He ran for cover behind the next tree, trying to catch his breath, but it caught in his throat when he heard her cry his name in return.

Risking another glance, he stuck his head out from behind the tree. "Hold on," he yelled. "I'm coming for you."

He watched as she struggled against the man's grip, thrashing wildly. The man's fingers slipped and she sprinted in Daniel's direction.

Daniel shot out from behind the tree, body slamming a rebel that moved in his path. Shoving him aside, he kept running, but stilled to a halt as the man caught her by the hair, wrenching her head back.

The force sent Staletta sprawling backwards onto the ground. Horrified, he watched as the man dragged her towards him with powerful strength. Digging her fingernails into the dirt and grasping at the grass to slow her movement, he watched as she lifted her head and screamed.

A musket ball tore through his shoulder, sending him to his knees. He grimaced, hefting his gun and firing back. When the shots ceased, he turned back to where Staletta had been, once again catching sight of the man wrestling her into a cart. And Archie. Archie was also there. The man hopped onto the horse attached to the cart, then slapped its rump. The horse reared, whinnying, then took off at a full gallop.

Daniel punched the earth, gritting his teeth with frustration and pain. He looked around quickly. Rebels were running around, scrambling to pick up parts of their camp and shooing the elephants back towards the trees.

With blood streaming down his arm, Daniel took advantage of the chaos and back pedaled, taking shelter once more in the trees with the rest of the men.

"You're hurt," Paul noted, pulling Daniel behind the tree when he came hurtling through the brambles. "We've got to retreat."

"The rebels are fleeing into the forest," Daniel reported. "We can't lose them now."

"You're injured," Paul repeated, then called over his shoulder to Peter, "We need to regroup."

Peter nodded, ceasing to fire. He called down the line of trees, "Fall back."

"But we can't lose them," Daniel breathed heavily.

"We tracked them once, we will track them again," Peter said, staring him down with a note of finality.

Feeling the pain worsen in his arm, Daniel slowly relinquished, and together, they retreated into the forest until the rebel voices died down and the rapid gunshots ceased.

Breathing out in relief, Daniel lowered his gun, and started to run with the others.

One last shot thundered through the night, and a split second later, Hamish fell to the ground, a hole in the back of his head.

64

Daniel stared at the crackling flames, one leg bouncing impatiently while the other remained steadfast, heel clenching the earth, reluctant to move. With hands clenching the opposite elbow, he sat hunched over, pulling tight to keep his stomach from total upheaval, and his chest from splitting in two. His eyes burned against the bright flares of the fire, but he did not care. He would keep staring. No one spoke that night and he needed something to distract his mind from the guilt.

That night they had buried their companion. He winced as his gut clenched something awful. It was all his fault. Feeling bile rise into his throat, he put a hand to his mouth and turned his face away from the flames, burying it in his shoulder instead. Eyes closed, he saw

Staletta dragged across the earth and saw brains oozing out of Hamish's head, and his stomach revolted, emptying into the fire.

Sweat on his brow, he sat back on the log, clutching his stomach, glancing up at Peter who stared at him hard.

"We messed up today," Peter spoke to all of them. "We will not let it happen again."

Daniel flinched as a hand landed on his shoulder and George lowered onto the log beside him. A flask appeared in his hand and Daniel took it. He hesitated for only a moment before unscrewing the top. He put it to his lips and tipped the end, feeling it trickle down his throat, relishing the burn. He handed it back to George, nodding gratefully.

George took a drink and lowered the flask. "I didn't see my wife today. But you saw yours?"

"I did."

"Then, perhaps, there is still hope for me."

"Eileen is strong," Daniel stared back at the fire, thankful that whatever was in the flask had burned off the taste of vomit in his mouth. "We'll get them back."

George fell silent, took another drink, then offered the flask back to Daniel. He took it, this time the drink filled his gut and eased a little bit of the churning.

"You are not a soldier," George commented as Daniel handed the flask back. "But you have become one anyway."

Daniel glanced at him, not understanding.

"A soldier bears the weight of many a burden all for the sake of the country he loves and for the family he loves. You are feeling it tonight, aren't you? Hamish's blood is on your hands, right?"

Lips thinning as his jaw tightened, Daniel nodded slowly, studying George's stone-like face, etched with lines from long years spent on the front.

"Let this ease your guilt," George raised a brow, held his hands out in front of him. "It is also on my hands." He pointed over to Peter and Paul. "And on the hands of the Burns brothers there. It is on the hands of the commanders, and on the white-gloved hands of the Queen herself." He paused, lowered his hands into his lap. "Don't let the guilt eat away at your gut, son. You are a soldier now. Put the guilt up on your shoulders and carry it, strong and true."

Straightening, Daniel relaxed his back and felt the tension release. He nodded, looking away from George to see that Peter had been listening intently.

"Tonight, we will also put our grief onto our shoulders as well as our determination. We have a battle yet to fight and we'll need all of our strength if we are to win. We may be few in number, but we are strong in passion. We fight for our families. No hidden tigers or rebel horde can stop us."

Daniel felt the wind refill his lungs and clear his head of its tangled webs, but a lingering strand of doubt yet remained. His knee resumed its impatient bounce. "How? How will we win this battle?"

Peter looked at Paul. "Do you remember, during the Siege of Sevastopol? The Great Redan?"

Breaking into a wide grin, Paul snickered. "Of course, how could I forget?"

Now widely smiling, Peter looked back to Daniel. "The Great Redan."

Eyes narrowed, Daniel shook his head. "The great what?"

"During the Crimean war, we attacked the Redan outside Sevastopol. We fought, unsuccessfully, for a whole year. No matter how hard we tried, we couldn't win it. Then one day, we tried a new tactic. A few hours later, the battlement was ours. The Russians fled for the north, tales fixed firmly between their legs." The grin broadened.

"Well, what was it? What was the tactic?" Daniel leaned forward, waving his hand for Peter to continue the story.

"No one may know of this. We went against orders that day. It is off the books, got it?"

Jack leaned back, slapping his leg. "I'm seeing a new side to you, Peter. You are more of a rule breaker than I thought. I won't say a word."

When everyone had granted their agreement, Peter continued. "We call it 'The Tiger'."

65

"Hiyah!" Khaneesh whipped his elephant, urging it even deeper into the trees as the rebel contingent pooled into the midst of the jungle. Crowded on a cart laden with prisoners, Staletta bumped and jostled as the wheels lurched over the uneven ground, even bumping heads with the lady next to her as the cart navigated over a clump of exposed tree roots.

With a sigh of relief, she felt the cart begin to slow as Khaneesh barked a command in his native tongue. Then the cart, with one last jolt sending her head whipping forwards, then back, came to a halt. She winced as the pain in her rear intensified from sitting on the bare wood of the cart for nigh on a full night and day.

Though it was late and dark, through the dim lantern light she could see the rebels that rode on horses, dismounting, and the rebels that had fled on foot, collapsing to the ground in exhaustion. Khaneesh came into view, calling out orders with a waving arm. The rebels scurried to pitch tents and light fires. Then he turned his eyes on the prisoner carts.

"Get out!" He shouted. "You have your duties, now get to them."

The bull hook he had used on the elephant came snapping out, banging on the cart and swiping at the prisoner's feet. Staletta pulled her feet in close as the hook narrowly missed her toes. Khaneesh stepped to the side, bull hook resting on the ground like a staff, his other fist on his hip.

Staletta scooched forward to the end of the cart while the other prisoners did the same. She swept her legs over the side, and pushed off. The other prisoners brushed their hands on their skirts and started to move off. Staletta moved forward to the do the same, but a hand clasped onto her plaited hair, yanking her out of line. As fiery pain ripped through her skull, she cried out, hands reaching up to claw on the hand that held her.

A powerful arm wrenched her head back and down until she collapsed onto the ground. Writhing to sit up, she felt the earth rub against her palms. Looking up, Khaneesh glared down at her.

"You had them attack us," he spat.

Shaking her head, she fumbled over her words. "No, I-I did not."

The bull hook came swinging down. She raised her arms to cover her face, pain spreading as the wood cracked into her forearms. Crying out, she collapsed onto the ground, curling into a ball.

Pain wracked her body as the hook bit into her back. Fingers clawed at the earth, trying to get away, but his foot came faster, stomping on her stomach. A stream of vomit forced up through her esophagous, spraying onto the ground at Khaneesh's feet.

Staletta panted into the dirt, seeing nothing but flames before her clamped shut eyes. "Please stop," she wept, tears turning the dirt into mud beneath her cheek.

"You knew someone in the contingent that attacked us," Khaneesh spat. "You brought them to us!"

Staletta felt the grass rub against her hair as she shook her head. Khaneesh straddled her, kicking her in the side so that she flopped onto her back. She opened her eyes, staring up at his scowling face. He slowly drew his sword from its scabbard.

Danny. She thought. She had seen him one last time, a little figure out there in the trees. He had come to save her. She smiled at the thought, causing

Khaneesh to scowl deeper. But her smile fell fast. *I will never see him again.*

Khaneesh brought the sword into both hands, lifted it above his head, and as the sword dropped, Staletta scrunched her eyes closed, throat too stuck with fear to scream, and held her breath.

A roar sounded through the jungle, quickly followed by a high-pitched scream.

Eyes snapping open, Staletta saw the sword in Khaneesh's hands had lowered and he stood twisted around, eyes peering into the jungle.

A second roar sounded, followed by another scream. This time from the south side of the encampment.

Khaneesh's head swiveled in that direction, moving his legs so that he no longer straddled her. Sword hefted, he eyed the jungle warily.

A third roar and a third scream. Khaneesh swiveled to the east, calling out in Hindi. His soldiers, now on high alert, hefted their guns and their sabres. Khaneesh pointed into the forest, calling out an order, and tentatively, a soldier went to investigate.

A fourth roar sounded, this time from the west. The scream that followed made the soldiers quake. Staletta raised herself onto her palms, squinting into the darknened trees, but saw nothing.

Khaneesh orderd more men to investigate. Slowly,

a soldier tiptoed to the edge of the encampment, gun shaking in his hands. He swiveled from side to side, looking for the tiger hidden in the trees or the bushes. Then, in a flash, a roar sounded and he collapsed, his gun firing up into the sky.

Staletta jerked at the gunshot. Heart racing, she looked to Khaneesh. His hand trembling, though he tried not to show it, he commanded his soldiers to fall in to the center of camp. But some of the soldiers were running away, fleeing into the night.

Then another shot rang out, and another, and another, and Staletta watched as the camp erupted into chaos, Khaneesh trying to rein in his fleeing troops, but half of them were already gone, running for their lives.

Breathing heavily, Staletta staggered to her feet, scanning the encampment for Archie and Eileen. As she moved into the center of the encampment, she called out Archie's name several times until his head popped out between the front flaps of a tent.

"Staletta, over here," Archie waved to her from the tent, Eileen appearing just behind him.

Clenching her side, Staletta winced, sucking in a deep breath. Willing her legs to move her forward, she kept one hand on her side, picking her way to them gingerly.

Halfway there, she raised her eyes to Archie. His eyes had widened and he raised his arm, pointing to something behind her. "Staletta, watch—"

A weight collided into her from behind, wrapping her in tight arms that inflamed the bruised muscles along her ribs and back. Her arms were quickly wrenched backwards and bound in rope. Then a knife was at her throat and a mouth breathing hot and heavy in her ear:

"Those aren't tigers. It's a ruse! They have come for you," Khaneesh hissed. "I should have killed when you I had the chance."

Staletta's heart pounded as his words sank in. *Danny.* Could it be true? Eyes open wide, she scanned the night, but could see no one.

Chest heaving, Khaneesh spitting in her ear, "I won't be making that mistake again!" Knife biting into flesh, Staletta closed her eyes...

66

Launching into a dead sprint, Daniel cried out as the rebel leader grasped hold of Staletta, holding a knife to her throat. *Faster!* Sucking in deep breaths, he ran, almost there, the rebel about to strike. *No! Not close enough. Faster!* No, *it's too late...*

Staletta clamped her eyes shut. Heaving breaths, Daniel ran faster, feeling his lungs burn, his legs flying. Then he kicked off the ground, tackling the rebel a split second before the knife would have cut deep.

Their bodies collided in a jumbled heap on the ground. Daniel grimaced as his cheek scraped across the ground, the impact rattling his bones. The rebel lashed out, grasping at his arm. Daniel writhed, wriggling an arm out of the rebel's tight grasp. Making a fist, he launched towards the rebel's face, but the man rolled out of the way.

Ignoring the pain coursing through his body, Daniel pushed himself to his feet, drawing a sabre from the sheath hanging from his waist. Gritting his teeth, he watched the rebel push to his feet, reclaiming his sabre from where it had fallen to the ground.

"You can surrender now, boy," the rebel smirked. "Save yourself from a grim death."

Daniel wiped his cheek, his sleeve coming away bloody. "Never."

The rebel took a slow step to the side, crossing one foot over the other, waving his sabre back and forth. "Why not? You are clearly no match for me. You are not in soldier's garb, so I presume you are no soldier. I outrank you, boy."

Gripping the handle of his sword even tighter, Daniel spoke through gritted teeth. "You were going to murder her," he nodded towards Staletta, his eyes longing to linger on her, but they quickly flicked back to the rebel.

The rebel chuckled, holding his arms out wide. "So I was." He glanced towards Staletta. "Your husband, I presume."

She nodded, frowning deeply at him.

"My deepest sympathies, North Star," the rebel fanned a hand over his heart. "I had meant to kill you first. Now you must witness the death of your beloved.

Alas."

"Enough words," Daniel broke in, hefting his sword.

"Eager for blood?" The rebel tipped his head. "Then I'll give it to you."

The rebel lunged. Moving his right leg back, Daniel leaned in to the blow, parrying it with his blade. A second blow quickly followed, and then a third, Daniel moving his arms quickly to block each one.

A lapse in the rebel's timing caught Daniel's attention, and moving on instinct, he attacked. He swung two times in quick succession, then leaped back, and forward again, offsetting the rebel, and pushing him backwards.

Daniel back pedalled, chancing a quick glance at Staletta. She gripped her hair, watching them wide-eyed and also scanning the ground as if searching for something.

Movement in his peripheral vision alerted him to the fact that the rebel was coming for him. He tore his gaze away from her, just in time to block a swing from the rebel, and return it with a desperate attack of his own, the strength coming from it enough to knock the sword out of the rebel's hand, then the blade continued forward, slicing a thin line down the front of the rebel's chest.

Growling, the rebel staggered back, clutching at his

chest.

Stunned that he had managed to land a blow, Daniel paused, staring at the blood line appearing on the man's shirt.

"You like that, do you?" The rebel, angry now, reached down to his boot, pulling out a small knife.

Cursing himself for not advancing his attack, Daniel fell back into battle stance. The rebel growled and threw the knife. Stepping quickly to the side, Daniel watched the knife fly past his shoulder.

"Daniel, look out!" Staletta screeched, causing him to look back to the rebel.

In that momentary distraction, the rebel had reclaimed his sword. Bearing down on him, Daniel tried to get his feet back into place, but the rebel was too quick, knocking him to the side with a heavy blow.

Disoriented, the blows came fast and heavy, driving Daniel even further out of balance. Daniel succeeded in blocking another attack, but the rebel was angry, quickly coming back with a fist to his face.

Pain exploded as cartilage cracked. Daniel staggered back, blood starting from his nose.

Not stopping, the rebel grasped his sword in both hands, advancing on Daniel. The sword flew from his fingers as the rebel came on with a strong back handed swing. Horror filling his gut, Daniel stared into the rebel's eyes, knowing the fatal sword blow was only seconds away. Worse, he had failed Staletta.

The sword fell, swinging quickly for his neck. Throwing up his arm to block...

A gun fired.

The rebel jerked backwards, eyes widening, sword falling from stunned fingers.

The gun shot still thundering through him, Daniel breathed out, lowering his arm from its defensive position just as the rebel collapsed to the ground.

Behind where the rebel had just been standing, stood Peter, a gun smoking in his hand.

Relief flooding him, Daniel's shoulders slumped and he breathed out a heavy sigh of relief. Holding his stomach, he shook his head, a nervous chuckle escaping his lips.

"Alright, Daniel?" Peter lowered his gun.

"Thanks to you," he nodded then turned to Staletta.

She launched into his arms with a relieved sob. He held her close. The feel of her against him almost enough to bring him to his knees. "Staletta, I'm so sorry."

"No, I'm sorry," she buried her face into his neck, squeezing harder.

A weight colliding with his hips, made him pull back enough to look down. "Archie!"

"I'm so glad you're here," Archie looked up at him.

"I'm just glad that you are both alright." Daniel

ruffled his hair and patted his back.

"Eileen!"

"George!"

Daniel looked over the top of Staletta's head, smiling as Eileen and George embraced, sharing a long kiss.

Then moving shyly came Peter and Paul.

"Staletta," Daniel placed his hands on her shoulders, moving her gently back. "I have something for you." He turned her around.

Peter and Paul took a step forward and then stopped. They looked at each other, removed their hats, and stood wringing them in their hands as they looked back at her.

"Peadar?" Staletta breathed, then flicked her eyes to the other. "Pól?"

Nodding, the brothers smiled and took another tentative step forward. Peter cleared his throat. "Réalta?"

Staletta nodded, looking from one to the other.

"Réalta," Peter's face crumpled and he rushed forward, burying her in his arms. Then Paul rushed in, throwing his arms around the both of them. They squeezed so tightly, Daniel thought she might melt under the pressure and heat of their bodies, like a lump of coal crushed under the weight of the earth.

Then the pressure released as they unfolded from

the embrace.

"Don't let go," she whispered.

67

"Sorry to interrupt," Daniel appeared at her side, placing a warm hand on the small of her back. "We need to be going."

Staletta broke away from her brothers, remembering they stood in the middle of the encampment. The noises of battle had ceased, but the shouting in the distance alerted them to the presence of the scattered rebels regrouping.

"Right," Staletta wiped away the tears in her eyes, her arms slipping away from the solid bodies of her brothers, her fingers tracing slowly over Peadar's, or rather Peter's, uniform collar. They were real. They were here. Shuddering at the thought, she smiled to herself, and drew close to Daniel's side.

Peter motioned to the other British soldiers scattered about the encampment. Some of the faces she recognized, such as Jack, smiling knowingly at the sight of her and her brother's reunion. The other soldiers lowered their weapons and trotted over. A woman that Staletta recognized as Bonnie from the medic tents hurried a group of horses out of a copse of trees.

"The scattered rebels are returning," Peter called, already mounting on his horse. "We have delayed too long. Make haste."

"Archie, Star, you ride with me," Daniel held out his hand and the boy ran to his side. Placing his hands under his armpits, he lifted the boy up into the saddle. Then placing his foot in the stirrup and swinging himself into place behind him, he reached a hand down for Staletta to grasp.

Staletta took his hand and placed one foot in the stirrup. A bugle coming from behind, stayed her from mounting up. Twisting around, she spotted Khaneesh's elephant trotting aimlessly around the camp, its ears flapping wildly while its head wagged up and down.

Staletta twisted, looking back up to Daniel. "Not without the elephant."

Daniel raised his eyebrows, lip curling with incomprehension. "The elephant?"

"He is a captive as much as I or anyone else in this camp."

Expression relaxing, Daniel nodded slowly.

A grin spreading on her face, Staletta twisted back to the elephant. She whistled twice and when the elephant spotted her, she waved him over. With cavernous mouth upturned in a smile and ears flapping enthusiastically, the elephant trotted over.

One of the soldiers grabbed the elephant's reins, bringing it into line with their small contingent. They had already grabbed an abandoned cart and in it were loaded all of the captives that they could gather. Eileen mounted behind George on a horse. Jack behind them. Peter and Paul at the lead. Smiling again, she took Daniel's proffered hand, mounting up behind him. "Let's go home."

"Everyone with me," Peter shouted, hefting his sabre, and pointing down the street. "We ride for Tirhut."

68

They arrived in Tirhut two weeks later. Peter and Paul were the first to enter the campground of the 19th Foot, followed closely by the rest. Daniel, Staletta, and Archie rode in leisurely at the back of the line, trying not to draw attention to themselves, which, of course, was impossible as Staletta rode atop of an elephant.

Peter dismounted quickly, passing his horse off to a soldier to take care of, and reported directly to the Commanding Officers.

"The renegade has returned," Lieutenant Colonel Cartwright stood, frowning deeply. "You have some nerve walking back into this camp."

Raising his head, Peter hooked his hands on his musket strap, setting his jaw defiantly. "I have successfully dispatched a contingent of rebels and rescued a host of civilians, Sir."

"You defied our orders and expect praise in return?"

Cartwright scoffed and glanced at Lieutenant Colonel Bright beside him.

"I have asked for no praise." Peter lifted his head higher. "I merely reported the facts, Sir."

Cartwright screwed up his lips almost as if to spit in his face. Peter stared him down, palms sweaty with nervousness. He had crossed a dangerous line. A line from which there was no coming back.

He swallowed, then continued. "I have done wrong and I will now accept my punishment, Sir."

Narrowing his eyes, Cartwright ran his tongue along his teeth, no doubt considering the worst punishment he could come up with.

Bright stepped forward, holding up a hand. "You forget that Officer Burns is in my contingent, Lieutenant Colonel Cartwright. Therefore, it is my duty to be giving the punishment."

Cocking his head to Bright, Cartwright scoffed, then straightened his spine, stepping back with his arms raised and his head shaking in disbelief. "My apologies."

Turning to Bright, Peter nodded. "I will accept any punishment without question, Sir. I only ask that you relieve the other soldiers. I misled them into believing that you had sanctioned the mission."

"I will consider it," Bright rubbed his chin, looking first at him and then the others that crowded behind him. "These are the civilians you rescued?"

Peter nodded. "We were blessed to rescue many camp followers, 18 in all, Sir."

"And did you have any losses?"

"One, Sir," Peter reported, wanting to look down at his feet in shame, but forcing himself to look the

Lieutenant Colonel straight in the eye.

Cartwright growled in his throat, stepping forward angrily. "The man went off on a suicide mission to save the lives of helpless leeches, and got a soldier killed in the process. Bright, are you really still considering his fate? Give him a court martial and let us be on with it."

A look of annoyance passed Bright's face. "Camp followers are hardly leeches. They do our dirty work so we can sit here, growing fat on biscuits." Bright picked up a biscuit, waving it under Cartwright's nose, and then dropped it back onto the table.

"They eat our food, slow our progress, and get in the way when skirmishes arise," Cartwright blustered, puffing out his chest and adjusting his britches.

"Thank you, Lieutenant Colonel Cartwright," Bright turned to him with a dismissive smile. "I can take it from here. I suggest you go for a walk."

Cartwright chuckled, nodding as he backed away. "Just wait until the Government House hears about this." Then he laughed out right as he disappeared into the camp.

Bright turned his attention back to Peter.

"I have considered the repercussions of your actions and I have come to a decision on your fate."

Peter sucked in his breath, expecting the worst.

"Congratulations, you have earned your promotion,

Lieutenant Burns."

The wind knocked out of his lungs. Peter stared at Lieutenant Colonel Bright. "What's that?"

Bright stuck out his hand for Peter to shake. "You have earned it."

"But I went against your orders?" Lamely, Peter raised his hand and shook the Lieutenant Colonel's.

Releasing his hand, Lieutenant Colonel Bright clasped his hands in front of him, looking at Peter out of the corner of his eye. "Funny, I do not recall ever saying no. Not in so many words." He winked.

The corners of Peter's mouth twitched into a smile and the weight of the world lifted from his shoulders. "Thank you, Sir."

Turning to the stunned crowd of friends and family behind him, Peter held a hand to his chest, sighing in relief. He started to walk away, until Lieutenant Colonel Bright cleared his throat and the group looked at him once more.

"I am not finished just yet. Officer Paul, will you step forward, please?"

Paul pointed at himself questioningly, then shrugged and stepped in front of Bright.

"You and your brother are inseparable, yet you two are as opposite as the sun is from the moon," Bright stared at him hard. "You are passionate which leads you to veer towards the side of recklessness."

Paul hung his head, shifted his feet.

"Yet you are fearless, precise, one of the best soldiers in the 19th Foot."

Looking up, Paul smiled, not-so-humbly shrugging. "Well, one does ones best, Sir."

"What you need is more responsibility, more structure in your life, I think." Bright nodded. "That is why you will also be earning a promotion to Lieutenant."

After smacking his temple with his palm, Paul reached forward to shake Bright's hand. "I won't let you down, Sir." He breathed in deep, filling his lungs with air, his chest expanding.

69

The campfire crackled, beckoning him to its side along with the laughter of his sister. He excused himself from the conversation he was having with a group of soldiers. Removing his hat, he peered over at the fire and paused, not stepping any closer.

It had been two weeks and yet the reality of having his sister back still had not fully settled in. His breath caught as he stared at her, sitting on the log next to Daniel, pretending to be a conductor as Archie stood, playing his flute. Their smiles and laughter put an ache in his chest. An ache he did not understand.

She had a family. She had a whole life. She would go off again. Return to London with them. They would go their separate ways.

But not for long. He drew himself up, taking a deep

breath. As soon as the rebellion was over. He would go to London. He would...well, he did not know what he would do. He and Paul would have to figure that out together. Unless Paul would also go his own way. The ache in his chest returned.

As if on command, Paul appeared, walking towards the campfire with Irene on his arm. "Stop staring, Peter, and let's go join them. Tonight, I feel like singing."

Peter smiled and tipped his hat at Irene. "I'm right behind you."

He watched the two of them take a seat around the fire and another pang hit his chest. His sister and his brother both had someone else. Someone other than him to take care of them. They could do just fine without him. Have families of their own. He sighed.

"You carry the weight of the world on your shoulders," a soft voice broke him from his thoughts.

He turned to see Julia drawing up beside him. He smiled and shook his head, then rubbed his eyes with his fingers. "I suppose I do."

"You are not happy?" She drew closer.

"I am," he looked down at his feet. "But I grieve the loss of my family even as I celebrate the finding of it." He scrunched up his features. "If that makes any sense at all."

She giggled and patted his arm. "It doesn't. Go and enjoy the celebration, and, maybe, invite me to come along?"

His gut clenched as she looked up at him through her lashes, her hand gently moving up his arm. No. He did not want to do this. "I am sorry, Julia, but I am not interested. You are, of course, welcome to join us, but between us there will be nothing more."

Her hand fell from his arm and a spasm crossed her features. "Very well."

Guilt filled his chest and he reached out for her as she solemnly moved to walk away. "Have you not met my friend, Lucas?" When she paused and shook her head 'no' he smiled. "I think you two will get along splendidly."

"Is he much like you?" She half-turned, raising her head slightly.

"No, he is much better," Peter chuckled softly. "He does not carry the weight of the world, as I do. He will be a much fitter companion for you than I ever could be. See, he sits there next to Paul," Peter pointed to Lucas, who was deep in conversation with Archie. "Allow me to introduce you?"

She smiled and shrugged. "He looks nice enough."

Peter sucked in his breathe as Staletta looked around and her eyes landed on him. She smiled brightly and waved for him to join them. Warmth filled his chest at the sight of her and he gestured for Julia to accompany him. "Shall we?"

She grabbed up her skirts, a smile once again on her face. "We shall."

"Play us a song," Paul leaned towards Staletta, pleading.

"Something fast," Peter added.

At the urging of her brothers Staletta pulled out her violin and stood up, launching into a tune. "I need my flutist to accompany me," she lifted an eyebrow at Archie.

"Yes, ma'am," he pulled out his flute, placed it to his lips, and followed her tune.

"I'm a deep water sailor just in from Hong Kong," Staletta sang, then pointed her bow at her brothers.

They drew in a deep breathe, then sang, *"to my way haye, blow the man down."*

Staletta nodded and danced around the fire. *"If you'll give me some grog, I'll sing you a song."* Pausing, she pointed back to her brothers.

The brothers bumped their mugs together and obliged: *"Give me some time to blow the man down."*

Laughing, Staletta danced around to the other side of the fire. *"'Lay aft,' is the cry, to the break of the Poop."*

Dramatically, she pointed her bow towards Daniel and Jack. They looked at each other, shrugged, then sang out: *"to my way haye, blow the man down."*

Staletta played faster and kicked out with her foot: *"Or I'll help you along with the toe of my boot."*

She indicated with her hands, encompassing the whole of the group.

Then they all sang: *"Give me some time to blow the man down."*

Staletta finished the song, taking a bow as the crowd clapped and cheered, none more loudly than her brothers.

Winded, she collapsed on the log next to Daniel, laughing as Paul jumped up to perform his magical tricks. For his first trick, he shook his arm, looked at it questioningly, then shook it again. He reached inside his sleeve, pulling out a small rabbit, shaking his head in feigned annoyance.

Irene squealed at the sight of the fluffy-haired, loppy-eared rabbit and he gladly handed it over to her. She cuddled it under her chin, running her fingers over its soft fur.

Peter shook his head. "Where in the world did you find a rabbit?"

Paul placed his hands on his hips, shaking his head, as well. "Where, indeed?"

Feeling Daniel's arm wrap around her shoulders, she turned her head to him, and smiled.

"Are you sure you are ready to return to London?" He asked, concern etched on his brow.

"Of course, why wouldn't I be?" She pulled back to look at his face more closely.

"If you need more time with your brothers, I would understand," Daniel rubbed her shoulder and pursed his lips. "Are you ready to leave so soon after finding them?"

Staletta sighed, dropping her chin in her hand. "I am," she said after a momentary pause. "They have their work to do here and we have ours in London. I have found them and that is enough for me. Plus, I am sick of this jungle. I want to go home."

Chuckling, Daniel nodded his head. "Are you sure you don't want to stay and get shot at some more?"

Nuzzling him with her head, Staletta laughed in her throat. "Oh yes, can we? Then I won't have to miss out on all the mosquito bites either." To accentuate her point, she started scratching a particularly large bite on her neck.

Daniel squeezed her shoulder, pulling her in close, resting his head on top of hers. "What will you do when we get home?"

Scrunching her brow, Staletta thought about that. Finding her brothers had been her number one goal for so long, now that the search was over, what would she do with her time? "I don't know." She sighed, looking up as Archie skipped past in front of them, playing his flute. "What will we do with Archie?"

"He will stay with us." Daniel replied immediately. "That is, if he wants to."

"I would like that," Staletta breathed in deep. "We will start a family. That is what we will do when we return. Family is everything."

Daniel reached over, fingers tracing her chin. "Agreed."

70

The day of departure arrived. They would caravan with a contingent headed back to Fort William. The trio had packed up and loaded their belongings onto Faithful, a name that Staletta had chosen for the elephant brought with them from the rebel encampment. All that was left was the goodbyes, which Staletta dreaded the most. As she had told Daniel, she was ready to go home, more than ready, in fact, but that did not lessen the fact she would miss her brothers.

She stood before them, admiring the men they had become. They looked dashing in their uniforms and she knew if their parents could see them, they would be proud. Tears popped into her eyes. She could not say anything. She threw herself at them, her arms wrapping around their necks.

After the embrace, Peter pushed her back and looked at her intensely. "As soon as we are deployed back to

England, we'll come visit you in London."

"You have the address written down?" She said, wiping the tears away with the back of her hand.

Paul patted the front pocket of his shirt. "Got it right here."

Peter nodded. "I've got it written down too, just in case."

"What?" Paul turned to him. "You don't trust me, do you?"

"I didn't say that—"

"You don't even trust me with a bit of paper," Paul continued.

Peter pinched the bridge of his nose and looked up suddenly. "You could take Paul with you." He smiled and slapped him on the back. "How would you like that?"

Staletta laughed, but Paul crossed his arms. "Trying to pass me off, aren't you?"

"A break from you wouldn't be all that bad actually—"

"Alright, you two," Staletta said, stepping between them before Paul wrestled Peter to the ground. "We're leaving, and you better not get yourselves killed between now and the next time I see you or I will be incredibly upset with you. Got it?"

"Got it," the brothers said in unison, giving her one last hug.

They each shook Daniel's and Archie's hands.

"Daniel," said Peter. "We couldn't have wished for a better husband for our sister."

"I still can't believe she's married," Paul said. "She

was only this tall when we last saw her." Paul held his hand up to his hip. "She'll always be that little girl in our eyes. Take good care of her."

"I will," Daniel said, smiling gratefully, then turned to help Archie climb onto Faithful. He extended a hand to Staletta and helped her up, then he climbed up himself.

Together they began the long trek back through the jungle, back down the Hoogly river, and over to Calcutta. On the promised day in October, marking one year since their arrival, they waited out on the docks for the *Redeemed* to appear on the horizon, and a dinghy to make its way to shore.

"Malachi," Daniel greeted, extending a hand.

Malachi nodded his head at each of them, and extending a hand towards the dinghy, he smiled. "The sight of you three weary travellers makes my heart rejoice. Can I offer you a ride?"

"Yes, please." Archie threw his bags into the dinghy and hopped inside. Staletta and Daniel laughed, clambering into the boat behind him. Malachi steered them towards the ship waiting out on the horizon.

Captain Alexander awaited them on board and as soon as they were on deck, he smiled eagerly despite a dark shadow of an albatross yet lingering on his features. "Did you find them?"

Staletta glanced at Daniel and smiled, looking back at Alexander, nodding happily. "We did it. We found them."

A look of serenity passed over his face and the albatross flew away.

Epilogue

Spring 1860, London

The wind had picked up and brought a different air to London. A new decade had started and left the old one far behind. Above all else there was a change in attitude, Staletta noticed, watching the faces of the people as they walked by outside the shop window. But she could not quite put her finger on what the change could be.

"Does it not feel different?" Staletta turned her head to Daniel, watching him staining the wooden top of a large desk.

"Hmm?" He asked, straightening, and motioning for Henry to hand him more rags.

"The people, they seem different. The wind feels different," she struggled to put her thoughts into words. "The world is changing."

Daniel wiped his hands on a rag. "So it has always

been and so it will always be."

Staletta bobbed her head in agreement. She found her hands moving to her stomach, where she held them there, her face pinched and thoughtful.

Sensing her unease, Daniel tossed his rag on the table and walked over to her. From behind, he put his arms around her, his hands overlaying her stomach, his chin resting on her shoulder.

"It's going to be alright," he said quietly.

"I know, I—" She sighed and took a deep breath. "I have a bad feeling, that's all."

"About the baby?"

"No."

"About Archie sailing with Captain Alex on the *Redeemed* instead of staying here with us?"

"No," Staletta sighed, narrowing her eyes. "There's something in the wind..."

Daniel shifted her around to face him instead of the world outside. "Whatever it is, we can handle it together." He brought her hands up and gently brushed them with his lips.

An intentional cough from behind reminded her Henry was in the room, a witness to their tender moment.

"Sorry, Henry," Staletta said smilingly.

A knock on the door turned their heads. "Ah, that'll be the post," said Daniel.

"I'll get it," Staletta said, letting Daniel get back to work.

Staletta opened the door, greeted the postman, and took the letters from his hand. Closing the door with one hand, she held the letters up with the other, examining them to see who they were from.

"Danny." She said excitedly. "There's one from Peter and Paul."

She ripped it open, letting the other letters fall onto the workshop table, forgotten. She scanned it quickly with her eyes, her fingers trembling. Now that she had someone to write to and receive letters from, she was glad Daniel had taught her to read and write during their three-month journey to India and three-month journey home. "They say they are well and that they are...Daniel, it says they are on their way to London." Staletta looked up to Daniel, beaming.

"An early discharge?" Daniel said, also beaming.

"It must be. They say they will arrive before the spring is out." She nodded, eyes bright. "I must go reply straight away."

Staletta had reached the bottom step when another knock on the door steadied her feet.

"I'll get it," Daniel stepped to the door, opening it to reveal a police man. "Good day, Officer."

Her gut clenching nervously, Staletta grasped the letter tighter, not daring to join Daniel at the door. Something definitely was not right.

"Is this the residence of Staletta May?" The officer drawled.

"May I ask what this is about?" Daniel placed a hand on his hip, stood up straighter.

"Answer the question," the officer replied in a deepened tone.

Swallowing, Staletta willed her feet to move closer.

Holding her stomach, she looked up to the officer's expressionless eyes. "I'm Staletta May. What do you want?"

"Staletta May, you are under arrest on the account of high treason."

Staletta's hand flew to her mouth as she gasped. Heart pounding, she shook her head. Daniel's arm flew up and he moved in front of her.

"Surely there has been a mistake," Daniel's voice cracked.

"Step aside," The officer placed a hand on the door, leaned in, cuffs dangling from his hand.

Daniel reached down, squeezed her hand. "But why?" He sputtered. "How? When?"

The officer moved into the doorway forcing Staletta and Daniel to take two steps back.

"It has been reported to us that whilst in India, Staletta May joined up with a rebel contingent, offering them intelligence into the Queen's army."

Staletta shook her head. "No, no, no, Sir, I was taken captive. I was a prisoner."

"Mutiny is mutiny, Mrs. May."

"But I'm not a mutineer!" Staletta pleaded into the officer's eyes. "You can't arrest me for being a prisoner."

"I have my orders," the officer frowned, taking another step forward. "You can plead your case in court, but for now, you're coming with me."

Staletta shook her head madly, grasping onto Daniel's arm as the officer reached for her. "But I did not join them, Danny, I was a prisoner. They can't put me in prison for being a prisoner."

"Star," he looked at her desperately as the officer locked the metal cuffs around her wrists. Hand grasping his hair, he mouthed words but no sound came out.

Her heart sinking to the depths of her stomach...the wind outside rattling the windows.

Daniel choked out the words. "Star...you'll be hanged."

THE END.

~If you loved by this book, please support the author by leaving a review – it helps more than you know!~

COMING SOON

FEAR
THE
WIND

FEAR THE WIND

This is not justice. This is corruption.

Staletta May has been accused of high treason. Pregnant and imprisoned, an appointment with the gallows looms ever closer.

A defense lawyer appears to be her only chance for acquittal. Notoriously corrupt and far too expensive, she struggles with the decision to hire one.

She pleads her innocence before the court, but her cries fall on deaf ears. Backed by a Lieutenant Colonel seeking retribution, the judge will not listen to reason, will not do what is right.

Friends and family must band together, must find a way for justice to prevail...and Staletta to survive.

BE THE FIRST TO KNOW WHEN IT LAUNCHES!
WWW.WENDYDOLCH.COM/JOIN-THE-CLUB

ACKNOWLEDGEMENTS

Capture the Wind is complete and I couldn't be happier. I have thoroughly enjoyed the writing of this novel and am pleased to present it to the world. It truly is a dream come true to have written two novels and to actually have readers that buy them, enjoy them, and leave reviews for them. A huge thank you goes out to every reader who has purchased or read my works. You are the reason I have sacrificed my time and money to produce another book. You are keeping the dream alive. You give me such happiness and my desire is to give you happiness in return. Please feel free to reach out via Instagram or email if you have any questions or just want to say hello!

This book would have taken me much longer to write (and been that much harder), if my husband, Jared, had not allowed me to have two months of unemployment after we were married to, yes, job hunt, but also work on drafting and editing. Those few short weeks off allowed me to dig in real deep, rewriting, and getting it all ready for my beta readers to critique. Thank you so much for being a good sport and allowing me two months of full-time author status! That was a dream come true, for sure.

And, speaking of beta readers, I would also like

to give a huge shout-out to my two wonderful beta readers: Katherine Schober and Joelle Roehrman. You might not realize it, but you two made a huge impact on the outcome of this novel. You answered all of my questions and brought up so many plot holes and questions that I never would have thought of. You have helped make this novel the best that it can be, and I am so so grateful for the time that you took to beta read this novel for me. I am truly grateful for your help and hope that you enjoy how the book turned out in the end.

I must also acknowledge MoorBooks Design for yet another great cover design! I love how it turned out and am looking forward to working with you on a third cover. As always, I would also like to thank my author coach, Bethany Atazadeh, and my business coach, Renae Christine. Again, writing a novel is a dream come true and I never would have stepped out to do self-publishing without your inspiration and all of the knowledge and information that you give to the world. Thank you so much for doing what you do!

Lastly, I just wanted to thank the writing community on Instagram. Since I started this journey back in 2019, I have met so many other authors who have written amazing works of art. Especially in the Christian historical fiction community, I have discovered people that truly care for one another, and that share a similar drive to share not only history and adventure, but also to share God's grace and love through the written word. You are all such an inspiration and encouragement. Let us all keep writing to the glory of God.

With gratitude,
Wendy Dolch

ABOUT THE AUTHOR

Wendy Dolch is a Midwest-based author of historical fiction adventure stories. She graduated from the University of Nebraska-Lincoln with a Bachelor of Arts in English with an emphasis in creative writing. Together with her husband, she now resides on a beautiful acreage in Iowa where she spends her days working full-time, gardening, sewing, cooking, and writing.

She would love to connect:
Instagram: @wendydolch
Facebook: @wendydolch
YouTube: @wendydolch

CPSIA information can be obtained
at www.ICGtesting.com
Printed in the USA
LVHW111227290921
699024LV00013B/585/J